ANTI LEBANON

Carl Shuker

COUNTERPOINT
BERKELEY

Library of Congress Cataloging-in-Publication Data
Shuker, Carl, 1974–
  Anti Lebanon / Carl Shuker.
     pages cm
  ISBN 978-1-61902-115-0 (pbk.)
  1. Arab Spring, 2010–Fiction. 2. International relations–Fiction.
  3. Middle East–Fiction. 4. Political fiction. 5. Suspense fiction. I. Title.
  PR9639.4.S56A84 2013
  823'.92–dc23   2012040545

Cover design by John Yates
Interior design by VJBScribe

COUNTERPOINT
2560 Ninth Street, Suite 318
Berkeley, CA 94710

www.counterpointpress.com

Printed in the United States of America

To my father

ACKNOWLEDGMENTS

I wish to acknowledge the Japan Foundation and the JENESYS Programme, and all the staff and fellow artists at the Tokyo Wonder Site. My thanks to David Cross and to Arts Council England for their support.

My deepest thanks to James Byrne and Sandeep Parmar, Ryan Skelton, Carl Patton, Bill Manhire, Jack Shoemaker, Glenn Schaeffer, Imogen Prickett, Nicolas Tillon and Mathilde, Harrison Mitchell and Fiona Lindsay, Tom Cunningham, Bruce and Barbara Smaill, John Hilton, Lucy Banham, Kim Ngoc, and my mother Dawn and my sisters Janine and Kathryn. Thank you to Jalal Toufic, whose (*Vampires*): *An Uneasy Essay on the Undead in Film* was a constant inspiration, and wherein he writes, "not only the murderer but also the victim return to the crime scene." To Gerry Judah, whose work adorns the cover. To Abu Michel, wherever he may be. And to my daughter Lotte, and always, always to Anna.

LOTTERY FUNDED

Supported using public funding by

**ARTS COUNCIL
ENGLAND**

The mechanism of Lebanon's amnesia was offered up in August 1991, when the government passed Law Number 84, granting a general amnesty for all crimes before March 28, 1991, according to specific conditions.

WALID HARB

Popular memory has no mercy.

WALID JUMBLATT

For the dead travel fast.

BRAM STOKER'S Dracula

in the anti Lebanon

1 In or near ruin

He came awake to a dead and freakish still.

The total absence of car horns or the squeals of tires on the cheap Syrian concrete with which they replaced the civil war roads. No voices, no music, no laughter, just the *hush hush hush* of the sea.

Then it was there, what had woken him, echoing through the sky vaults. The banal, far-off *dot dot dot dot dot*. The old taxi drivers onomatopoeicize it for the tourists as the *pah pah pah*. Ellipses in the silence; the ... .

He climbed back over the fence into the Luna Park. The Ferris wheel lights were down completely. The office was closed up. Samir had gone home. He could see the main gates to the amusement park were chained and through them no one down the length of the Corniche.

Another flurry of automatic gunfire came then. This time it was answered, in a different, deeper note, bigger caliber, and not stopping. The whole clip spent wild and wrong, rolling away over the sea:

... ...

... .

It was time to wake up.

—

Leon Elias—thirty years old, East Beiruti Greek Orthodox—is what's known as a losing stream. Despite the country's wealth in water, an undergraduate degree in hydrogeology doesn't take you very far in the Lebanon. Leon Elias's had taken him to an under-the-table security job at the Luna Park in Ras Beirut, an amusement park with 180-degree-plus views of the sea, but no roller coaster and little else—the largest ride they had was the Ferris wheel and it was dead. The night the Hezbollah comprehensively took over West Beirut Leon had no idea what was going on. Leon's closest friends, Etienne and Pascal, who had, respectively, a marketing diploma and a law degree, had found better work in the last few months, the only work available, at a security company called Falcon Group Limited. They now had real blue uniforms, militaresque insignia, a pay scale starting at US$300 a month, and they had a gig together in Minet el-Hosn for a stalled Solidere project, watching over the wasteland of the unfinished marina near the Hariri memorial. Pascal had a MacBook, a scooter, and a full $20 tank of benzene and Etienne had a richish family and a little apartment in Jtaoui and he was engaged to a good Maronite girl.

Leon Elias had no girlfriend, no company, a smock from a supermarket with the logo ripped off. He had his childhood room in his parents' old house in Achrafieh, and a mostly useless bus pass—no direct route—so a two-hour walk home, past where his father, Abu Keiko, did real security opposite the Place des Martyrs. The Davidoff billboard across the Corniche read: LUXURY STARTS HERE, but its beautiful Arab girl's hazel-brown eyes stared intensely away from here, over the amusement park and out to sea. The billboard was high above the empty tourist café where Leon still, even now with prices down out of season, could not afford the coffee.

Leon worked security for a Luna Park that was in bad shape. The bumper cars, some damaged since the car bomb and benzene-hungry, sat weird, scattered and silent, covered in canvas. Bars of neon on the Ferris wheel were missing or dead so even in stasis it seemed sometimes as if it were moving, or attempting the illusion of motion in deceleration, an optical trick: that reversed wheel-within-a-wheel. A rearguard action of which they all were guilty: putting on a cheerful face.

Welcome to Lebanon, we say, and smile our beautiful smiles.

They are often at their leisure when they die, these assassinated men. Men like the Phalangist Elie Hobeika, lady-killer, Palestinian-killer, whose fiancée was shot by the PLO at Damour in 1976, and who led the Christian militiamen into Sabra and Shatila in 1982 in long-displaced revenge, and went on to become minister for the displaced after the civil war in another kind of revenge, this one ironic. Hobeika was on his way to scuba dive, his car-bombed car full of wet suits and masks, oxygen tanks adding to the blast.

The car bomb that killed the Future Movement MP Walid Eido was before Leon's time at the Luna Park. It went off in an alley beside the park, behind the beach club where the MP came to swim. The explosion killed Eido, his son, two bodyguards, two members of the Nejmeh football team practicing on the pitch nearby, four other civilians, and as well as damaging several of the Luna Park's rides it destroyed its haunted house.

So many months later, there are no more ghosts there. All that is left is the scrap scattered in the haunted house's concrete foot-print. A shrapnel-pocked wooden ghoul peeking halfway out a barrel from which it will not rise again. A glowing plastic corpse whose light inside is dead, propped crooked in a coffin up against the wall. Their purpose and function now obscure, about them all in piles lie fragments of dusty engine, masks and pulleys, capes and curtains. Samir, Leon's coworker in the evenings, a silent African ticket puncher and handyman, had his leg broken in three places by the blast and was on crutches for a year. No one minds that he stays inside the office. Many of the Luna Park's rides were originally built in Italy fifty years ago and they are endlessly repaired: throughout the war, throughout everything. There is the Ballerina, a great torso of a woman twenty feet high whose fiberglass arms are outflung as if lifting her neck and breast into the brisk, warm Mediterranean winds. Her bright fiberglass skirts hold not secrets but little cubicles with seats and they spin and pleat to reveal not thighs nor petticoats but the greasy machinery within.

The original owner of the Luna Park built the non-Italian rides—actually built them, Frankensteined with scavenged parts, like the swinging ship, *el-Safina*, and the Russian Mountain, a miniature roller coaster of little cars on a gently undulating track inside a gaudy metal man-made maze. He built the full-size and silenced Ferris wheel too—an uncanny idealist, a dreamer, an entrepreneur and engineer, who made and maintained this tawdry, beautiful place for longer than anyone remembers. After the Eido bomb, he semiretired and brought in a new manager (a Christian who brought in Leon, in turn, as a favor to his father) and without him things began to slip, faster and faster.

What a trash, what trash . . . There are twenty-year-old punching balls with coin mechanisms that predate the hyperinflation. A spar would cost as much as dust. The stitching on the balls is burst, the stuffing leaks out, and the leather is so weathered they hurt to hit. Patchy Astroturf carpets the areas under the children's rides, as dirty and manged as the grass it might have replaced. The last properly maintained and functional ride left uncovered at night in May before the season starts is right in the middle of the Luna Park, surrounded by ribboned-off attractions that aren't attractive anymore. It is a child's carousel, a small, undecorated roundabout with five flaking horses and only ever turned on when requested, because of the price of benzene.

"Security," for this, in the off-season, in Beirut, is a joke. When the new manager finishes his half-day at half past four, it is left to

Leon and Samir to watch over the park as the sun goes down and the clouds go pink and purple and mauve, till darkness, till midnight, for that possible visit of three hopeful children a night. Leon is supposed to "walk the perimeter" for half an hour. Watching the scooters heading up to the Raouche. Watching for rich girls walking to their dates. The rich men coming to train at the sporting club. Watching bankers' wives with bandaged noses walk their little dogs and get some exercise—in the rush on plastic surgery in conflict when there's no society. That night, as any other working night when it was warm enough, he climbed the fence and went down to the rocks and smoked and ate his chicken sandwich from Makhlouf's. He drank his thermos coffee and listened to music as the sun set down the Mediterranean, like the last man in the last job, security for a dead Luna Park in a city about to fall.

At the Luna Park it was a guilty, wordless arrangement Samir and Leon had after the boss left: to keep out of sight as much as they could after half past four (as everything is kept shut down unless requested, for the benzene, anyway), and not invite too many random requests for visits by suggesting the Luna Park was much manned or secure. Morale was bad. They work together in silence, getting away with it, leaving on only the lights or what was left of them. Samir smokes in the corner of the office invisible from the street, his bad leg propped upon a stool, and ashes his full strength Marlboros in the corner of a cardboard box with a meditative caress, wiping off the butt's protruding waste on the rim like a skim of paint from a brush. Leon had left him there thinking, feeling the aches, filling his box of ash, and went out on the rocks to look west, watch the sea.

It was May so he could stay out there later and later. He didn't know anything much, really, about Samir. If Samir knew about him, or his sister, how she died, he didn't say, so, for a time, maybe four or five months, this thing they had: Samir's injury, Leon's languor: It had been okay. Summer was coming, meaning more Arab and Euro tourists despite the tensions. Pale Samir was okay, and so was their silence and their arrangement, but it was this situation that started Leon's real troubles. Out there alone, among all the cigarette butts and plastic bags and pistachio shells, huddled in a Leon-shaped hollow in the rocks, he had listened to his iPod on loop and fallen asleep. It only took a couple of hours. Asleep, he missed his phone, and missed the greater silence falling all around.

And then the shooting had started.

A fat-bladed helicopter roared down the coast, an old Lebanese Army Iroquois by the sound. He jogged home from the Luna Park down the middle of the empty lanes of the Corniche in the dark. The sea whispering to *hush, love* in the mossy lava rock beside him. The palms rustling above. The gunfire echoing up in the city. Whole floors of the apartments and the hotels around him in darkness. The salt-stench of the effluent pouring into the sea from the buried river in Ain al Mreisseh where the fishermen gather for pickings rich.

Leon was good at running quietly. He saw and skipped the patches of gravel, leaped scars on the road that would audibly reveal his footfalls. Scared, knowing that running, as well as standing still, made him a target for a chancer on a moped with a handgun making the most of the conflict. Along the waterfront he ran east, past the Hard Rock Café to St. George's, past the Hariri assassination rubble and holes, the cordoned-off hotel, then Downtown, to the Place des Martyrs and to the Christian East, and to his father.

Leon Elias's sister was killed in front of him because, his father would later say ad nauseam, she was too good, she was too strong, she had too much potential, the sun was white as her skin, the sea her eyes, and so forth, and everyone knew her and Leon knew his father felt, *she was just like me.*

She was killed by three Christian assassins in the street outside Makhlouf's, while inside Leon crouched behind a plastic chair pathetic, holding her chicken shawarma. Killed for her strength. Abu Keiko's hair went white overnight and now around his mouth the fringes of his beard and moustache are yellow with nicotine. He repeats himself, tells people, almost gleefully, his hair went white "in one second." But Leon was there; it took the terrible day and a night. Leon was also there when his uncle Joseph came to the old house, saying he knew the men who had done it. They were from the newly released Bcharrean Christian warlord Ja'ja', were hired by him or loyal to him. Leon's uncle knew who the men were, or said he did and seemed to, and he brought the SIG Sauer for his father to conduct his reprisal. Abu Keiko slowly shook his bent white head.

Keiko in militia fatigues sitting in the road outside Makhlouf's, the same age Leon is now, dragging herself backward on the heels of her palms away from the puddle and rags that was her foot, screaming at it. Neither his uncle nor his father looked at Leon; they knew, he knew, they all knew. What would or could Leon do? Leon wouldn't, Leon couldn't. But old ex-militia man Abu Keiko said there would be no reprisal. *We are Christian*, he said, and *here in my heart is love.*

Across the road from Abu Keiko's security post at the rich Kuwaitis' apartments opposite the Place des Martyrs, Leon has watched his father talk about her to the Lebanese Army soldiers who all "know" him and "knew" her and gather and sit and smoke in the glow of his charisma, bored on the overnight details. His papa always has his nunchaku tucked in his belt (three-times jujitsu champion of Lebanon during the civil war; when? who remembers; who knows now) and he never sits down unless alone (like he's protecting the soldiers). He makes the arms-akimbo gesture when Leon knows he's saying, "She was *stro-ong.*" The soldiers nod soberly and look at Abu Keiko's knees. Leon's father's post is only two blocks from Makhlouf's where she was killed. The soldiers love him like a mad old grandfather; they *know* him, as Abu Keiko is fond of saying, and he *knows* them.

But they don't see his coldness or his true oldness, they don't hear his screams at Leon's mother at night or feel his steel; although they might know what in the past he was capable of, what he has done. The balaclavaed assassin walked directly down the middle of the street as Keiko tried to drag herself away and he fired the weapon down at her barely looking and continued walking to his car and did not slow nor slacken his pace. The final shot that killed her was defined in the inquest as "a direct penetrating injury to the heart." Ja'ja' called for it in that terrible year because, like Abu Keiko had been back in 1989, she was with his rival, the Christian general Aoun, newly returned to Lebanon from his fifteen years of Parisian exile, and his Free Patriotic Movement party, the FPM. A lieutenant in the Lebanese Army, she had been favored and rising and her influence had been growing in the neighborhood. Ja'ja' had perhaps tried to recruit her and been refused.

Leon's father makes US$400 a month as a security guard. Ja'ja's men came to Abu Keiko two years after Ja'ja' had his daughter murdered and offered him that much a week to work for him. Abu Keiko had told Leon that Ja'ja' asked and that he'd turned him down. Leon didn't believe his father for a long time, that Ja'ja' would make that offer, but now it seems so ridiculous, so coarse and cruel, of course it must be true.

Ja'ja' funds surgeon's training in heart bypasses at the Orthodox hospital. Hezbollah provide heart pills and blood. Of the Hezbollah, Leon's father likes to say, "They are for the people and I love them." But he has a bypass, and has Ja'ja's money in or near his heart, even so.

Between their two massifs Leon is what is known as a losing stream. What you see is what is left of him. In the words of his hydrogeology text: *Secretive, irregular, branching. Perched in the epikarst; lost in the swallow holes. Coursing through the karst aquifers of the anti Lebanon, I deplete as I run.*

Up in Hamra, but that far east already was impossible, surely?—so close, maybe farther, with the echoes it was too hard for him to tell—he could hear the automatic gunfire thickening, clotting, periods without pause..... .. ..

Tout Beirut may have been calling, but not him with only two U.S. dollars' credit on his cell phone and only a few thousand utterly deflated Lebanese pounds in his pocket. The newly restored Downtown was empty. There were only the Lebanese Army APCs and soldiers reinforced at all the spokes of the wheel of new streets and unfinished alleys leading to the pristine Place d'Etoile and the Serail, the wheel's diameter a ring of rolled-out razor wire.

He slowed to a walk and greeted the first soldier he saw.

"What's up? It's Hezbollah? Amal?" Leon said as he came near.

The soldier stared at his face for a little too long. Then he shrugged amiably, hitched his M16 and boredly made two fists, sparring with one another.

Leon nodded as if a little skeptical or just cool, and walked past him. The U.S.-made Vietnam-era APC was mounted with a massive but ancient Russian antiaircraft gun and parked sideways forming a gate in the middle of the street's razor wire barrier. The three soldiers sitting around the big weapon looked down on him silently.

The empty boulevard ahead gently dipped and rose. The concrete barriers were pitted and paint streaked with old fights and accidents. They had been moved from the sidewalks to the parking bays, narrowing the road to a single lane. There was the fundamental-sounding *clump* of an RPG, which told him that what was happening had spread, and was in more than one neighborhood, stretching west-east but back in the city. The further he got from the sea the closer the sounds became. At the Place des Martyrs, the Green Line of wasteland-crumbled concrete began, the blocks of dead yellow grass littered with rubble and trash up to the car parks. The Green Line known thus not for any UN ruling, but for the quiet explosion of growth in the streets in the war. A hundred meters wide and nine kilometers long dividing the promontory between east and west, sniper deadly no man's land: a silent forest forming around the skeletal buildings. Under Hariri the remains—the old theaters, the machine gun nests, the tunnels and shops and blood-soaked stone and canvas—were bulldozed into the sea at the terminus of the Green Line to form the foundation of the new marina-corniche. No man's land reclaimed now lying doubly deserted in the aftermath of Hariri's death, and diffidently guarded by Leon's friends, with their law degrees, their marketing diplomas.

The gunfire shifted emphasis and pitch. Either the open areas were amplifying the sounds or the fighting was genuinely closer. It was less cracking than popping now, and there were no cars anywhere. No movement and little light, and above him the low poison-green clouds came in softly in strips like ragged sand dunes in a desertified sky over the wasteland to Mount Lebanon.

Leon felt a sick sort of relief approaching the Christian East and rue George Haddad; its unacknowledged and unspoken border, still in conflict de facto if not de jure. The Kuwaitis' apartment complex that his father guarded six nights a week looked emptily back over the Green Line toward the block comprising the Roman ruins, the Hariri mosque, the Orthodox cathedral, the Maronite cathedral, and the Virgin megastore. Hariri's monument to Lebanese solidarity past and present and future, now utterly empty. The sensitive Kuwaitis had all left Lebanon a day ago when Aoun declared the general strike. Everyone knew it was trouble. As Leon cut across, down to his left at the intersection of Haddad and Avenue Charles Helou, there were more figures than usual outside the headquarters of the Christian Maronite Phalange party, a large tan building archer-windowed like a citadel, beflagged with the Phalange cedar, presiding over the port. Leon could see thickset Phalangist men on the rooftops watching for developments, watching him cross the square and the Green Line too.

At the intersection by the Phalange HQ was a Lebanese Army APC with, pointedly, no AA gun. There was a jeep beside it and twenty men at least watching the Phalangists back—in the dim and the scattered streetlights it was hard to tell, but they were probably police not army. As if the army would or could, without falling apart, stop the Phalange or the Lebanese Forces anyway, if they came out in anger. In the old days the officers were all Christians trained at Saint-Cyr and the military *écoles* of France; the soldiers were Sunni, Shi'a, Druze. When fighting goes sectarian, uniforms come off and soldiers go home to their tribes. Everyone knows it's this way and it works. Farther up George Haddad was another APC and jeep, glowing orange-green under the streetlights like pollution or strange sweets, by the Paul Café on the rue Gouraud corner.

As he got closer he walked slower. He held his empty hands out from his sides so they would know he was unarmed. He could see the silhouette of Abu Keiko under the trees with a fat sergeant and some soldiers, laughing. Behind his father in the light sat one single plastic chair. Beside it was a paper bag and in it Leon knew was the fruit his mother packed for them both today, those black little bananas.

He crossed the road and approached the apartment terrace as the gunfire rose again back behind him. Another flurry of ellipses in the rolling stillness over the cape of Beirut, like bad memories in sleep, pockets of panic.

The fat sergeant was watching him. "All quiet?" the sergeant asked and didn't offer him his hand or cheek. Abu Keiko didn't speak, smile, or frown—his gray face was composed and still. As if preparing for a task that required all his faculties, a task not done in a while, and missed.

"All quiet," Leon said. The sergeant nodded and half-turned back to Leon's father. Three young soldiers, ten years younger than Leon at least, sat on the terrace's lower step, with the butts of their American M16s between their feet, watching him.

"All quiet," Abu Keiko finally spoke, without any tone of recognition or of intimacy, and with all the soldiers around him Leon realized what the expression on his face was like. It was the same as when he'd watched Keiko at rallies or talked politics in the kitchen with her in front of guests. It was pride, being with the soldiers again. He felt good with them.

"Go home and take care of your mother," Abu Keiko said, and there was a hint of a private look, then quickly gone.

The sergeant said, "The fighting's along the Corniche Mazraa. The airport road is still blocked."

Leon looked at the sergeant and after he spoke he didn't look at his father.

"Well there's nothing to do and nowhere to do it. I think I'll go and get a drink."

The sergeant laughed and one of the soldiers smirked.

"Have one for us then."

As Leon headed up the hill to rue Gouraud it was strange. There's a feeling, they say, of eyes upon you, but there's another feeling too, for which there is no cliché.

Leon could sense without seeing his father turn away from him, this night of all nights, and away over the waiting soldiers down George Haddad to the port, where out at sea there was maybe a storm coming. At the Luna Park, Leon had watched the clouds pile atop and rise in mauve and rotten apricot towers before the setting of the sun.

Rue Gouraud was dead. Of more than fifty bars honeycombing either side of the street he could see none were open. African waiters were outside Sinners hosing down the empty plastic chairs, and on a street jammed every night with Hummers and Audis and Lamborghini Diablos there was not a single vehicle moving.

Leon walked six or seven blocks to the fork at rue Pasteur near the Electricité du Liban. There the gunfire was distant, and the echoes were fractured and blunted by the buildings. Warmed by the walk, he took off his work smock. There was a *cromp* and a long high rumbling, and this last, he realized, was actually thunder following the RPG. A whispering bleak night of ghosts and soldiers and white-haired fathers, no one to talk with. He turned back to check the side streets—there was someone he'd seen leaning on a car and maybe he was a valet, so maybe there was something open.

At rue Youssef el Hani he saw him again: a young man, thickset, a black T-shirt, too big for a valet; he'd crossed the street. Leon approached him, walking openly in the middle of the road under the lights.

"Hey habibi, do you have a weapon?" was all the man said.

"No."

Leon raised his arms and the bouncer frisked him fast and firmly. Then he opened an unmarked door to a staircase.

"What's the cover?"

But the bouncer grinned skeptically and shut the door on him.

At the foot of the stairs the walls were papered in leaflets. A boy behind a school desk greeted him in French and waved him inside. In the tiny underground club, not counting the barman or Leon, there were only five people: two couples, a dark ponytailed businessman with a Filipina prostitute a foot taller than him, and a Chinese boy and girl, and at the end of the club was a DJ at a laptop and two decks playing something clicking and hissing.

Leon ordered the cheapest beer, local Almaza, and sat on a stool away from the bar, watching the DJ. Maybe he was good; what did he know. Was this one local or was he even famous and on tour, stuck in Beirut playing to him and a barman while the Hezbollah turned their guns on Lebanese in the streets a kilometer away? Leon had already decided to get fucked up. He finished the beer fast, waved for another, lit a cigarette. The DJ was his age, tall and bearded and intelligent looking, completely absorbed, watching the decks and levels on his laptop, not glancing up, shifting his headphones, not even nodding.

Leon had finished four beers when the DJ finished his set and left a track on repeat and went to the bar where the barman gave him a beer. The prostitute said something to the DJ and she laughed and he smiled and shrugged kindly, sipped his beer, looked around. Leon nodded to him.

"Good set," Leon said.

The DJ looked at him, then in a practiced gesture opened his wallet and placed an old and creased card on the table. It had a letterhead from the military hospital destroyed ten years ago. In Arabic, French, and English it read:

> My name is Frederick Zakarian and I have a form of speaking disability called echolalia where I may repeat your turn-final lexical items as a form of conversational repair. But I understand you and we can talk normally. Please be understanding.

Zakarian smiled and said, "Good set. But not a very big crowd tonight."

"Bad timing, I guess, habibi," said Leon.

"Timing, I guess, habibi," Zakarian said and smiled again and checked Leon's lips. "So what are you doing here then?"

"I got off work and this was the only thing going. You're finished?"

"You're finished." He was local, a strongish Armenian accent. "I'm finished."

"Things are a bit frisky. Do you live around here? Bourj Hammoud?"

"You live around here? Bourj Hammoud, yes," he said. "But I work here."

"So you can get home?"

"You can get home?" Zakarian thought about this and then laughed. "You? Can?"

"Yeah, I can. I'm in Achrafieh. Leon. Leon Elias."

"Leaning, a lie is. I'm Frederick."

There was a long pause between the repeat of what Leon had said and his replies. As Zakarian spoke he seemed to be thinking hard about something else.

"So you make a living off this? Are you famous?"

"No, I have a job."

"What's your job?"

"Your job," he said. "I am a jeweler."

Leon noticed he wasn't wearing any jewelry.

"You make your own? Like a designer?"

"I make your own like a designer, no . . . I'm . . . " He looked slightly pained as if this was always difficult to explain. "I work on pieces in a workshop down here in Gemmayzeh. In the Demolished Quarter. No one knows it's there."

"Wow. Expensive?"

"Wow, expensive, yes, some pieces for some wealthy people."

Leon could feel himself getting elevated with the alcohol, so he let the silence last a little. Zakarian began to smile. He'd decided to talk about himself.

"It's very frustrating because . . . we work on these pieces now, a set, necklace, earrings, cuff links. . . . It's incredible, very challenging work. A million-dollar set. They are finished now, just yesterday, and we cannot get them out. The buyers are from Iran and aren't in Lebanon and can't get in to see them. You know the airport's closed tonight? And the road north is closed, and the Beirut–Damascus highway is closed too. The pieces are stuck here."

"The Damascus road is closed?"

"The Damascus road is closed. So we won't get paid. For weeks. And these gigs don't pay. And it's going to get worse." He was grinning, excitable now. "This set is named after a figure in Persian mythology called the Peri. A supernatural being descended from fallen angels. She is excluded from Paradise until a penance is accomplished, the story says. She is a beautiful and graceful girl."

"You should steal her. Sell her." Leon smirked, then stopped himself. "Sorry."

"You should steal her." Zakarian watched Leon's face as he repeated his words as if he were speaking a foreign language, and he laughed far too late. Then he said, "My boss says the feeling is like you've built a Ferrari but you can't drive it."

"I don't know anything about jewelry."

"Anything about jewelry? Well, for this piece we have some exceptional super-ideal Ugandan stones with incredible depth and color sourced by the buyers. They've got really fine taste. We are doing a hearts and arrows pattern that's extremely intricate and involved. We've been working on the set for six months or more."

"Heart-shaped diamonds?" Leon was trying to keep his replies short. He could hear the preformulated, received patterns in Zakarian's speech. There was something about his vulnerability and Leon's mood that made Leon want to be cruel. He resisted it. Zakarian was starting to speak faster.

"Heart-shaped diamonds." He seemed to like that and smiled as he shook his head. "Heart-shaped diamonds, no, the facets are cut so that there's an appearance of alternating hearts and arrows, with a very fine and radical depth to the pavilion that's not been done much before except maybe in Japan where they pioneered a machine called an icescope—"

Leon signaled to the barman for two more beers, and offered Zakarian a cigarette that he took without looking up. The Armenian kept talking, confident now, borrowing someone else's words, someone else's conviction.

"—physics and the purity, and it's taken a long time and now the Hezbollah control the airport and the airport road. And you know what my boss says? I don't know anything about jewelry—"

The little repetitions could occur at any time, as Zakarian pieced together the things he wanted or thought he ought to say.

"—the Shi'a get proportional representation and Iran gets a *vilayet* on the Mediterranean he says all this is all gone, this is all gone," he waved generally at the club, "the bars, the music, the jewelry, the surgery, the clothes, broadband, kiss it all good-bye, he says."

"And the Damascus road is closed? That's unbelievable."

"The—the Damascus road that's unbelievable. No, no—"

Leon was half-enjoying, half-dreading what would come as he watched the autistic Armenian getting drunk too fast and quickly, visibly losing inhibition. Zakarian was shaking his head as he talked quicker, not even noticing Leon's reaction.

"—that is the . . . the Future supporters—they say they're stopping any fighters coming in from Syria to help Hezbollah in the Bekaa Valley . . . but they say they're totally disorganized over there and what they're doing is just burning flags and shooting at trucks and lobbing mortars onto the highway, surgery, the clothes."

"Oh man, yalla."

"Oh man, I know. And they say it is going to get worse. They say we are next. East Beirut. That it is a coup tour. That we are too isolated, too weak, too few. We have no money, no arms, no future."

"The Christians will never let it happen. We're strong enough. That is what you mean right? The Hezbollah will go after the Druze and then the east and the Mountain will be next? It will never happen. It's as my father says: They have gun; we have gun. It will never happen. Just another impasse."

Zakarian looked up at this, smiled, bloody-eyed. There was a long, dramatic, drunken pause.

"East Beirut. It will never happen? Do you really believe that?"

"Yes," said Leon. "I think so."

"So. I've got something to show you."

There's a thing they do in East Beirut to the unpopular, the competitor, to those they assassinate. To the billboards of political contenders despised or car-bombed mid-campaign, to portraits of murdered MPs and corrupt candidates, and to the memorial posters after. They do it with black spray paint and immense restraint.

A spray can is held well back from the image of the face of the rival and the dead; the surety and simplicity carries all the weight. A gentle press and a fine cloud of black no larger than that face or rather no larger than the features of that face, and the face disappears; all that's left is a name, a slogan, and a dark mist, a gray blur on the poster in a border of ears and skin and hair. Jean Wound, forty years old, educated at ENS in Paris and the Sorbonne, candidate for the chamber of deputies. Car bomb, twenty posters in a row, nice suit, salt-and-pepper hair, his face a hole, taken from him twenty times. Mikael Hawi, a Christian militia boy, only 1990–2008. A snowboarding picture on the posters and he's young in a bright red parka against the white but his face is not there. WE WILL NEVER FORGET YOU, it says in English. They let the phrase remain although the boy is gone. Walking poster to poster they erase them with a gentle press of an index finger — one eye, one eye, one mouth. Leon's certain it's done with some pitiful pious satisfied smile. Salman Nakano, car bomb, a leftist journalist for *An Nahar*. Nakano's friend, a writer, was first on the scene, ran down from their Hamra offices and into the smoking street. He thought Salman was alive because he could see his head and shoulders through the unbroken car window. But that was all that was left of him, roasted to the headrest. Later that week they grayed out his memorial posters and took his face from him too. William Habbab met with Damascene secret services and political oblivion. Michel Salama, the anti-war folk singer, who opened for a band that played a gig once in Tel Aviv. Concert posters from six months prior in Beirut Downtown, they fullstopped his face above the acoustic guitar.

Years ago, walking through Jtaoui with Pascal to a film, Leon passed three posters of his sister, Keiko, in uniform, pitch-black shaven hair, faceless; permanent twilight where her skin shone like sun, her pale blue eyes. WE WILL REMAIN HERE! the Aounist slogan under which she campaigned for one bright summer was allowed to stay beneath. The restraint is what weakens him. He couldn't tear the posters down because the glue had fixed them to posters of other dead, despised, and discredited beneath, and the glue-soaked paper was hard as plastic, hard as wood, and went up under his fingernails like splinters till they bled as he tore away at this freak, implacable monument of blank gray faces, Pascal looking away down the street for anyone watching. Years ago, back when they were twenty-seven.

Zakarian and Leon walked down to the Demolished Quarter (not accomplished but slated until Hariri's death when all the reconstruction stopped). The ruined empty Ottoman and Mandate-era buildings were eerie in the orange streetlights. Crumpled garage doors were jammed in hundred-year-old arches on the lower floors. Tiled stairwells filled with trash and rubber hosepipe and useless lumber. The lower sills of all the upper windows were slatted over with boards. This was because the walls beneath the windows were dissolved with bullet holes, where the gunmen on the street had fired wildly, aiming for the snipers' bodies, missing, knowing, or just hoping the old sandstone could be penetrated. There was a Lebanese Army tank parked silently back among the box trees in a vacant lot, sickly green in the orange light. Soldiers playing cards on an upturned milk crate paused and watched silently while they passed. Street after empty street, stinking of piss, feral kittens, the last ATM blinking with no more funds. No traffic sounds as they came near to Avenue Charles Helou just over the wasteland not far from his father's post. Leon had come around in a rough circle.

"It's over here," Zakarian said. He was walking unsteadily but the excitement, his glad dread, hadn't abated.

The vacant lot was opposite the Place des Martyrs. A missing building framed a view of the huge Hariri mosque. The four giant minarets were elaborately lit bright terra-cotta orange, and it towered utterly over the Orthodox and Maronite cathedrals. The lot was walled by two and a half buildings, and there was a scum-filled crater in the center. Frederick went to the wall that faced west, the wall that greeted those who entered Gemmayzeh and the Christian East, and he lit a match.

There was a great angel painted on a wall on the border of East Beirut. Some Shi'a kid had tried to paint and travesty a Christian icon. The angel was a death angel. It was frocked and winged and it had devil horns and folded arms of patriarchal patience. It was painted with the same black spray paint and terrible restraint; it looked ancient and brand new. There was a second smaller figure to its right, to Leon's left as he stood and watched it flickering in the light of the match. It was a creature of black flames and feathers; a familiar the size of a fist. The death angel dwarfed it. It was the size of a man, floating over the Quarter. The angel's face was made of three linked gray blurs in a greater blur; two suggestions of eyes and an open, speaking, cursing mouth. It had a confidence and knowledge though a crude attempt at Christian iconography. It was a warning to those who entered here. A curse, or a promise, rudely done in a kind of pidgin designed to speak to Christian ears, saying: *Something bad is coming.*

Zakarian was looking back at him as the match burned down. His face was a black blur, like the angel's, like the assassinated.

"See?" he said. "See?"

2 Take a deep breath and hold it

They walked through streets deserted, east. At the horizon lightning cracked a monumental wall of stone cloud with a filament of gold. They passed out of the Demolished Quarter and around the fringes of Gemmayzeh and then deeper east into the silent Christian Quarter where it was still safe to walk on a night like this.

The sounds of the Hezbollah and Future firefight dulled.

The two men looked up at a sudden bang—but it was followed by a long rumble of thunder, and they walked on in silence on the back streets of Mar Mikhael.

Up the hill into Jtaoui, on the way to Georges and Lauren's apartment, Leon stopped for more beer and cigarettes at Smuggler. The liquor store owner's son and his friends were playing cards around a plastic crate at the end of the counter and they smiled and sneered at Leon. The Elias family was far from rich but in the past it had been richer than some, and Abu Keiko and Keiko had once had a status Leon did not live up to. He took a certain amount of scorn and spite and casual hatred for his father's fall and for the decisions he'd made in his own life: the passive pacifism in a once-powerful family, for one. He typically took it with carefully measured rejoinders he'd calibrate slightly lower than the initial attack. He wanted peace.

In the past he might have framed the uncertainty like this: Was he evading violence through carefully showing just the right amount of weakness, or was he just the right amount of weak to evade his violence due?

But not this night.

———

Georges and Lauren's small place was a French-style apartment on the seventh floor. You reached it by an old shaking cage elevator with accordion doors and a broken latch. There were two bedrooms, a separate kitchen, a large living room, and a balcony off it that faced northeast over the rooftops up the coast to Christian Jounieh and along the million lights of the Mountain. When they knocked, the door opened a few inches and stayed that way. Etienne peeked out, unshaven, lazy-eyed, crazed, and languid, and he immediately did his Yasser Arafat impression in his awful English, making fun of the chairman he detested not from any memory but because his father did so much: sneering, angry, haggard, doomed:

"What's the meaning of their tanks . . . some meters far of here? Thirty meters—" His r's were rolled and husky, *thahrh dee-meetehrrs*, and he turned inside to his imagined aide, asking for the word, enacting a scene from an old TV interview, surrounded in his Ramallah compound in the second intifada, and back, a sneer and a snarl, sarcastic in their shared disgust with the language and the situation. "Ahp-*hroximedly*."

"Hello Etienne," Leon said and pushed at the door. Etienne braced himself and held it shut and snarled again, then saw Zakarian, the stranger. Etienne stared at him, clucked three times, opened the door, turned his back, and retreated to the living room without another word.

"Don't worry," Leon said. "Ignore him. Come in."

Georges and Lauren were in the kitchen, eating peppered pumpkin soup with sour cream and up far too late feeding their two children and Leon felt foolish with the beer and cigarettes in a dangling plastic bag. He kissed the orange-bearded Georges, holding the baby in his arms, and touched the crown of the head of little blonde pigtailed Hind who shrank under him. He turned to Lauren and kissed her too.

"Hello, Lauren. How is the baby?"

"Fine, fine. Is everything okay?" Lauren said, and her upraised eyes passed over him without purchase to the new person in the doorway.

"Yeah, fine, this is Frederick, a friend. Frederick: Georges, Lauren, that was Etienne. . . . " and he thought of what she might like and said, "and this is the most beautiful Hind, who is now . . . what are you, um, what you must be by now, is . . . five years old?"

Hind grinned madly up at the roof, and Georges said, "Oh!" one armful of the new baby, his other hand with a spoonful of refused soup in midair before the little girl. Lauren leaned to her and said, "Oh, my, *goodness.*"

"I'm . . . not five yet," said Hind deliberately. She considered a correction, had too many conflicting options for response, and accidentally accepted the spoonful of soup instead.

"How are you, Frederick?" Lauren said in English and smiled softly, slightly, and indicated the table. She was tired and wired, and Leon could see deep violet bruises of fatigue above her cheekbones. "Please, eat."

"Hello," said Georges, and Leon watched him frankly assess this new person, the two bearded men grinning naturally at one another. Leon saw Georges's charisma again, as always revealed by someone new, *just like Keiko.* And he thought, *When did we become bearded men?*

"How are you," said Zakarian, and he paused awkwardly, deleting his own first name and other inappropriate details. "Hello."

A sort of silence fell. Hind bounced three times in her chair, looking for what had gone wrong. Leon thought how he might handle this.

"Frederick's a DJ and . . . he has a card from the old military hospital. It's really interesting."

Leon turned to Zakarian, away from Lauren who was now giving him that look, that slightly disbelieving look somewhere ambiguous between appalled and quizzical, that always seemed to ask, and only of him, really, what kind of person are you Leon? What qualities are yours? He put the beer in the old fridge.

Zakarian fumbled for the card, held it to Georges who had no free hands, and Lauren took it, quickly read, and said, "Oh that *is* very interesting."

"What?" said Georges, and she held it up for him to read as Hind, abruptly bored, decided to bend slowly almost double, her face approaching her soup. Georges looked up from the card and smiled.

"Oh, I see. So do you like Cary Grant movies, Frederick?"

Zakarian smiled too and shrugged easily. Georges had this effect.

"We're having a Frank Capra session. Subtitled."

"Subtitled," Zakarian said, still smiling. "Okay!"

And they all smiled then and Hind sat up with a pastiche of pumpkin soup and peppered cream upon the very tip of her nose and they all laughed. Leon laughed too and went, then, his face changing in the doorway, darkening, to the living room, looking for the others, and for another drink, and hopefully some hash. Somewhere that he could hear and monitor the gunfire; adrenaline moving softly, silverly in him, obscurely or predictably, he never could tell.

There was a new poster in the living room, and nuts and fruit, pitifully little, laid out on the coffee table, curtains drawn. Pascal and Etienne squatted by the old laptop on a chair. They were trying to mirror the display on the TV.

"Hi Leon," said Pascal without turning.

"Hello, hello, hello, hash?" said Leon and half-lay on the sofa.

Etienne patted his jeans pocket. "We'll wait till the children go to bed. They can't sleep for the fighting or what? You can't hear it in here. Let those fuckers kill each other and be silent."

Pascal said, "It's probably the tension in the air. Children can feel it."

"The Secure Plus resistance has caved and they're moving on all their enemies now," said Etienne. "I heard they are besieging Hariri in Koreitem, and that they are already all over Ras Beirut."

Pascal hunched over the laptop. "Hind's bedroom faces west. Maybe she can hear it."

"She has a few questions even Georges can't answer."

Pascal said, "You see there is an option here to turn our laptop's display off, but it doesn't explicitly say it will send the mirror image to the other display by doing so. And though it seems like the obvious option and there aren't any apparent others, it asks you twice to confirm, so I would say probably—"

"Fatal," said Etienne. "If you turn it off you'll never get it on again. Pay attention to those warnings."

"Get a Mac," murmured Leon. Above the two men and above the television on the low credenza, where there was a carved wooden Saint Sharbel and rosaries draped around a Maronite cross, there was this new poster. It was a print of a painting of the frame of a mirror on a wall. The frame was elaborately gilded gold ivy, vines, birds, and angels, forming a triptych. The outer panels were narrower than the inner panel, and at the bottom the frame formed a small semicircular table extending out into a world outside the mirror, upon which sat a little dog.

Leon stared at it, slumped on the sofa, crashing. It was the sort of poster found in French head shops with old Tolkien and Paranoid King posters. There was something wrong with the optical illusion but it was impossible to say what was so eerie and unsettling and, yes, beautiful about it. It was only almost kitsch. The dog's back was reflected behind it, casting the viewer always to the left, and beyond that reflection was a room and not this room.

But there were strange darknesses on the middle ground of the implied reflection and wrong shadows and were there eyes? And figures of tall, ghostly men and women from a third reflection? And over it there was ivy, not from the reflected room and not upon the mirror, and strange stains too as if on the print itself and inside that the mottle and metallic pucker of an old mirror. The little dog itself had a superior, alien face, deformed or damaged—was it supposed to be real or supposed to be a figurine? It was laughing, looking up and left at the watcher, looking at Leon: a creature of this world and that. From Leon's angle the living room light caught it too, and the real reflection to the real world would have been northeast, the Christian Quarter, Beirut River or what's left of it, Jounieh, the Mountain, away.

"How's the Luna Park?" said Etienne.

"Oh, really busy," Leon said. "Full of Hezbollah boy scouts doing chin-ups."

"Mahdi scouts. Those little shits," Etienne said. "Pious brainwashed little shits. They have twenty thousand of them in the South. Beavering away. Growing up. Getting stronger. Always getting stronger."

"Is someone paying enough attention to that fact, I often wonder," said Georges from the doorway quietly. He bobbed the baby in his arms. Zakarian was in the hallway behind. "Is it working?"

"Not yet," said Pascal.

"The TV is only four inches bigger than the laptop," Georges said. "You realize that?"

"How is Falcon?" said Leon.

"We've been taken off the job since the strike," Pascal said, and smiled back at him. "Too young, silly, and educated."

"Starting yesterday they said they are only using the senior guys and liaising with the army," Etienne said. "Because if something really does happen that close they will probably just have to leave and anyway they don't want anyone . . . or want some *intellectual* with a . . . *college degree* trying to fight . . . for the . . . "

He trailed off, concentrating his disgust on the laptop.

"We are redundant," Pascal said.

"So you've no work?" said Georges.

"No work," said Etienne.

"No work," Pascal said kindly, and smiled again, and shrugged. Lauren and Hind passed by the doorway. The little girl was brushing her teeth and peering up at Zakarian and into the living room. Georges noticed Zakarian then and there was a brief awkward moment as he turned and tried to let the Armenian in the doorway, but there wasn't room with the baby in his arms, and Lauren stopped too, Hind between them all, and at the small domestic impasse Leon felt a great tiredness come upon him, falling from his shoulders and rising though his neck like heavy water, an immense heaviness and futility. And he thought of waking to darkness, running along the Corniche, the silence and the sea, his ghost and the volume of rock displaced for the unfinished marina of the new Beirut that his friends were no longer security for, and he turned away from that. Where was he now? The prospect of watching a Cary Grant film with this going on was like another sentence of absurdity and noise, everyone sick and scared, like being security for an empty amusement park with no power. All the impotence. Take a deep breath and hold it, they say when you cross what's left of the Beirut River near the Karantina abattoir. Take a deep breath and hold it.

We will always be here.

Leon slept. As the shooting in West Beirut began to quiet for the night, as the storm prepared to break. Piles of tires, to be "set ablaze," as the hacks would write in twenty-four hours, were gathered and heaped in the middle of streets as close to the Christian East as Marina Towers and St. George's. A memorial poster there to the Christian martyr Basil Fleihan, killed with Hariri in the assassination, was defaced, and Leon slept. The earth revetments on the airport road were doubled in thickness by Hezbollah flunkies and piously piled, and the strategy meetings of the three parties primarily concerned as the rout of the Sunni continued. Future Movement's Saad Hariri sat in conference isolated in his palace at Koreitem, his middle-class chino-clad base home, sipping tea and counting U.S. currency and deploring all this, as his pseudo militia, Secure Plus, abandoned the southernmost of their offices and fled through the empty streets. Hezbollah moved lithe and free along the Corniche Mazraa. Guerrillas trucked in over the Mountain from Baalbek were debriefed, and they communicated freely too, planning the operation via the contested private telephone lines whose attempted suppression by the government was the purported cause or excuse for all this. The Druze in the foothills watched closely the Sunni capitulation, having had reports of those trucks of Hezbollah, and reports of three guerrillas in Hezbollah tigerstripe walking the perimeter of a Druze village in the lower Chuf. Knowing their leader Jumblatt was besieged in Clemenceau in Beirut, they knew they would be next. And last of all: The bloodied old men of the Christian Phalange, backlit by flashes of the thunderstorm coming down the Mediterranean, strolled the roof of their east Place des Martyrs HQ with their big bellies, their secrets, and their basements, and stared west across the civil war wasteland and the Roman ruins, watching very, very closely.

3 Let your face talk

Leon woke. The movie had started. Coming up in the gentleness and dim to smiling faces turned to him. Emmanuelle had arrived, sitting beside him, so tall, so lean, and the others, all there, attentively round, and Etienne held out to him a little crumpled joint of hash. He took it in the spirit in which it was offered and had a gentle hit. The displays were mirrored, and on the TV black-and-white images, cartoons, of witches and a city, an arched-back cat and a fat watchful owl, wine and a jack-o'-lantern, and then a message in English and in French underneath.

This is a Hallowe'en tale of Brooklyn, where anything can happen—and usually does.

"Hell-oooo, Leon," whispered Emmanuelle gently and smiled—she looked different, her short hair shaved even closer.

Lauren and Georges faced the TV, Pascal and Etienne were lying on the floor. Etienne said, *"He's a madman,"* as Leon took the hit, and then, *"We have mirrored displays.... You were snoring, habibi...."*

Zakarian sat alone on the single armchair beside him and Leon passed him the joint. Zakarian seemed strange now, too tall, Herman Munsterish, foreign amongst his friends in this room. Directed by Frank Capra, the caption read, over bats pouring from a cathedral. Black and white flickered over the faces of his friends and this stranger and they seemed to move with the images on the TV.

"I need a drink," he said huskily, and Etienne lifted an Almaza from the floor and pushed it to him across the coffee table

without looking. He drank deep and Emmanuelle smiled and past her Lauren stared hard at the TV as if to scold him. In the dim and changeable light on the poster the little dog leered and in the room behind it he saw green eyes now, and how the mirror was divided into vertical panels too, over that room. So there were several layers to this picture, a print of a painting of a mirror within which nested three or more realities.

The film changed, a close-up of a face, a baseball game, unsubtitled, a man barking out at them, total absurdity as they all calmly watched and even as he felt this he felt the mediocrity of it, the stupid film, the garish music, the calm watchers of a barking American man and then a frenzied crowd of black-and-white Americans from 1940-something while a kilometer away in the border neighborhoods a part-time guerrilla with an AK-47 poured fire from a corner and a poor Sunni woman separated from her son crouched behind a retaining wall and slapped her thigh with her hand again and again in a muscle spasm of panic and horror at the sound, and screamed at her little boy to stay down.

He rolled over sideways in the corner of the couch, listened, a fight starting onscreen between two baseball teams and then everyone joining in, and Emmanuelle's hip was touching his. The hash's effects rolled sluggishly in, his eyes swelled, he squinted up at the poster.

"Leon doesn't like old movies," someone said. And then the music went soft.

Boy, I could sure use a drink, said a voice in English.

Looks like the same suckers get married every day. The soft laughter of the watchers came late, by a few seconds. They didn't speak English as well as he.

What's he hiding from?

Two by two, they come they go, hip-hip hi-yay!

Elaine Harper.

Mortimer Brewster.

Speak up, sonny, there's nothing to be afraid of.

I want to keep this undercover.

Love her? Of course you love her, you're gonna marry her, ain't ya?
More soft laughter seconds after.

*No, you don't understand. I don't want this to get out for a while. I'm
Mortimer Brewster.*

You're who?

Mortimer. . . !

Laughter, clatter. Some things happened, he lost concentration
over the loud braying voice.

Yes, Mortimer, a girl whispered sadly. *No, Mortimer,* a girl whispered sadly. The music changed, he opened his eyes slightly. On
the screen read: *From here in you're on your own,* and there was a
toll of a bell and a shot of a cemetery.

Leon looked up at the poster, and then he got up and walked
out onto the balcony. The soft orange of the streetlights lit the
high apartments opposite to an anti-twilight that was cast over a
two-story portrait of the Christ hung from frayed ropes. Above
that the Jtaoui hill fell away to a scree, a spangled dust of lights
from the coast to the crests of the Mountain all along the Jounieh
bay and to Byblos. He smoked and watched. A taste of salt and
exhaust. There was a constellation of lights moving on the sea—a
U.S. or Israeli warship out there; the *USS Cole* someone had said. It
was very quiet, and then a few, far-off, near-comical pops of gunfire that seemed to come from east of the city as they echoed off
the hills. He felt clear, empty, strong. He felt warm. It was strange
because he felt, for perhaps the first time since he quit his degree,
almost violent: viscid, lucid. The door opened behind him, gently
closed again. He stared into the eyes of the icon.

"I know it's bad," Lauren said without looking at him. She
moved up to the balcony rail beside him. He smiled, confused, and
grunted. "Just one cigarette?" she said and then grinned up at him.
"I know I'm bad."

"Oh." He gave her the cigarette and lit it for her and she didn't
inhale deeply enough; a little crescent glowed and died. He lit it
again. She exhaled and looked at the smoke, not the view.

"Is Hind asleep now?" Leon said.

"Finally, I think so. She was just lying in there singing to herself. She doesn't understand but then she will say strange things. She will ask Georges questions that don't make sense. 'Why don't we die?' she asked him tonight. And, 'What is under the floor?'"

"They're good questions."

They smoked. Then after a few minutes Etienne came outside too, and Lauren's brief softening changed. Something had been going on before Leon had arrived, some argument, some tension in them all beyond the obvious. Things like this usually brought them together, brought up the gentle, the quiet, the kind. But Etienne lit his cigarette and walked to the end of the balcony and leaned around to see the next apartment, then he strode back behind them, and looked down over the street.

"It's just *dead*," he muttered savagely.

"You should see Phalange HQ," Leon said. "Lots of blacked-out RVs moving very purposefully. Very far from dead."

"Doesn't it . . . doesn't it anger you? You don't get angry?" He stared at Leon, bloodshot-eyed, then, purse-mouthed, with a contemptuous *pah*, blew smoke over the neighborhood. "This . . . ? This?" He waved his cigarette at the silent and empty streets.

Pascal and Georges and Emmanuelle came out too then, the film abandoned, and it seemed like everyone was smoking tonight.

There was a sort of silence, then Georges said, "In Tripoli a funeral was fired upon. Three killed."

"Oh no," Emmanuelle said softly.

"So you're going up to the house in the Mountain?" Lauren said to Pascal, and everyone listened.

Pascal's uncle and aunt had a holiday house up in Mzaar, and, though they were Aounists, as Leon's father and sister, but as none of them were here, Pascal was going. It was a complicated and loaded thing. Hiding from the Hezbollah in the holiday house of Christians who, since Aoun propagated and signed the Memorandum of Understanding, in effect supported them. Pascal looked sort of blank, and there was a silence. Then he said, "Yes, we're just going up there for a day or two. They're family. Just until things calm down. Until they elect a president."

"A year or two then?" said Etienne. "A decade?"

"Why will they not let the army get involved?" Emmanuelle said. "Just *stop* it?"

Lauren scoffed outright, and Etienne laughed. Georges looked down and said, for her benefit, gently, "I hear they are, the Hezb, I mean, quite surgically and carefully taking over Future positions and then handing them over to the army. The government trying to control them is what has set this off."

"You've heard about these students getting attacked with sticks and chains at the LU buildings?" said Etienne.

Leon said, "That's just a total provocation and it should be ignored."

Georges said, "This is the beginning of Hezb ultimately making the complete transition from armed resistance to traditional political party proper."

Zakarian emerged from the living room to join the smoking crowd, an Almaza in his hand.

Etienne said, "By shooting Lebanese! It's that typical limp-wristed, willfully blind, defeatist, relativist bullshit that's got us where we are now." He waved his hand over the rooftops.

"Where's that, Etienne?" Pascal said.

"Fucking jobless, poor, isolated, weak, and ashamed. But with the best educations, the best libraries, and a couple of good clubs. The biggest waste of human potential while down there it's just a baby factory for their so-called resistance, their *militia*, in the slums. Look at us. We are *dying*. I'm *thirty years old*." Another silence fell between them. Give or take a few months, all of them were thirty. "We need to teach them a lesson. Show them Christian strength. Return them to their natural status in the hierarchy. Back to our shoeshiners and domestics."

There was a small collective groan, mostly Lauren and Emmanuelle and Pascal, and Georges shook his head and breathed out smoke.

"You're unbelievable," said Lauren. "You're such an anachronism. You're not *jobless*."

Leon watched Etienne's eyes—he wasn't backing down.

"Fucking Aoun. Fucking appeaser. *Traitor*. The Hezbollah are just pawns to Iranian religious primitivism. I'm a patriot. I'm a *loyalist*. We could have sold the Israelis our water," said Etienne. "We could act like a real country."

"Lower your voice and strengthen your argument," Georges muttered. They all laughed; the tension defused a little. "Leon is the one who knows about water anyway." Leon looked over the street and lit another cigarette as bearded Georges got diplomatic. "He has seen old prewar plans for dams in the Bekaa that would have provided us free power, irrigated the valley and the entire south. And still had excess to sell to Israel. Maybe even got them out of the West Bank. Or to Syria, to Jordan, whoever. And renewably. Our water and power bills are triple what they were. It's absurd. The constant blackouts. Gathering dust there right, in the water ministry? Those plans?"

They all turned to him.

"Yeah," Leon sighed. "Yes, I've seen them. Sensitive dams. They're pure genius. But they were based on a completely different political and sectarian reality."

There was a small pause. "Why didn't you graduate, Leon?" Lauren said. "Just finish the damned degree. How much do you even have left to do? The end of the dissertation? You had a good teacher and that's rare enough. Why do you just . . . " She was angry, but not so angry she couldn't edit herself. " . . . do . . . what you do?"

A great contempt; an awful-silver feeling.

"Well, they mercury-bombed the anti Lebanon aquifer, and my sister was shot to death," Leon said.

Lauren exhaled sharply in disbelief. Georges was shaking his head.

"Don't," murmured Pascal.

"I just didn't see the point," Leon said.

A long, chill silence. Leon almost laughed.

"Exactly," Etienne said in evident satisfaction, as if they were agreed.

———

It had been at the American University of Beirut in Ras Beirut that Leon quit his degree. He had arranged a meeting with Henri Fors, his professor through undergraduate and a year of honors, and his abandoned dissertation's supervisor (as if anyone cares about honors dissertations, anyway, he thought now), and his friend, a friendship he hoped or really felt he'd half-achieved but then had utterly marred.

Henri Fors, though an LU professor based at the southern campus, spent an inordinate amount of time at AUB, where he'd graduated before the war, dealing with a department with way more clout, prestige, history, and, yes, money than his, but in terms of employment remained closed to him like a clam due to a personal thing with the head of department. It had been at AUB one fine spring day that Leon had arranged a meeting with him at a bench in the gardens. The bench sat beneath some trees and overlooked through the gap in the foliage the steep bank down to the tennis courts, the Corniche, and the strip of pure blue Lebanese Mediterranean. There was a plate screwed to the wood of the seat he chose that read ABDALLAH SALAM 1909–1999, WHO LOVED THE VIEW FROM THIS BENCH. It was one of Fors's favorite places too, he knew, and it was years ago now he'd sat beside him on that bench and told Fors he was quitting.

Henri Fors had survived fifteen years of civil war as a civilian and academic and had witnessed, too, the end of every sensible piece of water management (through graft and cronyism and the *zaim* system and simple pure corruption) in a country whose wealth and waste of water were legend. Fors had catalogued every piece of failed pollution legislation; recorded throughout the war—a terribly difficult and perilous thing to do—the heavy metal deposits at every river mouth north and south.

It had been during his time under Fors that his professor broke the news, to a deafening lack of response, of the critical state of the Sidon rubbish dump, which had grown so big it qualified as a quarter of the town, high as a four-story building, before it collapsed into the sea. There in Sidon, where destitute fishermen, receiving fixed prices from a consortium of fishmongers, were reduced to destroying their seabeds fishing with dynamite. They often lost their hands and forearms too, in black accidents they could never remember, and had to live out the rest of their days in the coffeehouses watching the backgammon while friends held cigarettes and glasses of tea to their lips as they waited patiently and futilely for prosthetics. What fish they couldn't catch now strangled in the Sidon supermarket bags. *A land still bearing the imprint of its creator.* Fors, this man who'd recorded every calamity and every disgrace with resolve and good humor and a basic human optimism either blind or profound. Leon had to let his face tell this amazing man in short that just one dead sister and one ruined aquifer and that was it, another sinkhole of a losing stream, he couldn't go on, was quitting the program.

"Well, that's disappointing, but if it's what you feel you have to do."

Lunchtime in the great gardens of AUB with Henri Fors three years ago: sitting side by side on the old bench, their feet on the foot-worn and polished stones. The breeze had moved quietly in the trees and he had heard no traffic and nothing but the wind as a muffled shuffle in the leaves and all had seemed for a minute possible, before he said the words: substantial yet weightless: asylum and study, a future, endeavor and peace, as students and teachers strolled behind. He had imagined a man he never was and now would never be, a man engaged with the rock and water of his country, a man who made an imprint on that land, who was a repository of its past, its ills, and its potential, a man excited by the parsing of a problem. And he had been there that day to tell Fors it wasn't going to happen.

"Well, that's disappointing."

It was about money, it was about family, dead rivers and sisters and lost jobs. It was about his mother bent over Keiko's coffin with her palms upraised. About his father screaming in the bedroom. It was about a ball of lead in his chest he carried through the streets that seemed sometimes to crack and lighten, in places like that, on that bench, looking at that special view in the fluttering light of the trees' fantasy—but outside in the real world it found its form again. He called it reality. U.S. destroyers and Israeli Sa'ar class warships passed through that gap in the trees, cruising off the cape. As he had told Fors it was over, but not why, the beloved man seemed to be receding from him: Leon no longer, suddenly, could quite make out the features of his face, wrinkles that had once revealed facts to him like Fors's love of swimming, his long hours, reddened eye rims, and the cigars he loved and gave up. The professor receded and assumed a strange and human, vulnerable form, in mismatched jacket and trousers, a shining brown bald spot that seemed ready for some wound, chunky brogues, five foot tall, standing over there, walking, vanished, gone.

Leon's film, his only film, a film he made—*un film de* Leon Elias, *produit par, réalisation, musique, son, montage, montage son* Leon Elias and *avec* extras plus Keiko Elias or a photograph of her at least—was made after her death, after he quit Fors and university, with a borrowed camera and an old Compaq laptop and pirated Final Cut and Logic Express learned on the job. He called it *In the anti Lebanon* and subtitled it, after a poem by an Italian suicide named Cesare Pavese, *Death Will Come and It Will Have Your Eyes.*

His film was about his family and his sister and their history though he hadn't really intended it to be. He hadn't intended it to be well-received either: to secure, as it did six months ago, a berth in the short experimental section of the Festival du Film Libanais known as *"Né à Beyrouth"*—born in Beirut.

Cut loose from his degree, from Fors, life had gone quite silent. Leon had stayed home in the bedroom of his house of mourning and collaged: magazine photos and old *TIME/LIFE* photo hardbacks cut up and pasted on card over which he scrawled song lyrics ("those midwives to history put on their bloody robes") and taped or glued or sewed stones, cement, and tree branches. But the results weren't satisfying; he was blank in doing it and bored after and only later, finding the sheets of card beneath his bed, realized that he had been making sketchbooks for his film. He borrowed the camera from Pascal; from Pascal too he'd inherited the third-hand Compaq laptop (ca. five years old) and he learned to gently massage it into abnormally extended life: to use only ever one app at a time, to on a weekly basis faithfully defrag the disk and decant raw video to leave large tracts of the hard drive spare, like it was a sick old cow from which he'd get his milk or starve.

And what to do with a completed but hopelessly experimental short film? With a kind of contempt he submitted it to the Heritage section of the sixth film festival, which had been postponed from the year prior and its July War. The Empire Sofil Theater, the usual venue, had instead been used during the day for the children of southern refugees to make their own collages on trestle tables in the foyer, and Cannes Critics' Week films were screened for their pale insomniac parents at night.

He was informed by email that *In the anti Lebanon* was selected from only 190 submissions, and bumped from the Heritage slate. This was a selection premised on nostalgia and lament—it was dedicated to edited selections of dozens of old pre- and civil-war era 8mm family films rescued from the Sunday markets, implying to those who might have the imagination the varied scenarios of forced emigration and abrupt flight and washing of hands of Lebanon. *In the anti Lebanon* was bumped to a bushel of twenty-five short experimental works to be shown over three days in the graveyard morning slots of the festival. So, being now *un auteur*, Leon was awarded an AAA pass to all of the small festival's films and talks and seminars and lectures. After the screenings, serious, kindly Goethe-Institut and NGO staff and fest-associated friends and well-wishers—mostly, it seemed, impossibly chic and passionate women—congratulated the filmmakers and distributed information packs on film labs and script workshops, master classes and fellowships and readerships and all kinds of other ships to ports here and there: London, Amsterdam, New York. All the cultural sympathy votes and NGO goodwill hopelessly, steadfastly ranged against airburst, cluster bomb, flechette.

"There are, I think," the president of the festival had said in his speech, "very few films that capture a sense of Lebanon when there was no other war or catastrophe." When something happens, we all pick up a camera, he was saying. Leon felt his chances out there in this new world, where Lebanon meant only war and baffling religious complexity, were more or less nonexistent. Who would want a Lebanese filmmaker whose film tried to refuse coherence, let alone cognizance of what it was really about? He filled out the fellowship forms anyhow. He avoided most of the Heritage screenings and walked out of three short narrative films—at least in the experimentals he could tune out and be blank and think and be alone.

But atavistically, he wanted to hear something true. Reduced and desperate, he wanted to hear someone say something sensible, something frank, sane, and clear; to give him information. Really, he wanted to know how to live, to learn. In grief, believing no one and nothing and given this strange new opportunity he went looking—his guts boiling, chain-smoking and shy, blank-faced and angry, staring people down—for something to believe. In the stack of literature, the talks and titles were listed:

I Have No Scar, I Remember No Wound.
Towards a Foreign Likeness Bent.
Real Bombs in Imaginary Ruins.

He chose to go to a lecture in the west, held at the West Hall at AUB in Ras Beirut, and he chose it for two reasons. The first was the winning name: Witness Whores Collective presents Amr Saffari: *Since I Died Before Dying in the Interim Between this Death and the Last,* and the second was because he'd not been back to AUB since that awful day he quit, and as he would realize when Saffari said it, in his talk, aloud, *the criminal and the victim alike return to the scene of the crime.*

It turned out that the Saffari lecture at AUB had been a sort of analogical semifictional thing about vampires and violence, and he'd dreamed his way through it in a kind of agony (*the criminal and the victim alike return to the scene of the crime*) and he had left that early too, tripping on the stairs, to sit out under the trees on that selfsame bench, to feel the weightlessness, the shame, maybe to cry, to remember.

His film then, had originally been intended as anti-Lebanon; a twist on the antiwar: anti-recovery, anti-lament. The films of which he'd read and that he'd watched made by other young directors, especially do-gooding foreigners and second-generation émigrés, and the Lebanon they created—reproducing the failure of war-art; the volcano dormant or erupting; cycles of de- and reconstruction; ruined olive orchards reprised against; talking heads telling horror stories; tiny but "telling" details of trauma, judgment, and limping deliverance—he'd wanted none of it. If your Lebanese work was not about the war it was ignored outside Lebanon.

He'd made a film that wanted to be ignored, was defiant, that turned its head away. He'd sat above Rafic Hariri International Airport, with the West Beirut cape and the oil-fringed sea beyond filling the frame with mauve haze, and shot planes landing and taking off for hours. He'd shot flowers for hours and shot a photo of his sister. He'd composed a meandering story about the Japanese in Lebanon, told in voice-over from photo captions in his father's *Times Atlas of World History,* and from U.S. news reports from CBS and ABC in the '70s and '80s with their whitewashes, skews, and vicious Israeli torque. When asked what his film was about, he replied in an unanswerable non sequitur: "beauty in italics." He'd wanted it to be anti-everything obvious in grief, but somewhere, inevitably, it had slipped from his control and entered meaning. He had thought he wanted to be ignored; he got noticed.

He had recorded his friends' and family's conversations and stole aphorisms he cut into his monologue:

"With Christians, reach always exceeds grasp," someone says breathlessly at one point.

Abu Keiko intones, an attempt at humor at their dinner table, with some faux-drama, "We traded in shrouds; people stopped dying." An awful silence follows.

With venom Lauren mutters, about Aoun, "Tell him to wake up from his dream so we can wake up from our nightmare."

The large opening sequence of the twenty-minute film cut between the airport, the flowers, and the photo of Keiko Elias at twenty-eight. No uniform was shown, just her high, proud eyes hazel-brown, her fine eyebrows finely cut, expressionless, her dark hair shaved close and military. Neither beautiful nor unbeautiful—she was only a presence, completely calm; she was forceful; she seemed to see the photographer and his reasons, not his camera. Defiance would imply or connote some form of defense, some defensiveness. But she was an icon; impossible to imagine in motion.

Over her photograph, over planes rising and descending, Leon narrated selections from the books and TV shows, on the Japanese influence in the Lebanon. On the arrival of militant Japanese Red Army cadres in the early '70s, back when they were still sexy and exotic, before their utter fall from the small grace they'd gained, before the riots went bad, the murders and purgings in Japan. On the escapist middle-class beatnik hipness of the Palestinian cause to Japanese youth, and then the so-called "Second Wave," when hundreds of young Japanese descended on the Lebanon. Who were unlike those first pioneers who sought out the PLO and PFLP and trained and fought and organized and killed and died, however absurdly and futilely—as in the Lod Airport Massacre in 1972, the last successful terrorist act at Ben Gurion. Improbably, committed by Japanese—their victims: More than half of the twenty-six dead were a group of Puerto Rican Christians on pilgrimage. Leon recorded his mother telling him the massacre at Lod was lied about—that the Israeli airport security shot more than the three Japanese ever did. She said it with a little shame, though, as if it were slightly dubious or doomed, something to be looked away from. The second wave of Japanese riding in on this sudden infamy were instead revolutionary tourists—hippies—and largely assimilated as if baffled by the complexity, the changing times, sucked into the everyday, and gave up their Japanese identity, married, converted, contributed another twist to the plait of Lebanese beauty.

Leon and Keiko's mother, Junko, was a full-blooded Japanese and no-longer practicing Sunni Muslim married (in a civil ceremony in Cyprus) to an Orthodox three-time jujitsu champion of Lebanon and ex-militiaman. She'd come to Lebanon in support of Palestinians; she'd fallen in love and stayed as the wife of a Christian soldier in disgrace. The voice-over Leon chose stuck to the dry historical stuff, and dangerous pro-Israeli U.S. broadcast stuff, and over it played the soundtrack, just running water and the creak of the door of Keiko's ever-empty bedroom, opening and closing, which had sounded exactly like *Star Wars'* Chewbacca growling and had been a good joke between them as children for a long time, but that he'd treated and manipulated, sped up and down, so it didn't, and it wasn't, anymore.

So the first part of *In the anti Lebanon* was oblique, ironic, a hopelessly student film, coded for Leon alone, shot and edited in a bitter, extended blankness, a period he can barely remember, and almost bereft of any signification to anyone other than him. It was the part he most liked, for the blankness it enacted: somehow frightening to him, for all the unfrightening things it seemed to say.

Part two was what made the film popular with students, what got him some compliments at the festival, what spoke more readily in recognizable terms: Leon's satire of the local art films he hated. A car bomb near the ABC shopping mall in Achrafieh had led to the closing of Dolce & Gabbana. When they had gone, some students discovered shirts and dresses and suits and scarves left abandoned in the dumpsters behind the mall, and they donated them to the fashion school. Leon approached several patients in the serious burns unit of the Orthodox Hospital and asked them to model the clothes in waiting rooms of the day surgery unit. To his surprise, several said yes.

The third part of *In the anti Lebanon* was Leon's farewell to his degree and to a large extent a farewell to his ideals, the culmination of this, his tripartite farewell to the future. He took a bus over the Mountain and up the Bekaa then a taxi to the bombed aquifer, subject of his abandoned dissertation, origin of the mathematically beautiful losing streams of the anti Lebanon. He filmed the shining earth, the rising river's rime of quicksilver, the lobes of mercury rippling at the bottom of the poisoned cataracts, reflecting the refractions in the ruined streams above in their own slowed, dead, and deadly imitation, pulsing in a bitter sarcastic sympathy with what they lay within. It was all silver or was it all blue. Was this part of the film exactly about himself? Anyway, it ran in silence.

"Exactly," Etienne said. As if they were agreed. He dragged on his cigarette as if something had been won.

"No-oh," said Emmanuelle, smiling beautifully as if appalled, and shaking her shaven head, "that's not what he . . . " She stopped speaking. And then she turned and stared and smiled at Etienne as though her case was made.

"You're not the same, Etienne," said Lauren, and her voice was flat and angry.

"You're not saying the same thing," said Georges, and Leon saw him again as he was. Georges protected others from themselves; he did this now by keeping Lauren from speaking the truth.

Emmanuelle then abruptly stepped forward and hugged Leon; in her height her soft cheek directly against his. "Oh poor Leon," she whispered. "That was . . . so sad. . . . "

A long trail of gunfire echoed back off the Mountain. He could feel her short fine hair against his ear.

"Don't," he said very quietly. The hug was held too long—there was an awkward silence around them. They separated. Leon felt messy and hot. There was another spiral of gunfire, and they stared out east. Roughly, Leon said, "What some people think is that when your guard dog becomes too powerful you need to think about putting it to sleep."

"Yes. No," Etienne said, thinking, balancing the terms of the statement with his passion. "Yes."

Georges laughed loudly and Lauren looked out over the balcony disgusted.

"Speaking of guard dogs, Bashir is working for a Phalange MP down the hill," Pascal said. "He's gotten huge." Bashir was a Maronite from their neighborhood in Achrafieh they all knew as a kid; a bodybuilder now a bodyguard.

"See there—that's gainful employment, he's got a job that's just right for him," Emmanuelle said.

She was being completely sincere.

For a moment then, Leon let himself go, and he thought of being with her, of just trusting in her basic good-heartedness, her simplicity, her desire for children, a married life, a kitchen somewhere and a sink and a bassinet and services on Sundays (she was Orthodox too). He thought of forgiving the gentle shakes of her head and her exaggerated concentration during the TV speeches: the nodding, the way she hummed, the strange and infuriating laxity, as he saw it, and her willingness to understand, to be *understanding*, even when she was made fun of. He thought of not seeing people smiling kindly behind her in semi-disbelief when a chance remark like this showed just how much she didn't get it. He thought of wondering why he felt he had to forgive her.

And because she was long and tall and quite beautiful, and because he was angry, it was easy for him again to suddenly imagine sleeping with Emmanuelle, being with Emmanuelle. He'd for so long fantasized about her and he was instantaneously disgusted and bored with himself. Suddenly the end of years of low-grade sexual tension was there. He thought of her as a passive person, a compliant, an open and a steady person in the body and the face, right now in her youth, of a six-foot beauty, and she half-loved him or seemed to, and it had always seemed easy, picturing sex with her and her long thighs and the sensuality of her feet, as large as his own. He saw now how pitiful it was: just easy, just a relief, a lie, easier than really getting to know her, her family, convincing her to marry him, convincing them to let her, getting a life, settling down, settling.

Until payday he had about US$150. Marry *him?* A trap avoided or another door closed; it amounted to the same thing.

"Bashir," Georges said, and shook his head.

"I hate that man," said Lauren. "That awful big man."

Etienne stared at her.

"Let's get drunk," said Leon, "and hear what the new boy has to tell us."

So they laughed and they went inside and the movie was restarted but the light was left on and they drank and they talked. Something had been dispelled in that tense moment on the balcony, and then some fantasy had taken its place: a fantasy of friends discussing politics in a buzzy fug of beer and smoke, while outside didn't really matter; what you did or thought didn't really ultimately matter.

Leon let his face talk.

IN MEMORY OF BASIL the poster had read. There had been a poem to the left. *Do not stand at my grave and weep*, it began: the ubiquitous bereavement poem, selflessly secular here, and it was in English. The photograph of the martyr Basil Fleihan was from the waist up and to the right of the poem. The whole thing was screen-printed on a large canvas taut within a metal frame. It was mounted on the barrier by St. George's Marina opposite the Beirut Four Seasons, 100 meters from where Basil Fleihan was killed with Hariri and twenty others in the bomb blast that left the grand and ancient St. George's Hotel cordoned-off, hunched and drooping and hollowed out, an exhibit frozen and waiting, waiting for the UN Special Tribunal to rule, and in a peculiarly bitter further coincidence, waiting for Hariri's reconstruction company Solidere's claim on their equally ancient marina to work itself out and let them trade again. *Do not stand at my grave and weep, I am not there; I do not sleep.* Basil Fleihan was a Christian, and his face was Western. The next stanzas of the poem are lost, because the Hezbollah who that night came so far east, and built the barricades, burned the tires and slashed the poster, had followed Fleihan's hairline and torso with his knife, leaving just one arm, then dragged the blade left and hacked through the middle of the poem and grabbed a fistful of the poster and ripped it out. This left only those two opening lines and, beneath, a dangling fold of torn white canvas like revealed flesh, the blankness behind the dead man, and half the last two lines, *Do not stand . . . I am not there. . . .*

He isn't—beyond, through the hole, is the half-empty marina, the pleasure boats bobbing gently.

4 Une seule vie

"You always keep yourself apart."

Etienne said it.

"Like you think you're a peacemaker, but you don't get involved."

They were drunk now, walking down the hill from Georges and Lauren's apartment, just he and Etienne, and Zakarian staggering some meters behind. Over them the clouds swelled purple and the thunder banged malignant, rolled and rumbled like huge broken engines before the storm.

"Uh-huh," he said. "Do I?"

It was that time of a night when a certain drunken sweet spot hit. People began to say what they really thought, in the generous context of what they'd said that they didn't really think before and had gotten away with. When the smart and bored began to push the limits of what others would tolerate, and when abrupt furies and half-felt passions turned into speeches; whims turned accusations. And Leon's reaction to what he was saying was bearing out Etienne's thesis. They walked the empty streets beneath the walls of shuttered old Jtaoui mansions, towered over by bedraggled trees shifting in the uncertain winds of the coming storm and splattering the streetlamps' surreal orange light over their bodies like the shifting patterns of an elaborate tigerstripe camouflage. They both knew what they were doing: They both knew how Leon was playing the part Etienne accused him of. And knew they knew this: the odd old dance of the too-long familiar who must grow apart.

"It's alright. You're above it. But you *are* involved."

"I am not above *any*thing, Etienne," Leon said, and half-laughed. Then he had to check Zakarian behind. The Armenian was walking in a sine wave, his arms hanging, his face to his feet.

They'd played this game before—Etienne fishing for where he knew Leon's anger lay.

They'd not seen each other in a while. The security gig was part-time—soon Etienne would join his father's company, and despite his anger, Leon knew Etienne really was okay. Was set up for a life. That he did not really understand not having a future, and that he was a middle-class Maronite whose family connections would always protect him, here or in Paris.

"Why don't you just fuck her?" Etienne said.

Leon laughed and then didn't. Etienne was leaning down and leering up, grinning like a stranger, his eyes watery and loose.

"*I'd* fuck her," Etienne said. "I'd *marry* her."

"She . . . " Leon had already begun to respond before he could control this, could divert him, talk about something else that would make him just as mad. "She would never marry outside the church," he said lamely.

"Why not? I'm eligible."

"You're *engaged*, Etienne."

"Your *father* married outside the church."

"I . . . don't have any money." He felt sick and tricked as soon as he said it.

"You don't need any money. Just fuck her. Why not? If God didn't want us to get wet, why did he throw us in the ocean?"

"I think it's going to pour down," Leon said, but it was too late.

"You have to do *something*."

"We—right now—have to look after this guy," he said, gesturing piously, meaning Zakarian.

Etienne snorted. "Him—*whatever*." There was a rise in his voice. "Look—it's Bashir."

They were coming down a long sedate slope turning gently around the walls of a Phalange compound opposite an abandoned old mansion, and at the gates beyond the razor wire was a Phalange militia boy in fatigues and beside him was Bashir in combat pants and utility belt and a tight black T-shirt, and it was true — he'd grown huge. Big man before the storm in just a T-shirt, and his arms were thick and swollen, the latissimus under his armpits cartoonish, defined even under the fabric — his pectoral muscles were lit by the compound's floodlights, long and deep and immense, hanging over his tiny waist. He seemed suspended as if hung in a suit of body armor. Grinning too. He laughed as he recognized Etienne and spoke to the militia boy beside him. The boy went with his M16 into the sentry box as if sent.

"Bashir," said Etienne as if confirming the fact. "Look at this crazy guy," he called out loud. Bashir held the wooden frame of the razor-wire barrier and lifted it easily and stepped through onto the street.

"Lovely night for a walk," he said in a comically rich, deep baritone in which Leon could hear still his child's voice and remembered how not quite but almost bright he was. Leon remembered with a refreshed and tired dread Bashir's proud neighborhood stories of the size of his breakfasts; and how he'd once, at age twelve, after years of their low-grade abuse, half-nelsoned not one but two school bullies simultaneously. He had entered the new realm where force was currency and he was suddenly rich.

"Hi Bashir," Leon said and heard the tone of respect in his voice, the play old boys knew, and detested it as he detested this man but poor as he was could not afford to show it.

"Leon . . . Elias," Bashir said as if in parody of a man ruminating over a name long unthought of, and then literally nodded three times.

"Yes, yes," Leon said, fast, "a long time . . . " and then found himself absurdly holding out his hand to shake. *You're afraid*, he stated to himself, *and*, quoting his father, *like a dog you kiss the hand you dare not bite.*

"Yes, it has been a long time," said Bashir profoundly and reached out and held Leon's hand too hard and pulled him close to kiss cheeks and Leon flinched as his lips touched stubble.

What could he say next?

They stood there, the trees rippling in the wind. Bashir grinned. A ridiculous moment where, Leon knew, two dogs were sizing one another up though both knew one could eat the other like air.

"You've . . . " Leon tried to edit his obvious response, but was too drunk, " . . . become very big."

As if waiting for it and accustomed to it and seeing Leon beaten he didn't hesitate and kept his rapist's grin and said, "Yes. *Yes.*" Confirming the fact and the further facts of the militia boy, his job, his size, the Phalange, and his unspecified position within; his mystery. "What are *you* doing?"

"We've been watching movies at Georges and Lauren's," Etienne said, "and drinking large amounts."

"Who is that?" Bashir said. His tone and physical bearing changed, tensed. "Is he with you?"

They turned and watched Zakarian staggering down the hill toward them, drooped and strange, wavering over the road.

"This Armenian idiot is, unfortunately, with us," said Etienne.

They watched him cross the road and stand some meters off in the gutter. He was swaying, looking up at Leon with eyes half-closed, then down at the road again.

"A friend of yours."

"A friend of Leon's."

"A friend of Leon's," Bashir said and let that fact count.

"I just met him tonight," Leon said. "He seemed okay."

"Get him talking and you'll only want to slap him," Etienne said. "He is retarded. He repeats everything you say."

"It is a condition he has called echolalia," said Leon, feebly. "Repetition helps him understand the meaning."

They stood and watched him swaying in the road.

"Did you get him this drunk to shut him up?" Bashir said in his absurdly deep monotone. Leon remembered they'd used to make fun of his voice. Etienne laughed and Leon looked at him. Etienne knew Bashir better, and he was laughing at the banal statements Bashir took for jokes, and he was afraid of him too.

"So what is going on?" Leon said sharply. "Do you have any news?"

Bashir turned and looked at him until something ambient equalized.

"They have the west. They're taking on Secure Plus. You know that Future TV is on fire?"

"No."

"It is. RPGs and automatic weapon fire. Hezbollah teams are in Hamra as close as the Murr Tower."

"They *cannot* be that far east, surely?"

"They are."

Etienne and Leon nodded silently.

"You are the first people we have seen tonight. Though there have been firebombings near the USJ."

"I told you," Etienne said.

"Listen, I finish in half an hour, until the morning. Do you want to drink a bottle of something?"

Directing this only to Etienne, making things quite clear.

"What time is it?" said Etienne.

"Half past one now," said Bashir. "I am back on at eight but I cannot sleep. There's no point."

He was still looking at his watch and though the last words were deadpan, there was something plaintive. Leon looked closer at him, intrigued to see if Bashir felt pain, if he could see that boy, but the eyes of Bashir stayed piggy and black.

"Why not?" said Etienne. "But nothing is open."

"I have whiskey in my scooter," Bashir said. "We could go down to the Demolished Quarter, there's no one around."

Etienne turned to Leon. He computed the extra distance home, against the whiskey, insomnia, and tomorrow.

"Yes," Leon said with a sort of sigh. "Okay. But what about him?" He gestured to Zakarian, hearing something dead and distant in his voice.

"What about him? Let him follow if he wants."

—

They were halfway down the hill and entering the first narrow ruined streets of the Quarter, rue Sepile, rue Magenta, The Idler's Steps, Bashir puttering along on a squashed and straining Suzuki, the sound obscuring the gunfire, when the first fat and succulent raindrops spattered far apart with a patience and restraint that spoke of what the storm would hold. And that was when Zakarian said something for the first time in an hour.

"My workshop is just a few blocks away, in a basement. It is hard to find. But you can . . . we can shelter there."

They ran in the downpour down the muddy slick and darkened streets beginning to fill with runoff. They turned down an alley, along a long wall and there Zakarian unlocked two large wooden gates and led them into a courtyard of a dark and looming ferro-concrete apartment block spattered with bullet holes around the empty windows.

The yard was edged with swept rubble around old pots leaking dead plants. It was otherwise filled with Ottoman and prewar antique lattices and gates and doors lifted from their hinges and stacked in rows. As the rain became a deluge, Zakarian led them through the stacks of old gates to a long alleyway between the apartment block and the wall. Halfway down, the ferroconcrete met old sandstone blocks. There was an old stone archway there, gated twice, first with ancient brass bars and inside them a modern and ill-fitting garage door. The rain was growing immense, a roaring thing. They hunched in the alley and Etienne swore and Leon held his security supermarket smock over his head and Bashir wheeled his scooter awkwardly behind. Zakarian produced a ring of keys and worried at the big padlock connecting the new steel chain threaded through the old bars. He got the first gates open and there was a foot-wide gap before the rolling garage door rudely installed in the Ottoman arch. This unlocked more simply and he rolled it up, and they crowded inside the old stone archway into shelter, and Bashir pulled the scooter in sideways as easily as a bicycle.

Zakarian's drunkenness seemed to have lifted with the unexpected usefulness and a kind of competence discovered. Unless, it occurred to Leon, he'd been sulking, depressed, but Zakarian tried to stop Bashir bringing the muddy scooter onto the old polished tile of the corridor revealed within. Bashir ignored him and wheeled the little Suzuki past. They stood in a line dripping and panting in the silent, darkened hallway, the echoes of drops flat taps on the tile.

Zakarian went out to the gates and closed and locked them. Then he dragged the garage door down with a squeal.

With that an old hollow and echoing silence fell.

"Damn it," Bashir said. "Where are we?"

"It is just a couple of blocks off rue Mistral, isn't it?" said Etienne.

"Isn't . . . it . . . " tried Zakarian and Bashir's snort cut him off.

The corridor opened into a preserved internal courtyard and Leon stared up into the semidarkness. It was Ottoman. A few blocks east of the Green Line, it had survived two world wars, the fighting in 1958, and fifteen years of civil war, survived the Syrian bombardment, as little else around. As his eyes adapted to the change in light he began to see the remains of the old tiles on the floors, the mirrored writing and tesserae rendered mosaic by military boots and shelling vibration. There was a drained fountain in one corner, alcoves that once held trailing plants, one now home to a soot-stained Virgin.

"This was outside, once, wasn't it?" he said to Zakarian gently.

"Was outside wasn't it," he said, and his big eyes softened in at last some understanding, some recognized kindness. "Yes . . . "

"They built over it. Closed it up."

"Building over it. The French. In the Mandate era, my boss says. It was a compound of houses, they built the building over it into a villa, and . . . " He trailed off again searching for words.

"There are at least three layers to this."

"Layers to this, because it was bombed . . . "

He trailed off again, trusting in Leon, and they stood in silence at the edge of the old courtyard in the darkness underneath an Ottoman ceiling, Mandate-deco balcony railings at the mezzanine, and the Golden Age ferroconcrete block above: from a time when Frank Sinatra and Ava Gardner had taken taxicabs from the night-clubs here all the way to Baalbek under summer moonlight. Their sodden clothes dripped on the dusty tile.

Then Bashir's scooter fell over and something plastic shattered.

"Oh *fuck your mother*," he shouted.

"*Shhhh*," said Etienne, and giggled.

Zakarian was brightening. Leon thought maybe he'd never brought anyone here before.

"No, it's all right," Zakarian said. "The whole building is empty. It is gutted. There is nothing above us. We're the only ones here, in the basement. That is why my boss says that is why it makes the perfect workshop."

Bashir righted the scooter and lit his cigarette lighter to examine a broken indicator. In the flickering light, the Madonna's shadow in the alcove flexed and fluttered. There were mounds of candle wax downy with dust at her feet. Old rags of vines wound though ancient cigarette butts across the stone tiles, and dead ivy trails tattooed pillars up to the mezzanine galleries around. Halfway up the wall beside the alcove Leon spotted a graffito, a ghost of a dead militia. It was a slogan of Dany Chamoun's Tigers, from before Bashir Gemayel's purge in 1980 in consolidation of the Christian forces, and long before the final murders of Chamoun, his German wife, and two blonde children in 1990, machine-gunned in their beds in a mountain villa. The slogan was not quite finished—it read *only one life, only one: une seule vie, une seule . . .*

Bashir fumbled with the exposed wires of the indicator, the man bigger than his scooter. Etienne wrung out his shirt. Leon stared around him. Zakarian stared at them as if they were aliens, actors, models.

"Do you want to see the workshop?" he said finally. "We do not usually stay in here."

"I want to see that whiskey," Etienne said.

"This is going to cost me," Bashir said and stood. "I need a drink. We drink now."

Leon sighed inside and leaned back, staring up into the otherwise perfectly preserved ceiling with its puddles of black soot above the doomed militia's cooking fires. How many relics like these were really left here in the Quarter now? Three? What was the relationship between this thickset man and his need to dominate even those he considered friends and these ancient places? These places with their quiet, their urbane air of a time that did not know napalm or suction bomb, did not dream that in one hundred years politics would be conducted with earth revetments, burning tires. But Bashirs are always here aren't they, even here?

"Yes, show us the workshop," Leon said quietly and Zakarian stared right in his eyes, as openly grateful as a child.

Bashir searched in the pavilion of the scooter and as Zakarian led them back into the corridor Leon tripped, as if on a threshold, the high lip of an entrance. But in the dim he could see—there was nothing there. Zakarian continued, turning down a small set of stone steps in the near-darkness to a new steel door—he typed a code into a steel keypad and they entered complete darkness. Then Zakarian found the lights. It was a large workshop only partially underground—arched windows at head height had been rudely filled with breeze blocks sometime during the war and presumably left there for security. In lieu of natural light the lamps were many, high and elaborate, and the men blinked in their glare.

The workshop was divided in two. On one side an old red safe the size of a man sat against the stuccoed wall and two old partner's desks faced each other, one covered in paper patterns pinned to the leather, penciled outlines and sketches of rings and necklaces in huge scale, while the other desk was piled with files and pens, a laptop too, and a coffeemaker on one corner. There was a division of class and duty between this area and under the blocked windows where the workbenches were as high as his chest, with scalloped edges, one for each workman; old polished chairs sat oddly low and neatly aligned underneath the semicircles of their stations, and leather aprons tacked to the undersides of the benches to catch dropped jewels hung like crude blankets for old men's laps.

The tables were three, and catered for four workmen each—in the centers were four spindly tarnished brass lamps articulating over the bench blocks, and the tables were littered with needle files, drill bits, shears, and pliers of all sizes, and tiny hammers, calipers and rulers, cloths and pottery vessels, and there was a sort of metallic fuzz to the caramel old wood, a black static of filings and dust and grease that faded to the polished edges of the bench, and it was near-organic, fungal in contrast to the gleam and shine of the low polished chairs. There were newer things too—aluminum filing cabinets underneath, magnifying glasses, loupes and mandrels, head visors with brand names stenciled upon their brims, new rubber tubes leading to butane torches, and amongst it all, one to each station, a rabbit's foot.

Against the near wall beside them and the door, jewelers' smocks hung from hooks, high-collared and white as if this workshop practiced the strange rituals and awful pointless resections of a caste of passionate surgeon-priests. Etienne went straight over to a table and picked among the tools. Leon walked carefully between the two areas of the workshop. Bashir clumped down the stairs with a bottle of Jack Daniel's in his hand, picking at the perforated strip on the bottle neck's black plastic sleeve. Zakarian stood and watched them in his sanctuary, a little proud, a little scared, as if he might have made a mistake.

"What is this?" Etienne held up a rabbit's foot between finger and thumb. "They are everywhere."

"They are—they are everywhere," Zakarian said worriedly, "please do not, please put that back—because we each have, had them each one for a long time—for burnishing the silver, it is traditional—that is Mahmoud's—they are each—"

"Okay, okay." Etienne dropped it on the bench.

Bashir popped the cap off the whiskey and it spun into the corner of the room. As he drank, Zakarian went to find it, then he said, "So what is this place? Who is Mahmoud?"

"It's a jewelry workshop," Leon said. "He makes jewelry."

"Jewelry. God help us. Do you make a lot of money from that? Can he make me a cross? Make me a cross," he said. He drank again, and then he exaggeratedly burst air from the base of his throat, and then he belched. "Or I bet you only make jewelry for rich Gulf Arabs. Not for anyone who *lives* here. Who *cares* about the Lebanon."

Etienne took the bottle and drank too, watching Zakarian crouched in the corner searching for the cap. He held the bottle out to Leon. And the whiskey was good, sweet, smoky Jack Daniel's, and Leon drank deep. He watched Bashir flick through the tools on the workshop tables with his thick finger, push them into a pile. Zakarian came back with the bottle top and held it out to Leon, eyes pleading for something.

Leon gave him the bottle.

"Show us the Peri, Frederick," he said. "The one you told me you were so proud of."

"The one told me so proud of," said Zakarian, and he was too eager to please, too easy, and too easily pleased. He drank some of the whiskey, smiling, and passed the bottle to Etienne.

"What's a Peri?" said Etienne.

"It's a set of jewelry he's working on," said Leon. "Tell him."

"Tell him," said Zakarian, eyes rising again.

"Jewelry," said Bashir, and made a sound.

"Tell him about it."

"About it," Zakarian began, and warming to the theme, "this set is named after a figure in Persian mythology . . . " and he repeated the speech word for word and Etienne glanced at Leon and rolled his eyes and Bashir drank.

Zakarian came to the end and Etienne said, "Well show us what it looks like then." Bashir, excluded somehow, said nothing, and Zakarian seemed to come out of a reverie of half-remembered, tipsy, slippery, and complicated words. Gently, Leon said, "Show us." Zakarian smiled slowly as he understood what they meant.

He went over to the large safe. It was brick red with two immense hinges and two brass-colored circles high on the door, a keypad on one, a semicircular latch and handle on the other. He entered a code and the electronic lock hissed quietly.

Inside were several drawers rising the height of the safe, each front panel and handle made of polished dark walnut burled like shining desert topography. He pulled a lower drawer out in a practiced manner, right hand on the handle, left splayed beneath like a waiter. He turned with it in his hands and he laid the drawer down on the partner's desk, then turned back again to close the door of the safe. They gathered around the set.

Inside the drawer, arrayed on black velvet: a simple necklace, two earrings, a bracelet, an anklet, two cuff links, in matching white gold inlaid with diamonds. There was a strange long silence. Zakarian frowned down at the set, standing alongside them but facing them rather obliquely. Another seemingly practiced or trained position as a waiter stands patiently by a customer reading a newly offered menu. The necklace was a fine chain with a simple clasp and five large diamonds spaced around. The earrings were round diamonds in plain settings, near deco in their hard edges. The cuff links two nearly crude squares of white gold, the beveling almost rough, a dark burnish at the seams of the metal lustrous and deep like mercury; the diamonds set in the center likewise crude-seeming, old, disquietingly fine. There was further silence until Etienne and Bashir simultaneously lost interest.

They turned away and Zakarian looked after them, some strange violation of the ritual. Clearly his part in this act was unspeaking, and he seemed not to understand they were not customers. He looked after them, his eyes fixed middle-distance, a little reddened with the alcohol, and his beard and hair still wet with the rain. A pallid disheveled dyslexic in a T-shirt pretending to be of service. Then he looked back down at his creations, trying and failing to make the equation between this audience and his art.

"They are beautiful," Leon said lamely. "Descended from fallen angels."

"Hmm?" Zakarian looked up vaguely. He concentrated on Leon. "Descended from fallen angels," he repeated. And then he understood. He thanked him, and again it was in that practiced and distracted manner, that mien of service and restraint. Leon watched him, wondered who had trained him, who used him for this work, maybe filing away his wages, taxing them hard, and Leon was holding the whiskey, so he offered it to the echolalic.

"I only drink whiskey," Bashir announced. "Whiskey or gin. Beer will make you fat. I have got to stay in shape. Got to take care of myself." He touched his stomach and touched his chest. He prodded with three fingers at his pectoral thoughtfully, as if feeling for cancerous growths. "You can work with a whiskey hangover, because it makes you sharp. It keeps you mean."

Zakarian took only a small sip and passed it to Etienne.

Etienne drank and sighed. "Who's fat?' he said at last and laughed. "Come on, who's fat?"

"You, your sister, your mother, and your fiancée," said Bashir.

Leon laughed and Zakarian looked at each of them wearily, warily, baffled. "Who's . . . fat?" he repeated, trying to understand.

"Fuck your mother," said Etienne. "I'm not. I'm lean."

"Right now you are, but after thirty, a desk job, unless you work at it," said Bashir, and drank again. "You'll get fat."

Etienne considered and there was a pause. Leon could see him looking at Bashir's chest and composing a riposte, putting it discretely away. Leon laughed at him, and at this Zakarian laughed too.

Etienne turned on the echolalic. "Shut up—" he turned back to Bashir, "—*retardé*," and Bashir laughed, staring at Zakarian, as the whiskey seemed to center him. Leon watched as it happened right there in front of him; the whiskey coming on, the goofy boy in Bashir disappearing inside, the act of his new adulthood augmented by the drink.

Zakarian looked at each of them, his eyes now brightening again with this new half-understood camaraderie. "*Retardé*—" he said as if beginning a sentence. Etienne interrupted with a loud false guffaw.

"*Exactly.*"

"Exactly—"

Bashir was watching them, assessing them from far away.

"I am—" said Etienne slowly, nodding.

"I am—"

"Useless and *retardé*—"

"Useless and . . ."

"*Retardé.*"

Bashir started to chortle.

"*Retardé*—"

"Stop it," said Leon.

"Stop it," said Zakarian. He was watching the laughing faces, Etienne and Bashir, laughing, and at his reply Leon laughed involuntarily too.

"Who's fat then," Leon said to divert them. "Politicians."

"Hariri, may God forgive me, was revolting," said Etienne. "No, really. The size of his suits."

"Henri Boutros," said Bashir.

"Yes."

"Why are there no fat French politicians while there are hundreds of fat Arab politicians?"

"Israelis then. Ariel Sharon," said Leon, "was immense. There are those stories of him conducting his tactical briefings always on the ground floors. He couldn't get up stairs he was so fat. A wartime general. Lieutenants running up and down to the observation posts to tell him what was going on."

"Down to the—down the—" said Zakarian. He was getting visibly excited, trying to join in and articulate his thought.

Bashir imitated him again. "Down the di-duh-di-duh."

"He was tough though. People respected him," Etienne said.

"Not his own people," said Bashir. "The settlers celebrated when he went into the coma."

"The coma . . ." stuttered Zakarian, " . . . there was that story, that was—"

He was looking at Leon, trying to engage. They passed the bottle and waited for him to continue. He looked at each of them as if his story were finished. Finally, Etienne sneered and then sighed.

Zakarian tried again. "When he met Elie Hobeika during the Sabra and Shatila massacre, there was that story . . . "

Zakarian was eagerly staring right at Leon, and Leon began to feel uncomfortable.

"What's he saying?" Bashir said. "Leon?"

"I don't know."

"Because the Israeli HQ was on the roof above the camps . . . but he couldn't get up there . . . "

"Oh. In the Israeli invasion," Leon said. "1982."

"In the invasion what?" said Bashir. He was getting flushed.

"In the invasion what—" said Zakarian.

"*You*, shut up," said Bashir without looking at him, and held up his hand. "Just *shut—up*. Leon?"

It went very quiet and all of them were looking at Leon.

"The story goes," Leon said. The ground was very treacherous here. He suddenly realized how little he knew of Bashir's politics now, and how vehement they might be. How much his namesake Bashir Gemayel, and his death, the death of the Christian king, and with him, the better part of Christian hope, might mean to him or those who named him. Did Bashir even believe it was Phalangists in the camps? "The story goes, or went, that in 1982 the Israelis were headquartered on the top of a building right next to the Sabra camp. . . . " He reached inside his work shirt for cigarettes, but there weren't any left. "And the . . . massacre had started . . . "

"Massacre? So you are talking about the massacres of Christians by PLO? At Damour, and at Chekka and Mtein?" said Bashir.

"Massacre—" stuttered Zakarian.

"Shut up. What massacre? Why do you use that word?"

Leon stared into Bashir's eyes and saw all his glad resolve. Leon said, his tone flat and hesitant, "And they called in the Phalange to explain what was happening in the Palestinian camps. Hobeika was called in to see Sharon, but if Sharon could have just got up the stairs, he would have seen himself—"

"Seen what?"

A pause. Leon retreated.

"Seen inside. Seen into the camps."

"Yes? So?"

"But he was too fat so he couldn't."

"What massacre?"

"And . . . that it was only after this that the Israeli soldiers were ordered to start firing flares over the camp, because night had fallen, only so they could see what was happening. . . . " Now, trying to extricate himself, he realized he had made it worse. "Just . . . what was going on. It, it's said. Not to illuminate the scene or whatever . . . people said . . . you know, to kill more people . . . not to . . . *help* . . . "

"Help who? What?"

Bashir turned to face Leon squarely now. This was almost beyond control. Leon found himself completely lying. "So . . . the flares weren't to . . . lighting up the camps was not to . . . they were just only to help so the Israelis didn't . . . take sides . . . between the Phalange and the locals in the camp, because . . . " And then he gave in utterly and took the Phalange line. "Because some gunmen in the Mekdad family, some locals . . . were firing on Phalangists . . . firing on your men . . . "

Then, Zakarian, distressed and misunderstood, shaking his head, interrupted, tried to speak and he said, "The camp . . . were firing on your men . . . no . . . no . . . " and Bashir turned to face him.

"What did you say?" said Bashir.

"What did you say?" said Zakarian.

Then Bashir punched him in the middle of the face. Zakarian fell abruptly down as if he'd been turned off and his head hit the corner of the partner's desk with a quiet, hollow, fleshy sound and his neck crooked and he fell to the stone floor. He lay sidelong as if he were asleep. But his eyes were wide open and white and rolled up and his hands were in his lap.

It was very quiet for a long time.

"Oh, Jesus," Etienne said.

Bashir looked at the man, completely still on the rough stone before them, then up at each of their faces.

"*Yes.*" He went and leaned over Zakarian with one arm up, then straightened and turned back to them with a huge grin. "*Yes.* See that?" He mimed another punch; pulled it back. "*Bang.* One shot." Another pretend punch, slow and dramatic, as if in front of a mirror. "*Yes.*"

Adrenaline was silver as the river inside Leon, flooding him utterly, warm and singing.

"You fucker," Leon said. "You stupid fuck."

"Yeah?" said Bashir. Then he came right up to Leon, leaned down an inch from his face, and stood wider and taller than him, pulsing lightly on the balls of his feet, refined down to a monosyllable. "Yeah?"

"*You stupid fucker,*" Leon said again. "You . . . " he said, and then, "you stupid—" and in that moment, he heard the fall in his voice, and not striking Bashir at his most powerful, not striking, fighting him and dying, something in him crumpled slightly and it was seen and understood.

Bashir smiled into his face, leaned down closer. His nose was almost touching Leon's, his eyes to his eyes, no longer saying anything or needing to say anything; all dialogue over, pure power, he breathed whiskey tainted with him into Leon's face: sick and meaty, gamey, different to the taste in Leon's mouth.

And so Leon pushed him back. He stepped away from him, and then he walked away, circling him, to Zakarian on the ground.

"Oh," Etienne finally started up. He hiccuped, a gasp, then he laughed. "My God. That was *intense.*" He was full of some glee. "Like, something. Like just like in the *war . . .* "

Bashir turned and said, "Give me a cigarette."

Etienne fumbled in his pockets.

"What have you done," said Leon flatly, looking down at the man.

Bashir didn't need to say anything.

Etienne lit Bashir's cigarette and then he lit his own.

Then Etienne said, "He had it coming."

———

As drunken men do they did nothing, and then something that made only partial sense. They stood around for too long and stared at the boy and they finished all the whiskey in their different states of mind waiting for him to rouse and they smoked a joint of hash and they soon became very drunk and very high and it was then they found he wasn't breathing and Bashir made a plan. They would drop him up in the mountains by a road. But no one had a car. They argued in monosyllables and then in monologues. Flashes of a seeming pragmatism spoke profoundly. Etienne spent ten minutes wiping workbench tools he may have touched, and refused, point-blank, to ride the scooter. Bashir was too big to ride double with anybody else; it fell to Leon. He would carry the body through the empty streets and leave it in the west where responsibility could be deferred, the consequences displaced, the casualty mergeable with all those others; an accident, lost to the Hezbollah or a chancer high on hashish. They picked Zakarian up and took him to the doors of the workshop and then they put him down again. Bashir went and searched for the plastic remnants of the whiskey bottle's sleeve. They took the body out into the vestibule and then they put it down again. Leon began to move as if in a dream, in abrupt and inebriated flashes, wormholing through space and time, floating through the disaster, appearing in stages of the plan. The workshop roof's vaulted arches span around him, dreamed, and fell. Any purpose seemed a solution. At one point the men stood around the safe and pulled and speculated and entered codes, but it remained silent and unmoved. So Bashir took the necklace and the earrings, Etienne the bracelet and anklet, Leon was given the links. It seemed to make sense, and there was no capacity beyond what was required to do this action now to start another plan. Etienne even, in a stroke of selfless, mindful brilliance, volunteered to dump the drawer.

Outside the rain had stopped and Leon climbed upon the
scooter and Bashir lifted the body on the pillion behind him, and,
when some string proved inadequate, wired the body's wrists and
forearms together tight around his waist with coat hangers from
the jewelers' smocks. Then the head drooped back and the entire
thing sagged and dragged and began to fall until they wired the
body's belt loops to the pillion and feet to the foot pegs. It was
Leon then, floating in a purposeful haze of metastasizing disaster
that seemed to present its own imperative (solve *this*, now solve
this) and obscured any wider thought, discrimination, or alterna-
tive, who tried to ride in the courtyard through corridors made of
all those doors and the body's head fell back and pulled him to a
halt and the solution was to unwire its belt loops and retrieve the
helmet from the pillion and put it on the body and lean it down
on Leon's shoulder who then had to lean sideways to keep it
there, but the added weight kept the body forward and it seemed
to work. He sat in the courtyard with the body on his back while
Bashir and Etienne closed up the workshop, and though it was
possibly silent, it was just a dream, flashes of the pressure around
him, the wired hands in his lap, the metal dome against his cheek,
and they were able to make the entire awful stupidity inevitable
and ignorable and unreal. As drunken men do.

And the others appeared again then staggering red-eyed and
Bashir threw the keys away and Etienne swore at him but couldn't
articulate why he was angered, despite his complete conviction
that this was a stupid thing to do, and the burled walnut drawer
with its black and empty velvet tray dangled from his hand and
Leon couldn't turn around completely to see what they were
doing, hissing at each other. And then someone exhorted him to
go and then he seemed to go, wavering along the empty street
incredibly slowly, stopping and planting his feet and trying to
carry the weight of the body on his bent back on the unfamiliar
scooter and figure where he might be.

And the solution was, of course, speed.

He leaned under the body and followed the street west in a
hallucination of smashed sandstone, despoiled campaign posters,

closed shutters, wilted box trees, and orange lights that seemed to go forever and suddenly dissolved again, a darkness then emerging abruptly from rue Nahr Ibrahim by the Banque du Liban ATM and he came into the open. He was back below Gemmayzeh and the Place des Martyrs but all soldiers by the Phalange HQ were gone. The ring road down toward the sea was empty; George Haddad was empty. He could see up to the Kuwaitis' apartment where his father worked and for several insane seconds or even minutes he computed two choices: to cross into the west or to get help here. Some vestigial and nurtured part of him spoke loudly to not ruin this—he could picture Bashir but could not picture his father, who remained obscure to him, a shadow.

He rode out on the empty motorway and crossed four lanes and rode under the overpass and joined the ring road west, where he began to see that the thought of traffic seemed to be of *hiding* amongst traffic until he made himself think, *No the traffic will see*—it was a deliberate effort to understand this—and then the thought prompted the very sane thought that *just one car and you are dead, man* and so he mounted the curb onto the meager footpath where it seemed as if this could be less conspicuous, but the potholes and mess of the unfinished path slowed him down and the bike was jolting and jerking and the helmet was banging against his head, and his neck was crooked and hurting and the weight became immense and he realized how this was part of the same awful thought-trap that was associated with anonymity in traffic, how stupid this was, and for a partially sober instant saw himself as if from afar, leaned at forty-five degrees beneath a body, on a scooter puttering and weaving over the gravel on a little blasted sidewalk by the expanse of utterly empty four-lane highway, and saved himself, rejoined the road and picked up speed, his only chance to not be seen; to be lucky.

And this spur of sanity spurred a further instinct for survival and adrenaline competed with the whiskey and hash in his bloodstream and Leon tried to sit up straighter on the Suzuki, and he realized then, began to see or comprehend that the future existed and comprised, up by the marina under the unfinished Hilton, soldiers or worse, and that there was only one option and it had almost been missed: to cut a diagonal though the empty quarter of the Downtown redevelopment, amongst the skeletons of the unfinished resort hotels and the new souk unbegun, where no one was and there was nothing to guard, and to get the thing up to Bachoura or Zoqaq el Blat, west, further west, to somewhere under frightened curfew, somewhere tentative and teetering, plausible and liminal, a shifting threshold, and he concentrated hard, his back erect and leaned, and gently negotiated the corners though the empty streets and around the empty blocks, wasteland vacant lots where the souks once bustled earning paltry rents as car parks now, with individual spaces in the rubble marked by breeze blocks set on top of empty plastic drums, and the concrete barriers all around and the sedate slope up Avenue Suleiman Frangieh appeared before him empty and easy, Future TV up there, a danger area, it was working, he could see it all, see the future, and so he crashed.

The scooter simply skidded on the gravel and the body moved and again as if in a dream, a magical transference from man and body and bike moving in storm-cleaned night in long straightaways and abrupt shivers and straightenings to Leon sliding on gravel facedown, a massive weight around his back and stomach stopping their forward movement quite fast and the arm around him in fact protecting him somewhat until he tunneled again to find himself lying there tethered to the puttering scooter by the body, looking at gravel rash on the palms of his hands, just lying there.

His elbow was humming and numb, warm and distant. He looked down at it—a tickling drop of blood was running down his tricep. The elbow itself was crusty with blood and stones. There was a sting that was far-off. He lay there.

But it could not be impossible to move. This was not in the realms of what was permissible. He managed to get back on because one of the feet had come undone but Bashir had done a proper job with the hands and they stayed tied, so he hoisted the body on his back bent double, straddled then righted the scooter with just one hand and he got back on.

And he was up the avenue and the elbow was turning very cold and beginning to stiffen and he was passing the last dead and empty synagogue of Beirut then under the shadow of the scarred and disemboweled Holiday Inn and then he dissolved again and was passing under a sign that read ENTRANCE ENTRANCE ENTRANCE and moving though some dark and empty and thrown-stone- and cartridge-littered streets in Zarif or Patriarchate or any-where, a ghost city, who knew, near even the Corniche Mazraa, when the face of the body bit him on the neck.

This time there was no crash and it probably was the alcohol but the pain of the thing's biting was gristly and sharp and also distant and allied with the shock of the fall so he rode though it for it seemed several dozen feet—the most important thing was not to fall again. He came to a controlled halt, stopped the bike, and then over his shoulder punched the thing's face several times, his knuckle hitting soft then hitting helmet, and it bit again and this time harder and it stung and went deeper, a popping sound or feeling in his neck that suddenly got desperately deep and he punched again and then he rolled violently and writhed in the grasp of the thing they had created and he fell over deliberately, twisting so as to topple over sideways upon and hurt and stop the thing, and he hit the ground landing on its arm and this dislodged the biting helmeted head and he pulled up its hands and wriggled away over the concrete like his sister palming herself away from her disappeared foot and he scrambled up, and the thing just lay there inert and still, wired to the scooter in a position absurd, all tied up and crooked and ruined and wrong. He stood and held his hot neck looking at the fallen boy and then knew that someone else was there.

Standing down in the middle of the road was a man; a man wearing a black ski mask, in combat trousers and a T-shirt that read HOT HOT HOT, his face three pale blurs in the darkness, holding a samurai sword. Leon stared at him, swaying. He stared at his blurred face in the middle of the empty, littered street in the ruins, and the silence, just the blood thumping in his neck. The man didn't move, he stood there, feet wide apart, the sword hanging from one hand to the road. Leon waited for what seemed a very long time, watching the figure. Slowly, he then, too late, it seemed, crouched down by the body. He unwired the remaining foot from the foot peg and pushed the leg away. He righted the muttering Suzuki. He checked the street again. The man had still not moved. Leon got on the scooter and revved the throttle and skidded in a quick small semicircle, around to the way he had come, and then rode back down the hill, away, without looking back. When he did look back he looked back only once, in movement and at some speed, maybe fifty feet down the road. It was then he seemed to see that up the hill Frederick Zakarian was standing by the man in the ski mask and Zakarian had no helmet on and he was watching Leon go and as he watched Leon go his lips were parted and his teeth were there and dark and *he was hissing something* and then the scooter wobbled furiously but Leon held on and turned back and didn't look again and accelerated down the hill, east, away, home.

5 Under the promenade

The old house was very still. He lay in bed a long time, his hand on the bandage on his neck. His whole body ached. The light through the traceries of the windows was unbearable and bright but it was mercifully quiet. In a daze he rolled slowly sideways and groaned. His ribs seemed deeply wounded and he was forced to breathe in shallow inhalations; exhalations long and slow and controlled. He didn't move his arm. The elbow had stiffened completely. Even his teeth hurt. He reached to the bedside table with his other arm and saw two glasses of water. Only then did it occur to him he had made it home. That he had been so in another place he had poured two identical glasses of water for this hangover. He rolled slowly back and turned ninety degrees in the bed and curled into a quarter-circle like a tiny animal and seemed to sleep again.

In a dream that was given then Lauren was there. They hid together from camouflaged police in a video store with only a few video cases left on the thin shelves. A voice came from a blurred head on the TV screen suspended high in the corner of the store, and it asked of the viewers, "See? See?"

He heard the phone ring and church bells ringing out far away, whether in the dream or in reality, he could not discern.

———

He woke again when the light had shifted off the bed. He sipped a little water, held it in his mouth until it absorbed into the dry flesh of his tongue, and circulated it over his furry teeth and clotted palate, and swallowed.

From the living room he could hear a sound—a flat slap—every few minutes. Just like that: *slap*. It was late. He felt somewhat better. His ribs ached and his neck hurt badly and the palms of his hands felt raw and pocked but his legs felt all right. He attempted to bend the elbow through the stiffness, and it let him until the tightness gave way to a sting. This was enough to feel slightly better. *Slap*. A car passed outside. The light had turned the terra-cotta haze of afternoon through the tracery and the flimsy toile of the curtains. *Slap*. He lay in bed and examined his palms. They were grazed and one held a geometric dent colored deep purplish blue. He turned his head into the pillow and breathed deep through the linen and he remembered.

When Leon entered the living room, Abu Keiko was sitting on the sofa in his undershirt with several newspapers laid out before him on the coffee table. He held a damp tea towel with which he was slapping dozy flies as they settled on a distorted rectangle of yellow light from the balcony window. The rectangle of light extended to his sandaled feet across the scratched hardwood lines of the footprint of the old breeze-block barricade, built across the balcony doors during the war.

Abu Keiko turned to see him as he opened his bedroom door, and turned again to watch after he passed behind and went into the kitchen. Leon took the breakfast tray of hummus and olives and hard-boiled eggs from the old Kelvinator and put it on the kitchen table where there was fresh bread. Then he left it there and poured coffee from the percolator and then he went back into the living room and sat down in the armchair. There was a long silence and he sipped the coffee. Abu Keiko turned the page of *L'Orient-Le Jour* to a large photograph of a child holding his fingers up in victory signs in front of a mound of burning tires.

"Look," Abu Keiko said. "Tires, they write. But not burning. Not set on fire by orphans and idiots. Tires *blazing*. These hacks."

Leon sipped the coffee. Abu Keiko tensed and reached for his tea towel.

"Papa—"

Slap.

"Papa, please."

Abu Keiko looked at him and grinned.

"Brewer's asthma?" He turned the page of the newspaper and sniffed. "Smells like whiskey. Were you drinking whiskey?"

"Papa."

"All right, all right. Yalla." He laughed deeply in that distant, self-contained way he had when he disapproved.

"Can I see the news?"

Abu Keiko laboriously and ceremoniously raised the newspaper open and high as if showing it to some guilty observer outside the window, rebuking the world. He shook it briskly, realigned the creases, and folded it down onto the table. Then he shuffled out the inner section and folded the front and rear section precisely in half and passed it across to Leon.

Leon sighed shakily. A long silence then as he frisked through it all, knowing it was futile to look. But here were mortars and shooting in the Chuf. Here was Future TV gutted by the fire. Here were posters of the Syrian president pasted on the walls of despoiled Secure Plus offices in Ain el Tineh.

Slap.

"Papa, *please*."

"*Pardon, encore pardon.*" He bowed slightly, grimly grinning. "How is your headache, then?" Leon concentrated on an article. The words sunk in and out of focus, seemed to recede, merge with, and disappear into the grain of the paper.

"I'm fine," he said what he hoped was briskly.

"What happened to your neck or I suppose I am not allowed to ask?"

"Nothing."

"Of course."

Leon got up and went to the bathroom.

"Do you hear what Jumblatt is saying? He is the devil's cabana boy."

Leon closed the door and stared at himself in the old flaking mirror. He was as pale as the paper. His eyes were red and hunted. The bandage on his neck—a pressure bandage of self-adhesive gauze the size of a wallet—was rucked and crooked and one corner was peeling up. He pushed it down again and the burst of pain was intense and deep and ran down into the crest of his chest and up inside and behind his jaw. He gasped and breathed deeply and concentrated on the pain, on the wound, and on himself.

Then he didn't have to look at it or think about how it came to be.

From outside the door: *slap.*

"Leon, are you working tonight?" called his father.

Leon turned on the taps to drown it out and drew himself a bath.

"When Christian turns upon Christian," his father was saying, "that is the hardest. This? This is nothing." They were sitting at the dining table with Leon's uncle Joseph. "Nothing. But when Christian turns upon Christian they become deaf, as Leon's poet says, 'like an old remorse, or an absurd vice.'"

Junko was in the kitchen preparing dinner and what would be his father's late and meager supper and Abu Keiko was in uniform. He was sipping a Pepsi. He was on a twelve-hour shift tonight.

Joseph had come for dinner and sat in the fourth and empty chair at the dinner table. There were four more stained white polycarbonate seats for guests, rarely used now, and kept down in the basement closet with the weapons and the old mortar. In the closet there were also three AK-47s and a thousand rounds of ammunition in crusty boxes, their labels flaking like pastry. All that was left from his arsenal—there was a time before Leon was born when Abu Keiko sold an AK a month to feed his wife and young daughter. In the basement shelter too were couches and a daybed, covered in dust sheets, old whiskey bottles from before Abu Keiko gave up drinking, and there were Christmas lights and candles.

At the table Leon sipped a glass of water and unfolded and refolded a damask napkin. Joseph always became quiet and measured and smiling when Abu Keiko held forth. They all knew the old man was getting his energy up for a long, cold night out in the open, so they let him talk; hold forth. Joseph studied the tablecloth, smiled at Abu Keiko occasionally, smiled at Leon, and studied the tablecloth again. Dinner was breakfast: hummus and olives and bread, augmented just a touch with sardines in oil and coriander.

"Most of these troublemakers are just children," Abu Keiko said. "They use the children for the silly business."

"Yes," said Joseph patiently. "Just teenagers."

"Teenagers should get second chances. Men can only buy them. Leon," he turned to his son, "if you only knew, before—people were happy! People smiling. Now no one laughs, no one smiles."

"It is hard to smile when you're bashing yourself in the head," said Joseph.

"Hezbollah are for the people and I love them, but they are too frisky."

Joseph was looking at Leon too. "I saw your son today," he said. Leon looked up. Joseph was talking to his father but he was looking straight at him. "He was walking Place Sassine with a big Spinneys bag full of shopping and a long, sad face."

"Today? No," said Leon, confused. "No, I don't think so."

"You looked like an actor who had lost his movie."

Leon felt a momentary high panic. "No, I . . . that wasn't me."

"The government is a genie. Poof." Abu Keiko made an exploding hand shape with his fist. "A genie." He had turned in his seat and was addressing them all via Junko in the kitchen. "Where are their whispers and their pale faces now? And these people whose houses we guard—this Kuwaiti with his Sri Lankan maids—they rape them, you know that?"

Junko came in, arms full of plates of food.

"Abu Keiko," she said, "not at the table with your brother and your son." She began to lay the plates, frowning.

"Yes, they hold their passports, they beat them, rape them, they pay them a pittance. One of these Kuwaitis has three dogs. One of these dogs costs one thousand dollars a month for food and doctors. Not people. Dogs."

"Abu *Keiko*," she scolded him again.

"Here in my heart is love," he said warmly and touched his chest and beamed around the table.

"Junko," said Joseph, "this is too generous."

In the kitchen door Junko turned and stood at a strange angle, and met eyes with Leon. She looked hurt by the compliment, and said, just, "No, it's all we have." She went back into the kitchen. Joseph and Abu Keiko began to tear the bread. Leon moved some food to his plate, but his stomach felt vague and uneasy, and he sipped more water. He felt an urge to check his phone for messages, or to send a message to Etienne, or Bashir, as if they were businessmen, partners. He felt better when he knew he would not.

"One *thousand* dollars," reiterated Abu Keiko to his brother, who shook his head.

"It's terrible. A dog."

"A man needs a hammock in the annex with a view of the sea. This is what an old man needs."

"Mmm." Joseph looked up into midair and began to softly sing. "*I swear on my soul, to Sri Lanka I will go. From Sri Lanka I won't return, unless I kill or die.*"

"A hammock in the annex with a view of the sea."

"When will the election happen do we think?" Joseph said.

"Politics in this country is one long and very dangerous soap opera full of lies and repetitions and clichés. Every episode's climax leads to no resolution. We are in season fifty-eight at least, and few of the original cast remain. Apart from those grizzled old men—like me—who are typecast and cannot get another job."

Joseph snorted derisively—Leon could see him trying to steer Abu Keiko away from somewhere maudlin. "Who would employ an old liability like you?"

"Of course, indeed," said Abu Keiko, pleased, and serenely scooped hummus with a cone of rolled bread. "Junko, *ma belle*." She came out with a small bowl of salad and sat down and smiled at Leon. "*Ma chère*," said Abu Keiko. "Delicious."

"I'm ashamed to offer so little," she said, and smiled at the two men eating.

"Not at all, not at all," murmured Joseph. They ate in silence for a while. "And so what happened to you?" said Joseph. He gestured with a piece of bread at Leon's neck.

"We are forbidden to ask," said Abu Keiko solemnly.

"Oh, then a love bite. This is why the shopping. It was some gift—she is a fiery one."

The two men laughed and Junko laughed too and she ran her hand up Leon's shirt and scratched his back the way she always did, and Leon finally relaxed a little and let her, and ate a couple of olives. Abu Keiko was leaned back in his chair and he contemplated the table for a very long time and then he leaned forward and looked very intently at Joseph, then Leon, then back at his brother again.

"In the Lebanon," he whispered, "in the old days, there were many types of people. We came, after much bloodshed, to understand that only half of the people were normal people who could be relied upon to always tell the truth. The other half of the people, we discovered, were vampires. They *looked* like normal people. But they were vampires, and vampires never tell the truth. And what made everything more difficult was that after a time, a terrible time, half of the normal people became insane because of the situation and began to uncontrollably lie. And what made it even worse then after this was that after a while, a terrible, terrible while, half even of these vampires too became insane. These vampires were lethal but they told the truth. It was terrible and complicated. You see, normal people don't tell or believe in lies. But those who are vampires and the insane — everything they spoke and everything they believed in was a lie."

There was a silence. Leon's eyes felt wide and he was nauseous again. His mother's hand had slipped from his shirt and she sipped her tea.

"Yes?" said Joseph. "Believe it or not we're paying close attention."

"But who could tell, in those bad old days, when you spoke to someone or when you heard that someone speak, if anything, *anything* they said was true?"

Leon had a sudden, vivid memory of his father. In the memory he was in this same mode: playful, portentous, mock-profound. His father was slowly separating his thumb in two, just visible behind the screen of his fingers, hissing in pain though clenched teeth until he relented as if in defeat to this agonizing effort, and slowly returned his thumb and magically melded the joint again. All the while Leon and Keiko screaming, a silly trick made wonderful, with that hissing, with those clenched teeth.

"How could you tell between a person and a vampire? Or if a person was normal or if they were insane and spoke and believed in lies? Or if then a vampire had gone insane and spoke in fact, believed the truth? How could you tell?"

A long, long silence fell and Joseph studied the table and gamely tried to figure it out.

"You couldn't," said Junko, with great mock-sadness, barely distinguishable from the real. "Not *ever*. It's awful."

"No," Joseph said slowly, "You could ask him trick questions —"

"Could you? It would take time? Several questions?" said Abu Keiko brightly. "Suppose he was armed? Suppose he threatened to bite? Suppose you had only one question. Suppose your question to all those people of the Lebanon was, 'Are you to be trusted?' What would the answer be? Leon?"

Leon's neck was throbbing and his throat was dry and he took another sip of brackish warm water. "'Are you to be trusted?'" Leon repeated.

"Yes. 'Are you to be trusted.'"

"They would all say yes," Leon said.

"Ah." He nodded, pleased. "They would *all* say yes, wouldn't they?"

"So?" said Joseph. "Yes, I see. What do you ask then?"

"'What do you *ask*?'" said Abu Keiko.

"What do you ask?" said Junko. "How can you know?"

"My God," said Abu Keiko and suddenly he rose from his chair. "See how much time has passed. I must be off to work."

"Oh," said Junko and Joseph together in great mock-disappointment and fell back in their chairs laughing.

"Perhaps with time and experience you can parse this complex situation. Tune in to next week's episode. When all will be revealed. I promise. The government *promises*."

"Buffoon," said Joseph.

"No, a cruel man. A wicked man," said Junko, and she turned sharply, smiling, to Leon. Her face changed abruptly when she saw what he looked like.

"There are no real vampires," he said. His stomach heaved again and he turned sideways away from her and threw up three olives and a great clot of transparent bile in a pool on the floor.

He was put to bed—or did he just return to bed—and that night Leon dreamed hard and deep. He was inside a vast, empty hospital, with a rumor of evacuation having gone on while the structure was still under construction; the air of a set not quite broken:

the neglected empty wings and crushed and empty cigarette boxes lying on the floor, unfinished doorless elevator shafts, a massive auditorium with no seats, just wide shallow terraces descending to a vacant dais, dust and offcuts of fiberboard lying scattered everywhere.

He passed through this auditorium and out and under a broad, new, elevated ferroconcrete promenade leading to the beach. Over rocks he climbed and down under the promenade where there was an empty, man-height space hundreds of meters wide and lined with brand-new concrete barriers to no apparent purpose but frustration, lines of them like hurdles stratifying the space between here and a fine line of blue sea out there. Wires and tubes hung from the promenade's raw concrete underside; trash and rubble littered the ground. As he began to climb the first barriers, an old woman walking a dog passed him by, and the dog barked at him, and its bark said the English name *Neville*.

At the edge of the sea on the littered beach a fight began, with professional villains, or perhaps police or worse: *deuxième bureau* or Syrian *mukhabarat*, mixed among the crowds of workers walking to regular jobs—he wrestled a knife from a villain's grasp and the man patiently offered his neck up as, slowly, so awfully slowly, Leon cut his throat and rooted around inside for a reluctant artery. It was awful, too awful, and morphed rapidly then to the hospital room where he was having sex with Emmanuelle on a gurney, him licking her as she lay back with her legs resting against the aluminum railings, their bodies draped with blood-filled tubes dangling from IV sacs that hung in superfluous numbers all about them, an orchard of blood-filled sacs for this Adam and Eve and she was smiling down at him and very turned on, and after a while he was lying beside her and his leg rested on her long maternal thighs familiarly, and she was so very long—and it was so, so hot, the bright hospital room filled with light, the debris swept thoughtfully into the corners, and they lay quietly together and watched and waited for someone to pass the open doorway, a doctor, some advice.

The dream changed down a gear: The doctor appeared, Abu Keiko, but younger, in a high-necked white jeweler's smock, impatient, desperate, distracted, and he checked the IV sacs and left again wordlessly. They began to have sex again, guiltily, frantically, and without sensation, Leon over her, but there was suddenly an awful, personal tug at his arm and a chomping sound, and his arm was whipped off by something, a flurry of his blood spattered her body and he lost balance and fell beside her, and snuggled in, an amputee, amputatedly.

He bled to death for a long time—this was in his dream an apparent fact bereft of any feeling or much consequence, and the blood filled the bed till it was hot and soggy, and he turned to Emmanuelle. She was covered in blood and she smiled at him, maternally, in pleasure, pleased this had come, and she murmured, *Oh là, très, très gentil.* Leon then rose from the bed, the job was done and the operation complete, he had to leave. He heard the words of the Dismissal as he stepped out into the corridor and under the promenade again, *To the Father and the Son and the Holy Spirit, now and forever and to the ages of ages,* and he saw it was the marina, the new Corniche, he was beneath and within the Green Line's oily debris swept down into the sea, all that bloodied earth, and he moved through it like a ghost.

6 At AUB

What is an aquifer? Scratch the back of your hand deeply with a fingernail. The stones are flesh and water rises like blood floods the pale meat of a shallow wound. Ninety-eight percent of all freshwater is stored underground. Rivers are rivulets, scripture; aquifers are the book.

He woke in his own bed to darkness. There were faint sounds of gunfire, confused in their echoes. He checked his phone and it was three in the morning. It was time to act. He sent two text messages.

To Etienne: *Hallo?*

The second was to his professor: *Dear Professor Fors*, it read quite formally. *I am in need of your advice. Might we meet sometime today?*

Within five minutes Fors had replied, *Leon, up late! As bad luck would have it, I am too. We are stuck at AUB where they were good enough to offer us beds. If the situation improves tomorrow we can have lunch in the gardens?*

The reply came from Etienne half an hour later as he lay on his bed in the darkness wide awake; but there was no message in the SMS; empty, it read only, *From: Etienne Suleiman*, the time, and the date.

He messaged Etienne back. *Message is empty.*

Leon's phone lit again. He picked it up and there was a message this time: *Hey. It's late. I saw you at Spinneys today in the frozen foods section. Called out, waved. You didn't wave back. . . .*

Leon messaged him: *That wasn't me. I haven't been out. What's happening?*

The reply from Etienne: *What do you mean what's happening? It's late. Nothing's happening.*

In the dim he messaged Etienne again: *This could be really bad.*

Etienne messaged back: *What could?*

What we did.

What did we do?

You know.

Know what? What do you mean?

You know. What I did.

What did you do?

With the boy.

Well, it was just a fight. You took him home.

. . .

Didn't you?

At AUB the trees blew gently. Fors was sitting on Abdallah Salam's bench, his feet up on the smoothed stone. Beyond him in the gap through the trees a gray patrol boat passed. It was quiet, a *hush,* a *hush, hush* as the wind moved though the branches, a spring day in May. The campus was empty, the street outside full of Lebanese Army there tacitly by Hezbollah permission. The sun shone on Fors's bald brown head as Leon approached him from behind and he seemed so small.

"Professor, peace be upon you."

He stirred and turned.

"Ah, Leon." He smiled. He looked tired, his eyes more than usually red. It was very quiet. "How are you?" he said in English and rose. They kissed cheeks, Leon leaning down to him.

"Fine, and you?"

"Oh fine, just a little frustrated." He laughed to himself and paused, looking at Leon's face for just an extra moment. "Well, here we are again. Shall we sit?"

He sat and they looked out over the sea as the patrol boat passed from view. Leon placed his foot on the marble-smooth stone and let it fall again. Fors was waiting for him to do the speaking. He made to say something small, or something about the Hezbollah taking the Druze village in the lower Chuf, sniper fire and mortars, or how relations were with the unpredictable head of department, or a question about the Litani research, no doubt suspended again, any kind of something that might amount to nothing.

"Have you heard of a . . . *Peri?*" he finally said.

Fors crossed his legs, looking up into the trees. "Now that you mention it . . . but remind me."

"It's a fallen angel in Persian mythology, something . . . " His voice seemed not his own, yet his tone entirely appropriate, as if this were another of himself, the connection between these selves this quiet man.

"Oh . . . "

"Not a . . . " The words seemed difficult and foreign. "Some kind of perversion of a Christian angel, I think, a Persio-Christian hybrid, I don't know, some kind of mistake, or distortion."

"Yes, isn't there something? Some English poet wrote a long thing called something about a *Peri?* Was it Swinburne or Rossetti? No. But some nineteenth-century poet or other wrote on the subject, I seem to remember."

They, Leon realized, were now looking directly at one another, side by side on the bench, turned to one another. This was an image of a memory: how the awkwardness between them—Fors's coolness and composure, and Leon's love for him he couldn't find a way to show—dissipated when they shared a problem or a question they could be lost within, and how these blank selfless moments were the warm, mute root of their friendship.

"Yes, I bet, some kind of nineteenth-century quasi-colonialist invention." He laughed. "Some tourist composing pseudo-Orientalist poetry in the lyric mode? Thomas? Campbell? No, Thomas Moore? That's the one. Not the bloodthirsty saint, though, ha ha. An

Irishman. With the references to Baalbeck. *Lala Rukh*. And am I remembering correctly a Gilbert and Sullivan musical too? What is it, the political one? *Iolanthe?*"

He didn't like his own construction and laughed again a little embarrassedly.

"Are you . . . " Fors tapped his brown neck and nodded at Leon's bandage. "All right?"

"Yes, I'm fine. Just . . . " Leon realized he was smiling painfully, stretched cheeks aching. "An accident. Professor . . . "

Fors furrowed his brow, a gesture too, a sign of willingness, engagement.

"I . . . " There were too many ways to say anything. A long silence.

"How is your father?" Fors said quietly, finally.

Leon sighed. "He's fine, thank you."

"And your mother?"

"Yes."

"Good."

"I'm . . . " Leon felt nauseous again, small and cold. "I'm sorry for how things have turned out."

Fors looked intently at him. Frankly, he said, "Yes. It was a pity. But it was a decision you had to make and you made it."

"Yes."

"How is the filmmaking going? Your film did well?"

"Yes . . . "

Another pause.

"I seem to remember . . . " and then he mentioned several names in the communications department, people associated with the festival, London, Tokyo, New York, scholarships, fellowships, all the other foundering ships. Leon was breathing shallowly and his heart beat high, just beneath his wound. It throbbed and the pain was good.

" . . . you may hear about that soon? Something rather grand to look forward to."

Long, slow waves from the patrol boat's wake had at last reached the mossy rocks below the empty Corniche.

Then there was some gunfire and the two men paused, looking either way like the walleyes of a wary face. It was far-off, amplified by the silence. They turned back. A long coil of fire unwound and a low thud of an RPG.

"I might be in trouble," Leon said.

Fors sat very quietly waiting for him. Leon said nothing. Eventually Fors spoke. "What kind of trouble? Would you like to smoke? I don't mind. In fact I might join you if you have a cigarette spare."

They faced each other obliquely, elbows on their knees.

"One night ago," Leon said. He gave Fors a cigarette. He lit it and then his own and breathed the smoke in deep. "One night ago, the first night of the . . . the events. I think I may have been involved in something . . . bad."

Fors smoked in shallow, cosmetic inhalations. A ladybird moved on Leon's sleeve. The birds were not perturbed by the firing or anything and sang on. *Hush*, said the trees.

"What sort of thing?" said Fors.

"A death. A . . . death, maybe."

Fors sat silent, looking, Leon could sense, at his profile, as he himself stared at the sea, feeling that he was solidifying, warm, a growing strength.

"It was not my . . . " he groped for the appropriate word, "not my . . . *doing*, but I was involved."

"I see," Fors said. He too had assumed his own dimensions, and Leon saw now in their true selves they were no longer together or connected. Fors had shrunk. Fors dropped his cigarette and stubbed it out with his foot. He stared at the crushed butt.

"What do you plan to do?" he said.

"I don't know."

"Are you in danger?"

"I don't know."

"I . . . " Fors looked up and out through the foliage. "I honestly don't know what to say to you. I don't want to recommend a course of action without . . . does your father know?"

"No."

"If you need protection, I understand your father is a well-connected man."

Leon looked up at him—was there sarcasm here? The bitterness of the unconnected, or clearly he didn't know about Ja'ja' and his sister, and the offer of work to Abu Keiko just twenty-four months after her death, as if that were an appropriate amount of time to wait, to let them grieve. Was there bitterness or didn't he know about bitterness?

"I suppose he is," he lied.

"You've considered turning yourself in."

"In the middle of . . . this, I don't know if that would be a . . . smart thing to do."

Fors contemplated this. He had receded so far; the bench, so small and confined when he had sat down, had widened, was huge; that little man down at the end, his watery eyes, what use was he to him?

"Whose is the dead man?" Fors asked. "Who was he with?"

"There may be . . . there may be someone. . . . "

Leon looked at his stopped watch, broken in the fall. The ladybird crawled inside his sleeve. *Hush.* "I have to go," he said and rose. A sparrow slipped on the smoothed stone.

Fors stood too.

"Well . . . " he tried.

Leon's eyes felt stretched and overexposed.

"Well, thank you," Leon said briskly, and turned and walked to the gates, not looking back.

7 A simple demonstration of power

He walked down the center of rue Bliss outside AUB in clear view of the soldiers ahead. Grouped around the front of their APC behind a razor-wire barrier, they watched him expressionlessly, turning like sullen automata as he passed by and through the gap in their barrier. The streets were dead, silent. He waited ten minutes on rue Clemenceau. When nothing passed he walked a few blocks to rue Hamra. All the shops' barriers were pulled down, nothing moved. A new Syrian Social Nationalist Party sign commemorating the killing of two Israeli soldiers in 1982 had appeared, its swirling swastika bolted to a NO PARKING sign. He walked another five minutes and a lone taxi passed and he hailed it.

"*Service*, Achrafieh," he said simply. "To Mar Louise. That okay?"

The wizened old driver refused to look at him and said miserably, "There's no *service* today. You have to hire the whole car. Look around you." Then he turned at last to Leon. He took a moment, weighing the potential fare against this pale, bandaged young man. "I can take you as far as Mar Louise. You'd be a fool not to. The West is not safe."

"How much?"

"Seven thousand five hundred LB."

"Come on."

The driver shrugged.

"Five thousand," Leon said.

"You must be joking."

"Six, then."

"Seven, then."

He got in the front of the car and they crossed through several blocks of the silent, deadened, empty West where the traffic jams were usually legendary, spectacular, hooting, shouting, crunching, stinking things. His phone beeped and the driver sighed, leaned wearily against his door. Etienne had messaged him again: *B mssgd last night. Wants the bike back. His number is 3 475136.* Leon sat by the sad and muttering driver and stared at the screen. Then he replied.

I can't remember where it is.

You better. He's mad. And he's scared.

And then they came to an L bend in the road turning left, and there were several different vehicles approaching. The driver sat suddenly upright, and pulled the taxi over into the farthest, deepest corner of the L and came to a halt.

In the bright Beirut sunlight there came the Hezbollah convoy down the street: three dark SUVs in front with open decks and masked and scarfed guerrillas in tigerstripe in back with AK-47s, those seated at port arms, those standing with their weapons pointed to the sky. The masked faces turned blankly and mechanically as they passed the taxi and the eyes of the faces stared in at the taxi driver and at him. The driver stared intently forward at his dusty windscreen; Leon stared at the dashboard. The fourth and fifth vehicles were white SUVs with closed canopies and tinted windows and on the passenger seat windowsill of each a guerrilla sat with one hand on the roof and one holding his weapon free. And then came three more open-topped SUVs with their trays full of small squads of four or five guerrillas, all the vehicles moving quietly and steadily through the middle of the empty streets at a moderate speed, and all impassively watching as they passed the lone taxi and its silent, frozen occupants parked facing a fence, as if it were an exhibit, a broken display in a gutted haunted house. And they kept coming in frightening numbers; the central section of the convoy comprising a loose and frayed array of guerrillas on scooters riding one-handed to keep their weapons free and pointed to the skies in a small and simple metaphor for the point of this exercise. Leon and the driver didn't move and didn't move when one of the last of these scooters with a passenger on the pillion peeled off and came toward them, pulling to a halt just meters from their car.

The two guerrillas dismounted—one was in civilian clothes, jeans and a country and western shirt beneath his webbing; the other in tigerstripe, both in Oakley wraparounds. As the civilian guerrilla approached, the old taxi driver wound down his window, and he said in a pained and cheerful, generous voice, "Peace be upon you."

The Hezbollah man replied, "And upon you," in a rich, confident monotone, and hitched his weapon upon his shoulder and bent down to their window.

Leon leaned forward to show his face and show his smile.

"Peace be upon you," he said. The Hezbollah didn't reply, and examined them both silently for several seconds, his partner standing off the front quarter of the car with his weapon held down by his side. Behind them the convoy rolled on in a steady flow of sobering numbers and sober deportment, a complete absence of horns blowing or voices calling, a queer antithesis to the usual brio and grind. Leon looked fixedly at the strap of the man's weapon where the buckle sat at his collarbone, the scuffed plastic cliplock, and above that, his small ear, his closely cut hair, and unshaven jaw. He avoided his eyes, and allowed the Hezbollah to examine him, a gesture like presenting the back of a hand to a big dog to let his scent be known.

"Where are you traveling to," the Hezbollah said as if it were a statement.

"Sir," said the driver, "I am taking this fare to Achrafieh."

"Achrafieh. What are you doing here." He said it again like a statement; a monotone of power.

The driver turned sharply to Leon, facing down into his lap with anger. "*What are you doing here,*" he said sharply, urgently. Having achieved some kind of neutral alignment, he shrank back in his seat.

Leon leaned forward and to the window, over the driver's lap, showing his face clearly and openly, his hands on his knees. The convoy continued on, scooters and yet more SUVs, most of them dustless, brand-new, engines silent, later models than the vehicles of the Phalange; blank, implacable, without relent, shining in the sun.

"Sir, I am a student. I was visiting my professor at AUB."

The Hezbollah's Oakleys returned Leon's pale, pathetic, eager-seeming face to him as his heart began to beat high, as if beating at the top of his chest, almost in his throat, the upper ventricles pumping hard, his wound throbbing with each pulse audible in his ears like a hollow *blom blom blom*.

"ID," at last the Hezbollah said flatly and without implication. Leon produced it from his wallet. *Leon Elias, Achrafieh, Mar Louise, Bldg-Albert Moujaise, Greek Orthodox Christian*. The guerrilla read it thoroughly, and hitched his weapon on his shoulder again. This mild, irritable, homely gesture touched Leon strangely then, as if watching and knowing this closely—his observation and understanding of this man's physicality, his tiredness, and total focus—might prevent arrest, detention, a shooting, a killing accidental or otherwise. As if knowing the nature of this man's body might prevent politics from happening. It was the same buckle and strap as one of his father's weapons.

"It doesn't say that you are a student." His eyes were made of Leon's distorted face, lit ribbons and blurs; Leon looked steadily back at his wavering self. The taxi driver leaned further away from Leon, into the corner of the car seat and the door toward the guerrilla.

"I was . . . I had . . . I dropped out."

"That's not good," the guerrilla said. Leon's heart was like something long and hollow knocking. The guerrilla contemplated him. Then he tapped his neck.

"What's that?"

"Uh, an animal bite."

"An animal bite. What kind of animal?"

"A dog."

"Did you get a shot?"

"Uh . . . yes."

"You have to be careful. Dogs can be dirty and carry communicable diseases like tetanus and rabies."

"Yes, you're right, thank you."

"Who exactly is your professor at AUB?"

Leon controlled his breathing. "Henri Fors."

"What department?"

"He's actually from LU. In physical sciences. Geography."

"He's *not* at AUB?"

"No. He's from LU, but he was visiting."

"Visiting."

The Hezbollah stared at the card and thought. Then he straightened and walked over to the other guerrilla with Leon's ID in his hand. As they spoke together the last three SUVs of the convoy passed and the street behind them lay empty. The taxi driver muttered something. The second guerrilla made a call on his cell phone. The taxi driver lit a thin-rolled cigarette, struggling to ignite his lighter, his fingers' skin like yellow caramel, polished, shaking, shining and hard with nicotine and age.

The second guerrilla spoke on his phone. Then he spoke to the first guerrilla. Leon watched the man hitch his weapon again and could almost feel the weight of it in his own hands. The first Hezbollah looked up, past at the receding convoy, then started back toward them. The driver hurriedly dug his cigarette into the cluttered ashtray on his dash. The Hezbollah leaned in the window and, without looking, boredly said, "You can go," and moved away again.

And the driver briskly said, "Thank you very much, sir," and started the car, and they crept slowly around the two guerrillas and the scooter in the middle of the intersection.

As they pulled away down the bare and dazzled, emptied street, the driver muttered curses, hunched at the wheel and scrabbling for another cigarette. Leon turned back. The Hezbollah hitched his weapon again, and both guerrillas looked down at what he held in his hand. Leon hissed between his teeth.

They had kept his ID card.

It had grown hot as the sun went down and the wind died and Leon stopped the taxi on the edge of the East on Avenue Charles Malek and walked up to the Jardin Saint Nicholas opposite the Orthodox cathedral. In the square of the little garden the man-sized statues of Greek goddesses had all lost their heads and their hands in the war, and they presided over the bright blue mosaics in the shallow pool, where a flat page from Friday's *L'Orient-Le Jour* lay against the tile at the bottom of the water. The paper rippled gently in sympathy with the water of the scarred old pool; the patterns of the tile beneath were visible through the newsprint. Rendered transparent, the headline read, *hallobzeH el remraséd ruop «etneloiv non érueirétxe noisserp enu» sap esoppo's en riefS hcrairtaP.*

Patriarch Sfeir does not object to "nonviolent external pressure" to disarm Hezbollah.

He walked blankly, aimlessly around the pool and over to the garden against the steps. There a little birdhouse sat at the foot of another headless statue. A caretaker sat on a polycarbonate chair in a little nave, watching Nasrallah give a speech on a fourteen-inch TV. Leon sat on a bench and messaged using the number Etienne had given him, a simple, *Hello Bashir. It's Leon.* The message came back instantly. *This number is no longer in use.* A sonic boom from an Israeli jet rolled across the city.

He continued up the avenue, past the empty blinking ATMs, the sun falling, his feet aching. Up ahead was a Deek Duke and he realized he had not eaten since yesterday. Inside were only four or five people, outnumbered by the staff, and from the door came the smell of oily chicken and the sickly stink of roasted garlic. He walked on; up ahead was the bridge to nowhere at the junction by Spinneys supermarket and the Greek Orthodox cemetery. The apartment buildings on the hill above the cemetery glowed a bright and ancient orange in the failing sun: The unfinished bridge over the intersection hulked in shade, just an archway now, the on-ramps never built, all graffitied, weeds growing from its stump, flags and faded banners drooping from its parapets. Here everything temporary is permanent.

He turned up the hill and crossed the road to Spinneys, still bustling inside despite the silent streets. Just for a snack, some fruit, maybe even just a little water. But inside the bright light hurt his eyes and he walked the depleted shelves without choosing anything. The women eyeing the roasted chickens and pastries and the precooked kebabs stared through him and through each other, totally focused on their family's menus for the next uncountable number of days, what to buy if tomorrow they could no longer leave the house. And at the deli he thought supplies of food must have been delayed or cut off or had simply run out, for Lebanon's glory was in ruins. The remaining lettuces were leathery and dry to him, and the puckered and dusty grapes full of rot. The oranges looked big and overbright and alien in color, waxy, man-made, juiceless. A man his age, two-thirds along the queue of shoppers along the deli's sloped window, met his eye, lifted his hand, and slowly waved it side to side, questioning and shy. Leon didn't recognize him — his face strange; scarred or recently operated upon; asymmetrical or swollen — but he didn't look away. Leon turned sharply left in to the meat aisle, grabbed a tray of minced kofta lamb, and paid and left.

Outside the people bussing their trolleys murmured and sighed. Off the jumble of glowing golden apartment blocks came a rumble, gunfire, or not. Then the convoy of Lebanese Army APCs came into view, grinding over the old, worn, and corrugated concrete, loud and rude, with their brutish half-turns, their broadsword of the track, and the shoppers held their ears as the APCs passed by and out of sight to take up their posts for the night.

Up above the cemetery and the church, at the roofs of the apartments on top of the hill, stone crucifi and steel television aerials glowed gold alike as they caught the last of the sinking sun.

———

Leon climbed up onto the bridge to nowhere. On top of the bridge he sat by the railing looking west into the sunset, and there he punctured the corner of the Saran Wrap on the polystyrene tray and sucked a little juice from the meat. It was thin and watery, a touch of saltiness that made his hunger rise, an awful emptiness, but then he was suddenly nauseous again, and the gray cooked meat in the dying light looked dead and revolting to him, the smell was sour-sweet and thick, and he dropped it on the concrete with a flat slap. They had taken his ID and everything was ruined. The rumble of the APCs ebbed, and no longer shielded by the sound the gunfire rose again, and it was closer now. He realized he was looking directly down the hill to where he'd ridden or he thought he'd ridden two nights ago, ENTRANCE ENTRANCE ENTRANCE, toward Zoqaq el Blat and from there God knows where. Something had to be done. He shivered slightly.

Within ten minutes he'd reached the gentle slope down toward the Jtaoui Phalange compound. As twilight came on at the razor-wire barriers of the compound coming into view was a young man still in sunglasses with a walkie-talkie and military webbing over civilian clothes, an M16 hanging behind his back. Leon waved over-cheerfully. The guard beckoned him closer with a slow flat hand as if Leon were a backing car.

"*Bonsoir,*" Leon said.

"*Bonsoir.*"

"My name is Leon Elias. I'm looking for our friend, Bashir Feghali," he said.

The guard contemplated him.

"Wait here."

He went into the sentry box and spoke on his radio. Leon waited outside the barrier.

The man came out again. "ID," he said.

"I don't have it. It was taken from me by some Hezbollah this afternoon."

"You said your name is Leon Elias?"

"Yes."

"You have to come inside," he said, and opened the barrier without looking at him at all.

8 Monsters are among us

Leon was led down along a long, winding drive, pitted here and there with plate-sized holes from the Syrian bombardments. The drive was set in retaining walls lined by jeeps and above them the gardens were old and lush and dark. At the house, rebuilt, three stories of louvered armored windows, several militiamen and bodyguards stood outside the garage doors, smoking, watching him come.

He was searched thoroughly by the first man, who then entered a code on a keypad. Inside the garage three black RVs were parked and he was taken up a pale blue carpeted staircase and into a waiting or meeting room like that of a patriarchal hall for supplicants and arbitration. It was vast and empty but for large vacant wooden chairs lining the walls, a steel crucifix on a sideboard, and great portraits all around above them: Pierre Gemayel, Bashir Gemayel, Amine Gemayel, Pierre Amine, Sami Gemayel, a fly buzzing against the glass of one of the famous men. At the far end, the Phalange cedar, the abstract: three quadrangles and a triangle atop made the tree. The guard told him to wait, knocked and opened one of the three doors in the wall opposite, and Leon had a glimpse of an office, a large desk, and a bald, emaciated man with sunken eyes looking up in tired and patient irritation.

Leon stood awkwardly in the windowless hall and waited in the scents of spice and incense and ancient cigar smoke, staring at the portraits.

"Sit. *Sit*."

A thick, throaty voice. Over in the doorway to the office a short, stocky pale man with pale blue eyes and white thick hair in a light khaki canvas suit was smiling so wide and confidently that Leon immediately sat, in the closest chair, then stood up again as the man closed the door and approached.

"*Bonsoir*," said Leon, and in French continued, "I have lost my ID card, I'm very sorry—"

The pale man's eyes closed in mirth and his head rolled back as if at the insanity and gaucheness of the proposition and he flapped his arms.

"No, no! Sit, *sit*," he repeated, and his short legs seemed to bring him across the floor very fast. Leon sat and the man sat beside him, grinning at him, looking him over, pleased and paternal, until he saw his bandage and his expression changed to one of great concern.

"*Vous êtes blessé?*" he said. "You are wounded?"

"No, no, it was just a bite, a dog."

"A dog then?"

"Yes."

The pale man stared at him intensely, grinning again, quizzical and playful.

"My name is Leon Elias, my ID—"

"Oh yes, yes, we know who you are. We know your family."

Leon looked sidelong at him, a snap-glance on an impulse he couldn't stop. The pale man nodded.

"Yes, Abu Keiko. Didier Elias. 'Didi.' Of course we know him. A brave man. He defended the pharmacy of Abu Murr in 1976. He participated in the Karantina operation with distinction. A brave and ferocious man." He sighed theatrically and looked around the vast empty room papered with portraits. His back was erect and his hands on his kneecaps. "They were special days. Years of humiliation we had suffered through. Our children . . . our children lived in the environment of war with trepidation and with all its dangers. Our children lived in constant danger of *extermination*. . . ." He added a strange emphasis on the word. Leon's armpits were wet and cold with sweat. "I am quoting there. Sheikh Bashir. It has not been put better. But you. Please let me bring you something to drink. Coffee? Tea?"

"No thank you," Leon coughed and repeated it.

"You're all right. A little pale though." He burst out laughing. "Yes, I remember suiting up with your father for Karantina. Just down the hill there! Can you believe Palestinians there? In our area? Killing our people? We were just boys, then. It went on for many days. We would prepare each evening at Phalange headquarters. Can you imagine? Young men taking back control of their neighborhood, their city, their *country*. Smoking, dressing, blessing weapons, trading stories. 'Going down to the party.' That's what I vividly, *vividly* remember your father calling it. 'Are you going down to the party?' He loved to kill Palestinians! You weren't even born. We knew we were few. If we only knew how few there would be. All those bright Christian eyes. We were just boys."

He sighed again and pondered the empty seats. Leon stared at them too, watching the man peripherally.

"But then ten years later your father made a very bad decision. He chose to side with General Aoun in a futile action, and he chose political oblivion. Now. Now there is you," he said. "What can we do for you?"

"I was looking for our friend Bashir Feghali, who works in security for the party."

"Feghali. Yes."

"That's all. I was looking for him. I know he works the gate sometimes."

"And your family is well? In these troubles? Your mother, I hope, is fine?"

"Yes, sir. My mother is fine."

"And you?" He beamed. "You're fine?"

"Yes, sir."

"Fine."

"Yes, sir."

"They are well."

"Yes, sir."

"Abu Keiko is fine."

"Yes, sir."

"And tell me what is your father now?" He smiled kindly. His tone had not changed at all. "A decadent in his pitiful boudoir? Sitting around in his underwear?"

Leon felt the ambient pressure increase.

He felt a force on his head and neck, pushing his head down, his very vertebrae compressing.

He took a second, stared at the carpet.

It was very wrong.

He could only control himself.

With a series of three long breaths he straightened his spine and stared across the room, focusing in on a flaw in the wood of the opposite empty chair.

He turned to look the pale grinning man in the eyes.

"No," Leon said. "No, that is not right. My father works for a security company."

"Ah," the pale man said quickly, and stared Leon right back with great benevolence. "I see. A security company. The son walks in his father's boots." He sighed again like a bad actor or an actor playing at one and he looked over the empty room. There was a long silence. "You know," he gestured at the portraits of the dead men, "when I was young the elders chose who was to come up. They were very old to me. It seemed unfair! I wondered why it had to be that way." He grinned. "Later I realized that without their seniority, nothing had any meaning at all."

A quizzical, sad look.

"Let me try and explain what I am trying so laboredly to say. Often, tourists who have not come to Beirut before, who have seen the footage of the independence intifada and have come to take a sip of Lebanon, will come to the Green Line and they will make an error and assume the whole area, from the cathedral to the sea and right across, is our Place des Martyrs. But the Place des Martyrs is very small. It was only a small, pretty city block. We remember it. Now there are no distinctions, just a few wrecked curbstones: first the snipers, then the artillery of decades, then the renewal—it is all conflated, all the lines are blurred—the old Phoenician village and wall, car parks and tennis courts, roads and emptiness, it is all wasteland now. One cannot see the real city without knowing the city's past. The borders and the thresholds, the distinctions are in history and they are only in the mind."

He grinned and turned to Leon.

"Are they in *your* mind?"

Leon didn't answer.

"Monsters are among us, Leon, this much I believe is obviously true, but what is their relationship to us? A provocation? A secret? A parentage? How shall we respond? How do they know our sanctuaries and how do we not know them?"

He grinned more brightly.

"Coffee? Tea?"

"No, thank you."

His grin finally faded and his eyes took on the dead quality of a pig.

"The body of our soldier Bashir whom you seek was found yesterday in wasteland near Mkalles. He had been bled to death in *ballanco*—you know this torture? Hung by the wrists tied behind his back. His arms were dislocated and broken. He had been bitten and burned. When his body was examined in our morgue, it was discovered a boiling egg had been forced into his anus. These are old, classical *deuxième bureau* methods. This is a signal, a communiqué. Now we ask you to stop mocking us."

Leon could not get enough air though his nostrils and realized his mouth was wide open to breathe. With his left hand on his knee, unconsciously imitating this man's pose, he pushed his forefingers hard and deep behind the ligament to keep his focus.

The pale man leaned forward slightly, looking Leon over.

"Antoine Harb Jewelry."

Leon shook his head slightly.

"A necklace. One million U.S. dollars. Earrings, five hundred thousand. Anklet and bracelet, four hundred thousand each. Cuff links, four hundred thousand each. We have been approached"—he sneered—"by the *Armenians* to make these inquiries. They have lost someone too. The clients for these pieces are Iranian with not insignificant financial and political influence over our Shi'a friends who so easily liberated you of your identity today. There are many interested parties. Without protection— without *representation*—you may find yourself in such a position again. Floating free. No one. Alone. Your Aounist leanings will help no one here. We ask you to stop mocking us."

Leon straightened his back.

"I would like some tea now, if that's possible, sir," he said evenly.

The pale man seemed very pleased at the opportunity.

"Of course. Call me William."

Tea was brought for them both on a gaudy silver tray and placed on a small carved table. William took his with sugar, sipping just once for the courtesy. He waited patiently now, feigning the air of a man fascinated by all human interactions and the potential of each who came before him. Leon took two sips and gently placed his cup down.

"My father," he said, "fought for us, for this country, for"—he used an old formulation—"the cedars, the cross, the cause. I know he made a choice, maybe a bad one. He made many sacrifices, and now he is old and his heart is not good."

William seemed to grow almost merry with interest.

"I don't understand what was happening in those days. But you parted ways."

William's feathery eyebrows raised and he nodded slowly as if his sympathy was great. "Parted ways?"

"He chose to marry, to raise us, to care for his family."

"A family man."

"My sister was a patriot too, but she came into conflict with"—he hesitated, edited—"she came into conflict. She took one road. I took another. It is hard now, in this country, to get ahead on the way I have taken. But it is hard for everyone."

William nodded slowly. He seemed of great cheer.

"Whatever it is you think I have done, I am not guilty of it. I am not political. I am just a failed science student with a bad job."

"You *are* quite mad, aren't you," William said softly, reassuringly. "Your sister was a bad one. What has happened to you, my son?"

"No, sir. I saw Bashir two nights ago, the first night, and he loaned me his scooter to get home. I was too drunk and I lost it. I do not know why this has happened, and about these other things, I don't know. Don't know anything."

William's face had grown grave and thoughtful, and he reached for his tea to sip once more. He leaned back in his chair.

"And your friend Suleiman. He will back up this story?"

"Yes, of course."

"A peaceful science student, a failure. Abu Keiko's son, the ne'er-do-well. Not involved."

"That's all, sir."

"This is your little story."

"Yes, sir."

"My son, if you don't start telling the truth, there are many in these events who have no history with your family, or care for your welfare. When you do not pick a side, you pick a side."

"Sir, I am telling you the truth."

"My son, we were looking for you. But you came to *us*. Not to the Aounists, not the Party of God. You were drinking beer at a British-themed pub named The Frank Gour in Gemmayzeh until the early hours of Friday morning. When you could have been home with your family, crying over your bitch sister. How you live or do not live this life is your own decision, but our comrade is dead. Where was he going? Who was he with? What is it that you want? Tell me what you know, or *I will fuck your God*."

"What—" Leon reached for his cup of tea, and then didn't. "I don't—" Bewildered, there was the stink of a dead thing, his armpits cold and clammy, sweat rolled down his stomach. "I have not been to that bar. The last I saw of him was when we walked down to the Demolished Quarter and . . . he loaned me his scooter."

William stared at Leon, all merriment and theatricality gone. His face was iron and Leon saw that he was to William as meat, something to be carved and served or thrown away.

"He simply loaned you a scooter and disappeared. Poof. Like a genie."

"Yes, sir."

"You cannot deceive me, my friend. I know too much and my horses are swift."

"Yes, sir."

"To be dead in Mkalles. A spoonful of quicklime on your tongue. How would that be?"

"No sir."

"A dog, ah, yalla—" He sighed and he rose to his feet, his thoughts visibly moving to other matters, and he patted his pockets. "A dog will always be a dog, even if raised by lions. Get out."

9 Labyrinth

There were flowers everywhere outside the Jtaoui compound, all floured white with dust from the street. They grew from cracks in the road and the sidewalk. They grew through the dagger-crucifix of an LF graffito painted over the seams of degraded mortar in the sandstone garden walls of the ancient, empty mansion across the road. The old house, built in the *hara* or old high-vernacular style, lay back in the overgrown grounds, gray and white in the moonlight, silvered with dead ivy like Abu Keiko's stubble. It was flat-roofed, high and triple-arched on two floors, not visibly damaged by shellfire; a French-Arab aristocratic family home long abandoned, dreaming vaguely, like an Alzheimer's patient, of their return.

Leon crossed the road toward the house. He started back up the hill then stopped. He turned back down the hill and stopped again. The guard's walkie-talkie crackled from the darkness of the compound drive behind, and at this Leon stepped away, into the shadow of the huge and unruly trees of the perimeter. He leaned there sidelong against the wall. Above him the twilight was finally dying, and the moon's light loped over the trees through the weary wisps of cirrus laboring south toward the Hezbollah.

Leon took a handful of flowers, purposefully crushed them into a fist, and released them. A paper coffee cup knocked and skidded loudly down the road in no apparent wind. He looked up the slope, then down, then toward the compound.

Then, in one brisk movement, he swung to the top of the wall. He paused a second there over the pitch-black tangle below, and dropped down into the garden.

It was completely, unanimously overgrown. Only the larger structures of what had once been there showed through the tangle, all dusted silver and gray by the moon. There was a vined pagoda, and the vast and fusty hump of a stone fountain producing an explosion of bastard honeysuckle. There was a series of great trees tracing the barely palpable circuit of what had been a wide path meandering around and alongside the mansion, and beyond the trees were huge mounds of dark foliage and they were sufficiently high to obscure a full third of the house.

Leon stood silently in the tangle, poised in the dark, up to his shins in thorns. No further sounds came from the compound; nothing from the house. He waded forward through the vine and branches. The great mounds were trash; the grounds had been used as a dump but had grown forth such a militant and energetic display of dirty, dusty brush and vine that the trash beneath was obscured. But it gave and subsided beneath him and here and there were alien traces: By a winding multifarious stump an old plastic lemon squeezer and boat lay, opaque with scratches. A scatter of rusty shotgun shells. A fossilized diaper. The stock of a rifle. The punctured wing of a light plane forming a sedate ramp bursting with weeds.

Cicadas masked the sound of his progress across the exploded lawns. He passed the fountain and into a deeper strip of foliage, man-high and mutated from the house's border gardens, and an eruption of white butterflies burst before him and enveloped him completely in tiny, dusty caresses. He span around, his hands half-rising, to watch the rabble split and consolidate into gangs of four and five chasing one another in drunken spirals up into the moon.

He emerged from the treewall of the garden proper and approached the house along a clearer path of crooked tiles, under a long, elaborate, and blasted Francophone arbor lined with dead vines as black and weathered as the wrought iron. He approached through the arch, passing a bucket of composted clothes pegs and dead leaves sat to one side—the arbor had been used as a clothesline.

He entered the house at the right and doorless front archway. Inside, the vestibule was completely empty and it gave onto a large gallery. In the center was a great stone bath and everywhere around a spatter of trash and inches of dust, cigarette butts and cartridges, and no fewer than four great winding staircases led up and away before him, bookended at each side by two descending. The high roof of the gallery was blackened by fire and paint hung in long dark lunes revealing pale sandstone beneath. It had not escaped the shelling. In three or more places—under the first right ascending staircase winding out of view—artillery had penetrated the interior of the house and left rough new archways in the two-foot walls. It was raw and utterly ravaged: no memory or clue to inhabitants or purpose. There was only one graffito, in small white letters, on the bath: BIENVENUE DANS LE LABYRINTHE. But there was contour and texture and peace and a great reptilian familiarity. It resembled a medical engraving, an internal space, a seared lobe, organic, complex, dead on the page. SOIXANTE JOURS SOUS LE BOMBES, it read beneath. He hunkered down on his haunches and watched the staircases as if examining the moonlight's many angles. Then he rose.

The left-of-center staircase held a smattering of burned boards and a blackened dinner knife, and he stepped quietly and decisively round the bath toward it. The sloping, winding wall above wound left, pitted regularly with small holes from which a banister had been torn. Letters in mosaic still visible on the tile: CANAL ANTÉ— Moonlight showed in the upper reaches sloping out of sight. He climbed the staircase, running his fingers through the hard flakes of burned paint, and the muted cicadas outside grew dimmer; his loud footsteps, the scrape of grit and stone. There was a landing then, and there two charred theater seats, just rusty springs and wrought iron, sat for some burned spectator to contemplate guests ascending the final flight. The stair wound up in a great and sedate three-quarter circle, and he slowed as he approached the source of the moonlight on the next floor, the brightening, the rising again of the whine and rattle of cicadas. There he walked up into another large and empty gallery, four more staircases rising to his left, another great matching stone bath in the center. And he stopped there at the topmost stair, checked back down the way he'd come, then across to the left-of-center staircase and its stack of burned boards, its black dinner knife. He walked around the bath and grinned at the message there: BIENVENUE DANS LE LABYRINTHE. SOIXANTE JOURS SOUS LE BOMBES.

Outside the triple archway through the vestibule the garden glowed and hummed.

He had come back to the beginning.

This time he chose the staircase right of center. He wiped off the tile to read CANAL POSTÉRIEURE, and he scraped his feet at the first landing to mark his passage in the dust. At the second landing halfway up the stair a dark opening presented itself, above it a bent rail and empty dangling curtain rings. Within, a pile of more burned theater chairs formed a man-made barrier to an actor's entrance, the wing of a stage. He pressed on up and entered again the same gallery he'd left—the boards, the dinner knife, the bath, and cheerful welcome. BIENVENUE DANS LE LABYRINTHE. SOIXANTE JOURS SOUS LE BOMBES. At the top of the stair he stopped and looked back down to figure the trick, where the disorientation had begun. But the curves were too gentle and restrained; from no point could he ascertain where things had gone awry. He walked out into the gallery again and sat on the edge of the bath. There was a soft growl from the vestibule and he full-body jumped.

A shadow in the doorway. A small shape. A dog.

He didn't move. After the first exploratory growl the dog waited for developments.

Leon was very still and he watched it; both animals frozen until the moment grew long. Then he shifted a foot and the dog tensed and growled again. A hollow, sloppy snarl.

"Good dog," Leon said in French.

It growled again and stopped, but something was odd—it wasn't facing him. Its small dark body was at an acute angle, in his approximate direction, but it was not facing him. Leon silently raised his arm. There was no response. He silently stood. No response. He deliberately shifted a foot loudly in the grit, and the dog growled very low and backed off a step, its back arched and tense. He pulled a cigarette lighter from his pocket and at its scrape and click the dog growled again. But in the light the little dog was the same as the dog in Georges and Lauren's poster, though this one was blind and deformed, its eyes were pale with cataracts or wounds, its teeth were mangled, a piece of lip missing, its tongue slipping in and out to lubricate the scar.

"Good dog," said Leon again. "Old friend."

This time the dog barked.

A man's voice called from the street beyond the garden wall.

"*Allez,*" called the voice. "Harold, *ça va?*"

Leon stepped back away from the doorway and the moonlight. The voice was joined by another, and the dog, caught between them, ceased its growling but did not move.

A brief conversation was held out at the wall. Then a little whistle.

"Harold, *allez.*"

The dog barked; a sloppy, urgent slur.

"*Harold,*" called the voice.

Leon backed toward the second staircase, his footsteps echoing loudly in the empty gallery. The dog barked again. There was another brief exchange of voices out at the wall, then silence, then a crunch and the crash of a man's fall into the dried foliage of the garden. Leon carefully backed down the staircase until he was out of sight.

The sounds and echoes were too bright and tinny: the crash of the man's progress toward the house through the ruined garden, swearing in French, the dog's cheerful pant. Leon had reached the blocked-up door and he stepped inside and grabbed hold of the wrought-iron handrails of the highest theater chair and tried with all his strength to lift and extricate it clean and quiet from the barrier but it was caught, welded on to another in the intense heat of the ancient awful last stand and made a noise and footfalls in the vestibule above were amplified to intense volumes and then came a voice—

"Hallo? Who is in there?"

—at the top of the stair the guard and his weapon appeared in silhouette, and seeing him the guard lowered his weapon slightly. He said, "You. How did you get in here?" but then he seemed to shiver all over, danced and rippled and moved wrong, snakelike and sexual and he seemed to reach for his crotch, thrusting his pelvis and he grunted obscenely, he gibbered and hissed and a liquid shadow spilled from his fly like a disembowelment and Leon quickly wrenched the two chairs down with a crash, and things scuttled in the darkness beyond and then the dog started barking crazily and the guard said something urgently in a language Leon didn't know and he got a foothold and climbed up, raised one leg over and through the hole, and a nasty tug in his inner thigh ripped and spread and settled and the intense stench of old burned fabric rose and enveloped him. He climbed through into a faceful of spiderweb and ash and utter darkness. He blew hard through his nose and mindless of the rip and tear at his ankles he stumbled through low wreckage in the corridor beyond, stepping like a drunken man, all deliberate strides and bizarre and contemplative pauses. He blundered down the hallway until he could no longer see the light in the hole in the barrier behind him or hear anything at all but his breathing and his pulse, and he stood on the invisible rubble in a wide, blind stance, his hand upon a banister or something that felt like one.

He listened. There was nothing. So he went on, with his hands out like a crucifixion, stepping slowly until the air went suddenly cool. He stepped on nothing and dropped and fell into the thick and icy water rising fast through his shirt and jeans up to his chest, surfaced with floating objects bobbing up into his armpits.

The angles went wrong; the smell intense, unnegotiable. He couldn't come out of the darkness, couldn't wake. The smell of shit caught and bit in the crevasse.

He waded a few steps forward. The walls had gone. He waved his hand ahead and hit his nose, a sharp pain followed by rising tears and a shudder and the need to sneeze. Following the contour of the ground, he thought he could see a shape of the wall ahead but the lines turned inky and malevolent, chaotic and fat, pockets, twists, airless and suffocating—the fear grew. The cold grew and stank of burned benzene. The silence and the shiver, the labyrinth pubic and beautiful.

He stepped forward again and struck his forehead on a sloping surface he hadn't sensed.

He stopped. This time he closed his eyes to concentrate, to listen, and to wait. The cold was there—but it would be minutes before he became numb. The laps and drips of his movement subsided. And there was nothing. He spread his hands upon the surface of the still water of the sinkhole and let himself feel it and he waited. A long but unremembered period passed. In time he opened his eyes and there was nothing. He stepped forward again through the psychotic space as if it were his own and it let him, accommodated itself to his progress gently through the thick flood, and this time there were no objects beneath his feet to turn his ankle, and the thick stink faded into a thin nothing, and he waded through the still chill water until he knew he was approaching the end of the cistern. He raised a hand as if to salute the rough stone wall of whose civilization and raised one foot through the thick water to mount the stone stair smoothed by whose feet and he climbed from the well up the stairs emerging from the water.

At the first landing he reached up to grasp what he could not see, a sconce with a dead electric bulb bent in its socket, and a spider-webbed and dustlagged wire led from the light. He followed it up the wall. The stair went left and narrowed. Seven steep wooden steps up and then he was on a wooden landing, and climbing over piles of lumber and coils of electrical wiring and then there was carpet. He was passing through a corridor, and then soft fabrics brushed his shoulders, and swung easily to let him pass, creaking softly. At the end of the corridor at last the scotoma faded from his eyes and he watched himself emerge dripping and dark through racks of suits, his reflection coalescing. A plateglass frontage floating over streetlights and the flittering sea beyond.

Stenciled letters in backward cursive on the window—*inoirB* —*dnik a fo eno eb ot*—floated enshadowed on his chest, transposed, as if an imprimatur. *To be one of a kind.* There he stood, the sodden bandage dangling from his neck and on either side of him like bodyguards for a Bcharrean warlord stood two headless mannequins on low pedestals, a male in a pale blue summer linen two-piece and a female in white tennis-business. He peeled off his soaked shirt and took the male's jacket and walked over the gray slate of the store to the entrance. Outside, a Lebanese Army APC was posted—he was Downtown, at the foot of the redevelopment, overlooking the new, unfinished Corniche.

The doors opened easily for him and he stepped out into the cool May night. A flash went off; maybe lightning, maybe a journalist's camera. Spanning the road there was, no doubt, the journalist's shot: a still-smoking barrier of burned steel-belted radials sprouting strips of red-hot metal like the fine rib cage of a metal phoenix birthing slowly from a carnage of thick and rough black rubber.

Above St. George's Marina, the despoiled commemorative poster for Basil Fleihan flapped idly. *Do not stand. I am not there.* He turned and walked through Downtown following the smoke blowing east, at last at home. Beneath the skeletal shadows of the unfinished hotels, his own shadow long on the concrete barriers. His shadow passing over the painted billboards shielding from investors the piles of concrete and drainage hose. A Banque Libano-Française poster read: *build, it's possible.* A series of artist's impressions of high shining towers over the Mediterranean showed no rebar, tanks, or razor wire but Lexuses and one-child families strolling the boulevard in bright day.

He began the long walk back, crossing the Green Line to Gemmayzeh, to Mar Mikhael, to Jtaoui, and to Emmanuelle.

10 Emmanuelle

Her nose was ugly. It was far from perfect. It was long and it had facets, a fine V and a cleft at the tip. And her apartment was as bare as her head. She shaved her dark and wild hair in the July War and never grew it back. She had told everyone the facts, appalled, obsessed, like statistics of the dead, wounded, bridges blown: Lebanese women spent on average US$200 a month on haircuts, waxings, eyebrows, manicures. It was another thing, a simple thing: It could no longer be borne. In her apartment there was a bedroom open to a kitchen and living area and it was bare but for an armchair, a yoga ball, and a credenza with a television, a cross, and above it a poster of Catherine Deneuve. She wore a cross at her neck, at her chest. She was six foot tall.

Her nose was ugly, and it made her perfect. For she had clean icy blue eyes wide and open to injury, and in the July War and now, beneath her eyes the skin was soft, tender, and inflamed. Old men on the street sighed irritably and shook their heads and remonstrated with her for shaving her hair, and called her ugly, and asked why she made herself so ugly, she could be beautiful, and she was made more alone. Her imperfection drew attention to her perfect teeth, to expressive, lush lips, to a lack of self-consciousness, especially of her looks. Her size gave pause and drew attention too; six foot, and arms and shoulders strong from the yoga she practiced alone. In the July War, she said, she slept two hours a night in her armchair, and stopped yoga as it opened her too wide and she couldn't stop crying. Georges used to say, when Lauren got angry at her, "Emmanuelle is on a different gear to you, that's all."

A perfect skull was revealed when she shaved her head. It made her face explicit and raw and she came out from behind her eyes like a nun or a saint. She lived alone and volunteered for a Christian aid agency in Bourj al Barajneh. She was patient and inquisitive with old people — crying on the steps of the Place des Martyrs monument with a meeting of the Mothers of the Disappeared after the Syrians left. She had a little dog and believed deeply in Jesus Christ and war and despair went straight through her eyes and her family was rich enough to be in Paris and campaigned endlessly for her to leave: to marry well or leave. Wars made other people tired or hungry; with her it went in without a ripple and sunk deep and glowed. Older people thought her special, angelic; those her own age thought her naive, dyslexic, touched, even a little pitiful. She would talk to Lauren about not remembering her dreams and setting the alarm to wake at strange times to retrieve them before they fully flowered and died in her singular subconscious. Lauren, a new mother then, listened and made faces as if Emmanuelle were some kind of traitor complaining of the many rigors of spying: appalled and disbelieving. Emmanuelle would never notice or not care, so wrapped inside her own mind and tending to its gardens. Once upon a time Leon saw them both clearly.

He knocked at her door. Inside there was music, and he felt and heard the faint tremors in the floor of her coming down the hall, then the clicks of three locks disengaged. The door opened and she was there in track pants and a T-shirt and unsurprised. Just as tall as him, barefoot and slimmer, more frail than he remembered.

"O là, Leon," she said. "You came." She examined him briefly, checking his eyes. There was no model or precedent; he didn't say anything. She had been crying. He half-raised his arms in a strange and robotic gesture, and she seemed to check his neck and then check herself. Then she hugged him, came into him from hip to shoulder tight and matching, her arms over him, and he shuddered. They hugged in the doorway in the scents of old wood and dust and her pulse beat fast against his neck and they hugged until it slowed.

Urgent gunfire came again, echoing through the open balconies of the stairwell, not automatic but fierce, the fire of indiscipline and fear. It rose, continued, and coalesced like dazzled applause and she winced and turned toward it.

His hands on her hips, he pushed her inside, and closed the door and it grew quieter. She pulled away from him and locked the three locks, at the base, the top, and latch, and then turned and pushed him against the wall and brought her face so close to his her breath was on his cheeks, and she seemed to examine the crest of his chest and then they kissed and he grew hard against her instantly. The smell of her was like faint tea and protein, elusive and fading. She seemed to feel him hard against her; in her height he was pressed against her pubis, and she pushed back on him.

Other sensations came, anonymous and extra-real—the light switch against his back, the clammy wet jeans, a button of his fly painful on his erection as she pushed, the creak of a flawed floorboard, and that his body was only a connection between wall and floor, an abstract thing, a piece of light. Destroy the wall, and destroy the body. They kissed and then she backed away from him abruptly.

"You're all wet," she said, and she looked down at him. "You're soaking."

"Yes," was all he could summon, and she placed her hand on his bare chest in the Brioni suit jacket. She walked away and into the bathroom.

The hallway seemed to hum, to fill up with the need for destruction, joints to rip, nails to scream and bend, ruin to transpire and vines to slither and gather and fill the walls. A roar of white noise came as she turned the taps of the bath on full.

She came out of the bathroom's sliding door, its stained glass tracery dark already with mist, and she said, "There are towels in there." She disappeared in the door beside, closing it behind her, the empty living room.

He went into the small unfinished bathroom, and there was bare fiberboard everywhere, a bath, a mirror, a simple vanity. He took off the jacket and his soaked sneakers and stripped off the wet jeans and his boxer shorts, and in the misted mirror he was just a vague and narrow pale-brown thing. He pulled the bandage from his neck and examined the shape in the mirror. There was no detail to the image. He touched the wound—there were puckers and ridges beneath his fingertips but now no pain at all. The bandage itself was clean. He dropped it in a small wastepaper bin and he was beginning to shiver with cold and he touched the water and climbed into the bath where he sat and hugged his knees like a small boy. He listened but could hear nothing but the faucet's rush. The scratch on his inner thigh stung a little. But it too was healing fast. He hugged himself until the bath filled and he warmed and he leaned back.

The living room door closed and the bathroom sliding door opened and Emmanuelle came in wearing a thin gray terrycloth bathrobe. She stood over the bath and examined him slowly. She was bereft of affect, abstracted. Then she said very quietly, "You have a body like Christ." She untied the belt of her robe and knelt down beside the tub. He sat up. The echoing of the pouring water drowned out the gunfire. They kissed again and she put her hand in the water on his stomach and up onto his chest. They kept kissing very gently, exploratory and careful like children pretending to kiss, that there was nothing else. Then he reached to touch her breast and she shuddered, and shivered, and said, "Oh you're still cold." Like she cared for him, maternal. She stood and dropped the robe from her shoulders and contemplated him in the bath. She was like marble and he saw the ribbons of muscle at her hips, saw her long nipples in shallow aureoles hardened in arousal or just in response to his cold hand. The fine dip of deltoid on her upper arms, a faint down of hair from her belly button to her triangle, the rhythm of her muscle. She smiled down at him, misled, and stepped into the bath, either side of his hips. The slip of her foot in the narrow bath made a squealing sound underwater, and she settled onto him.

"Oh, you're still *cold*," she whispered differently, and then they kissed again. He felt her pubic hair against his penis. The tiny rough tugs of skin on skin in the water. They kissed for a while and then he stopped her and said, "I can't, it's too hot."

She said, "Okay. Do you want to get out?"

"Yes."

"Okay."

She stood above him and stepped out of the bath and was paused there, her shaven scalp gray, her long back touched with moles and freckles and the high rounds of spinal column catching the light at the nape of her neck, a beauty she would never see. In the mirror he could not see himself, just her, lost in the selfless knowledge of her back and hips and ass, long, like an icon, paused in this moment, he was not there, and the faucet suddenly choked and stopped. Gunfire rose again, muffled but absolute and seeming all around. She hunched her fine head.

"The *stupid* water," she said, and half-laughed and then sighed with a tired shudder. He stood. They dried each other gently with the rough towels. As he dried her back the faucets shuddered and coughed and began to pour again. She closed her eyes and pressed her body against him and he felt in their exact height and in the bath's dissolution of her smell he was making love with himself, something innocent and primeval and religious though separate and abstract, his penis still soft moving in her sparse wet pubic hair as they toweled each other, completely asexual, an indication of sex, an image.

"You're *still* cold," she said, scolding, joking.

"I don't feel it," he said.

She took him by the hand and naked they seemed very child-like and pure and they padded through the hallway and into the living room where her little dog, invisible in its cane basket, shuffled with a crunching sound and sighed.

She led him barefoot, simple, and he saw the moles on her back, dark and rough against the skin like cocoa powder, and he saw the ripple of the flesh of her ass cheeks and he began to grow hard. Some trauma lifted and simplified: He wanted to fuck and only to fuck, and it would be okay. She opened her bedroom door and inside just windows on the eastern wall and a double bed and nightstand. A candle lit there swaying in the breeze of the door threw the shadow of the Christ-hung crucifix above the bed over the wall and stretched it till it snapped. He stopped her at the foot of the bed and pulled her round and kissed her and let her feel his erection. She kissed him and then said good-naturedly, with a kind and condescending humor, just, "*Oh*," and looked down at him for just a second and then kissed him and his hands went straight to her ass and pulled her to him and she raised one leg to let him between her thighs and then lowered it again and held him there where he could feel her pubic hair against him.

They lay down on the bed side by side and he rapidly moved his hands over her, from her ass to her breasts to her stomach and triangle, urgent and silly like a boy checking everything. She seemed patient, decided; holding his hips and concentrating on the kiss. He moved his cock to the lips of her pussy and pushed, too prematurely, he knew but could not stop, and she was very quiet, very patient, and opened her legs, drawing one foot up the blanket. Their kiss separated and he pushed desperately and she began to breathe deeper, hot into his chin.

"No, wait. Wait."

She licked her fingers and reached down between her legs and touched herself, then took him in her fist. Then she looked him directly in the eye.

"We can't do that, Leon, you know."

He didn't say anything.

"I'm a virgin, Leon. You know. I can't do that. I have to wait. I'm sorry."

Her eyes were very open, waiting for understanding.

"Okay, okay," he said. "It's okay."

She licked her fingers again and she drew up her leg and took his cock and moved her smooth and shaven head into his shoulder and cheek and pressed his cock against her. This time it felt different, stronger and constricted. He reached down to feel and he could feel her pussy above the base of his penis and he realized what she wanted and a strange sort of shock paused him there, knowing what he was doing. She wanted to remain a virgin but there was this other thing. She responded differently when he moved inside her. She was more tentative, more open and more self-absorbed, her eyes tightly closed and far away. There was a sudden strange rage and frustration—he pulled out of her and turned her on her stomach and entered her again on the awkward angle, looking down as he fucked her at her cool skin, her cocoa moles, the strange shapes and lines of her bare head. Trying to connect this sex with her beauty and her passivity, her meekness, willingness, as if he were committing an alien act on a perfect simulacrum, a body of silence and sadness, an inarticulate stranger from a darkened valley country he was not to know. It made him fuck her harder, feeling it was useless, and she said only "oh" quietly into the pillow and it was wrong not to be gentle, but that was useless too, and he stared around the room as if waiting for the vines to rise and foliage to grow, waiting for the butterflies and rust, the burst of scorpions, the mercury to swell from the stones, the alien lice in the water of the anti-land to come, the sad convoys of Christian refugees heading north filing past the ruined reservoirs sunk in Roman stone, but saw only himself in the mirror of the window to the darkened east, her body by the blanket obscured—just his face and torso and it was he, the alien thing, faint and pale and prickled with lights of the Christian East all the way up the Mountain. He fucked harder to escape the feeling and be away from it in pleasure, in that simple moment in the hallway, but the lubrication was not there and he was still hard and dead to the sensation so long looked for. He pulled out of her and wiped saliva on himself and she made a sound when he entered her again and coming to the end of something at last he came, a tiny click of pleasure and a sting, not all that was lost but all that was not found. It was a relief for it to be finished. He knew that it was not for her. He put his hand on her hip and drew her over with him as he lay down on his side, to not be abrupt, to try and be kind again. He was somehow disgusted at himself, the act. He thought to clean himself. She murmured something and reached back to pull him close to her.

Over her hunched shoulder he could see the rectangle of light of the open door reflected in the window's mirror, and a shape at its base, a darkness. He turned.

In the door her little dog had come to watch, and it was the same dog as in the poster in Georges and Lauren's apartment, the same dog as from the garden, deformed and hurt, blind and white-eyed, softly drooling, licking his lip, but otherwise sitting quietly in the doorway.

He might have fallen asleep. If anything a sort of half-doze, disturbed by the fizz of insects dying in the candle-flame, and just like fireworks the sporadic shots from afar. She was asleep and he watched her: flat on her back, facing just obliquely away, as it got very late. Her soft sounds, her shifts on the hard, strange bed. She, dreaming, was gasping or kissing, light lip flexes, urgently, testing; twitching, parting into the kiss, and out.

He woke definitively, from a dream of terrible escape, crawling through a construction site, a tunnel that narrowed and aged and clogged with spiderwebs until it was all he could do to part and pull them in order to breathe. It wasn't dread or panic; what was it? A terrific sadness and waste that this was what he had to do, negotiate this tunnel; he alone, and there was worse to come. He woke in the dark with tears cold on his temples like the arms of cold glasses, to no idea of where he was or why.

It was a strange miracle to roll over to her and to come slowly into the knowledge that she was gentle and meant no harm to him. He watched her through cold-teared eyes and then saw the shine on her cheeks. She was crying in her sleep too. He moved into her, splayed his hand on her stomach. She moaned a terrible shuddering moan as she came out of her dream, and she shuffled back into him like a weary child. He felt her shudder again, and then sigh, and subside.

He used the balls of his knuckles to wipe the tears off her cheeks. She curled up. He felt the soles of her feet on his shins, and rough skin at her heels catching in the hairs of his legs.

Then she made another sound, incidental and unsad; a bare interrogative. She stirred and slowly disappeared underneath the blanket. He felt her hand on his knee, then down to his calf. Then a little hair-sting.

She came up again and murmured, her hand on his hip, then finding his. Taking his hand, pressing it in, a gift, a reminder, from the garden, with a tiny murmur, a burr.

He slept again and had a dream he was eight years old with Keiko ten or thereabouts. Sitting on the carpet down in the bomb shelter and playing with the AKs as they were absolutely forbidden to do and had done. His had no magazine; Keiko had confiscated the boxes of bullets and kept them safe in the crotch of her crossed legs. Superior, she pushed cartridges one by one into a chipped clip, put the clip in the weapon, cocked it with a *clack-click*, leering, put it under her chin, and pointed it at him. He raised his empty weapon in defense, and then pulled the trigger to show he was at least her equal, in daring, insolence, and rage. It went off in a clap of darkness and a change in Keiko. A burble, a giggling sound, and he woke up in an airless paralyzed gasp.

Keiko, changed by death, but still around.

He lay and watched her alien head and the furthest fine peak of her eyebrow for a long time until his heart slowed again. He used the sheet to gently wipe the cold sweat from the backs of his knees; gently so as not to wake her. Then when he had calmed he watched her. The good pale skin, the bruises underneath her eyes. Another tear was forming in her eyelashes, rising, squeezing from her frail, inflamed eyelid, tentative and exploratory. Like the soft birth of some new being so sensitive and barely made and surely doomed before the hard creatures of that other land. It gave out and fell and the losing stream made a line of shine over the bridge of her nose and she wiped it away with a balled fist and another sigh and she too was still awake or nearly.

He thought, *I shall not sleep again*, and there was fainter gray at the window, and it was quiet now. What would happen tomorrow?

He thought, *I shall not sleep again*, but he did.

———

A single line of dawnlight ran down the blanket and across the floor to the foot of the door. His hand was on the cheek of her ass. The skin there cooler than her hip and his palm was dry and slid over her skin lightly and easily. He ran his fingers along the cleft between her cheeks. Down between her thighs his fingertips touched short, prickly hair and she shifted slightly and the bedsprings made a sound. There were strange mottles of light on the ceiling from the tracery of the window and he pressed his fingertips in harder and the hair was stiff and short and warm and a tiny touch of wetness deeper inside. He felt her draw her leg up. She grunted softly when he slid his finger into her. After a while of what he did she rolled over, flushed and very wet, and she pushed his fingers out of her and she whispered harshly, with her tear-swollen eyelids closed, *If you're going to fuck me, fuck me now.*

The next morning he made breakfast with what she had, eggs and toast and cucumber and yogurt. They listened to news on the radio until the blackout came. He'd drunk only coffee and they lay on her bed with the curtains drawn. "There's going to be a protest today," she said. "At the Electricité du Liban." She looked at him.

"That could be . . . bad," he said quietly at last. "I don't know. In a Christian area now. Things are very uncertain." He could hear his father in that phrase. They were talking, suddenly, after long silences not unpleasant, as if nothing had happened, as if they were like they always were—she was just interested in what he had to say. He was not. He tried to break the change, return to their future: He laid his hand on her thigh in imitation of that miraculous moment when a man knows he may. Her smoky gray-blue eyes and a smile that fit him. She didn't smile and she didn't move and watched the wall. He took his hand away. His stomach rolled. She looked down the length of his body.

Then she said, "You look really pale, Leon. O là, you look so thin," and her voice seemed filled with love and concern and she pushed the breakfast tray away. She hugged him, naked; she seemed so frail and endangered and he realized maybe he was just there, just someone to love against this.

And he thought, *I should be the same way.*

"You're not yourself, are you?" she whispered, and didn't seem to need a reply.

The power didn't come back on. But the Beirut afternoon was still, and even a little traffic passed for a while outside. She fed the dog and she came back to bed. They smoked and read.

The dog harrumphed and sighed and the cane basket creaked.

"What's your dog's name?" he said.

"Harold."

"Harold?"

"Mmm."

"I didn't know you had a dog."

"Mmm."

"What happened to him, Emmanuelle?"

"He was hit by a tank."

"Really? A tank?"

"A BTR. The one with wheels. When the Syrians were here."

They began to grow restless as twilight came. She washed dishes, and bathed in cold water. He came in to her in the bathroom and she shivered and he hugged her and her head fell, and she said, "I'm so tired . . . of holding myself in." They touched each other against the wooden vanity, and it was quick and then they sat in different armchairs in the living room as it darkened, and then he said, "I should go," and she looked up as if panicked and said, "No," and came over to him and sat in his lap and said, "Men always want to leave. Why do they always want to leave?" and he stayed.

He tried to read three-day-old newspapers, and he petted the dog and they waited for the protest and for the fighting to start again.

"I'd like to take the dog for a walk," he said.

"Are you sure?" she said.

"Just a short walk. I'll come right back."

"Okay?"

"Okay."

The dog went very still when he picked it up and affixed the leash and it stayed very still in his arms.

He carried it down the stairs, with the plastic straw she'd given him tucked in his pocket, grit on the concrete under his feet. At the street he put the dog down and it began to sniff around. Across the road a butcher's was closing up and outside the window was the last skinned and flystruck head of a red-eyed pig on a hook. Leon could smell urine and flowers and paint — and a man.

In the alcove of a door of the shuttered store next door, the thin old man, devastated and grave, in suit vest and odd trousers, stood with his hands held behind his back, assessing the street. He didn't look at Leon but watched the dog.

A rooster began to call from the backyard through the alleyway.

"*Bonsoir. Ça va,*" the old man said looking down at the dog.

"*Bonsoir,*" Leon said. The street was far too empty. A long pause. "Why," he said, "is that rooster calling at dusk?"

"The rooster is mad and has lived too long," the old man said and made a deliberate and minor gesture of disgust at the street, then reclasped his hands. "He went mad in the Hundred Days' War, in 1978, from the artillery. It's one of those things."

Leon watched the dog.

"You visit with Emmanuelle?" The old man was looking at him now. "Do I know your family?"

"My family?"

"Yes, your family. You are an Elias, no?"

"What's the lifespan of a rooster? How old can he be now?" said Leon.

The old man looked at Leon's midriff.

"I don't think of foolish things like that."

"Maybe you ought to," Leon said in a voice that did not sound like his own but like his father's, viscid, lucid, and clear, "and wonder why old things don't die at their time."

The old man looked away as if familiar with defeats and cruelty and shows of strength, familiar with responsibility. He looked at Leon's midriff again, then murmured a flat, blank good night and went back inside.

At the end of the street Leon stopped by the stone fountain papered around with Phalange posters of Pierre Amine Gemayel. The dog snuffed sibilantly at their urine-tinged paper, and sat down obediently at the sound of water. Leon dipped the straw in the water halfway, sealed the end with a fingertip, and lifted the half-strawful to release onto Harold's tongue. The dog lapped at the little trickle, but his tongue was crooked and drooped from some busted nerve in his cheek, and water fell in his fur. So Leon repeated the process four times, watching the shuttered windows, the closed-up shops, Harold's white eyes. Then he led the limping dog down the street, along a block: a vacant lot, an abandoned home, a potter's, an art gallery displaying Phoenician ships in gaudy frames and portraits of Saint Sharbel behind steel mesh barriers, past an old woman sweeping her stoop.

He turned up a zigzagging street leading up the hill, its fringes ripped up for roadworks. He passed the Phalange memorial, a stone, a plaque, and in relief a man-sized kneeling boy saluting the cedar. Occasionally on the hill the dog paused, exhausted, to sniff the ruined gutters, sniff the air, half-sneeze, and splutter. At one point Leon crouched and gently groomed him, with a finger-pad softly tugging half-hard spheres of ivory sleep residue from the moist corners of his pale blind eyes. Patiently, numbed to the world by his wounds, the dog let him.

He led him on up the slope, walking very slowly, and eventually to his left and right the old trees rose, a sandstone wall gathered from the rubble, the dagger-crucifix painted there, and then the razor wire of the compound. The dog stopped again and snuffled up at the trees toward the old mansion, did confused things: He looked back then tottered forward, turned a full circle, checked the breeze, and sneezed. He was excited by the scents of the garden.

They were on the hill above Mar Mikhael and over the rude apartment blocks the floodlit hump of the Electricité du Liban buildings hunched like an abandoned steel factory below them, above Avenue Charles Helou and out there the darkened sea. The guard's walkie-talkie crackled at the compound gates. Leon led the little dog on and the guard strolled into view from the sentry box, sunglasses on, hitching his U.S. M16.

"Hey yalla," said the guard.

"Good evening," Leon said.

"Hey, you know you're not allowed in there," he said and took off his glasses, nodded toward the mansion. Leon looked at the man. He was a young Christian boy, strong and curly-haired and aggressive, with fear and defeat and churlish resentment around his eyes. He seemed suddenly very vulnerable and Leon stepped toward him into the light of the Phalange floods. The guard stepped back and reached to the stock of his weapon.

"A dog likes a walk," Leon said.

The guard contemplated this, his hand still on the butt of the M16.

"Just the dog then. Not you this time," he said.

Leon said, "Of course," and the dog, oblivious, followed him over the road, slurping at the air as the whir and click of cicadas rose like a wide machine. He released the leash and let him into the gardens through a low hole in the wall, and listened to the soft crackles as the dog slowly nosed his way through the dried foliage.

Leon heard the guard come out from behind the razor wire then, and cross to the middle of the road.

"Hey. Hey."

Leon came out into the streetlight.

"Hey, someone said you know Feghali."

Leon watched his eyes. "Yes, I know him."

"You know what happened to him?"

"Yes."

He crossed himself.

"It's wrong. It's really wrong. He was *strong*."

"Yes."

"They don't even—they say not to do anything."

He lit a cigarette and never looked at Leon, furtively checking up and down the street. He fell quickly into confidence. He was perhaps only nineteen or twenty.

"People are leaving already." The sentence echoed in the still street. "Because there is this protest tonight, and they're saying it is a pretense. And some of them are arming in the hills, getting ready for war, but they don't tell us anything. I don't know. Hey, is your dog all right?" The dog was barking over the hum and whir of the garden, hollow and echoing.

Leon looked away over the empty sea, down the hill. "His name is Harold," he said, as if scripted.

The young guard went over to the wall, was too short, and jumped several times to see inside. "*Allez*! Harold, *ça va?*" He turned back to Leon. He was excited, distracted, impossibly young. "Is he all right? What's in there?"

"A mystery," said Leon.

The boy turned to the wall, whistled, and shouted, "Harold, *allez!*"

Nauseous, now, chill and empty, Leon watched the boy search for footholds in the sandstone wall. He took a step toward him. The dog barked again urgently.

"*Harold.*" The guard turned back to him, one foot wedged in a hole. "I'll get him. Watch the gate for a minute. I think someone's in there."

"I think you're right," Leon said.

The guard put his sunglasses back on, climbed the wall, and dropped down inside.

After a moment, Leon followed him.

All across Beirut the loudspeakers in the minarets began to click and pop. One by one the muezzin cleared their throats, murmured a muted *Allahu akbar*, began to cough and call.

An unremembered time passed. He had talked to Emmanuelle about Keiko, watching the candle tremble and hiss. He had told her a story about how at their *école* he'd had a vest like that old man's, hand-me-down and tailored for a boy, and how he always lost it, and how Keiko came home and laughed at him and sighed and told Junko and Abu Keiko how embarrassing he was, because they broadcast his loss over the loudspeaker for the *n*th time and appealed for its return, and the children of her class turned to smile at her. Why did he always go to the office, she complained. The vest was always where you left it. And he had wanted to say and explain what it felt like, that there were always two places; there was always the odd mad possibility he had conjured but which felt so real, and there was always the inevitable and eventual rude fact that coalesced, and left the vest flattened and flecked with mud in the corner of the courtyard where he could near swear he'd never been. If he couldn't remember leaving it there, was it really him that did? *Monsters are among us. This much is obviously true, but what is their relationship to us?* He left the guard in the corner of the garden on the border of the labyrinth, wreathed about with vines and flowers in a bower, peaceful, his sunglasses on and his pale hands clasped upon his chest. The protest against the blackouts and the price hikes brought good Muslims out into the streets of Mar Mikhael, claiming the Shi'a southern suburbs had their power suspended while the Christian East was left live. Behind closed Christian doors this was called *a provocation.* Two Druze villages had been overrun in the lower hills of the Chuf near the borders of the Dahiyeh, street fights, young Shi'a boys on mopeds openly armed, and a stabbing in Ain el Rummaneh. *A provocation?* Semi-unhinged single Christian men, living alone in brutalist concrete boxes on the borderlands with their rage and a shrieking TV, a simonized gun and a cross on the wall, were approached and made use of. Aries, Andromeda, and Perseus slowly wheeled across the dead guard's sunglasses. Christian snipers took positions around Mar Mikhael overlooking Electricité du Liban. *A secret.* Leon, labyrinthine, tunneled from shadow to shadow. *The criminal and the victim alike return to the scene of the crime.* Would the Israelis come? The taste of blood was hot: There was juniper, vetyver, and chypres too, copper drying down to a powder, wealth and breadth of deathless rivers in endless cycle, over centuries, aeons, untouched and untouchable: Nahr al Kalb, the dog river, collecting on its rock walls the signatures of dead empires: the steles of Ramses II, Nebuchadnezzar, Napoleon III and Caracalla, General Gouraud and *The XXI British Army Corps with Le Détachement Français de Palestine et Syrie occupied Beirut and Tripoli: October 1918 AD*; and Nahr Ibrahim, the blood river, which flows red: iron-rich soil rusting, seeding red anemones of the rebirth along its banks. The land still bearing the imprint of its creator, still running with the blood of Adonis in cascades; cataracts of rust. The march crossed the exact point on the Green Line where the Black Saturday ID checkpoints were erected once upon a time and to cross was to have your ID checked for religion and your throat cut in the passenger seat, watched over by Phalange HQ, past Makhlouf's sandwich store—his weakness, his frailty. He told her about the last shot, what he alone saw: that the assassin didn't even look as he ruined her; as he ruined him. He told her about his dream of guns. Emmanuelle came to him and she sat down in his lap and she kept repeating as if scripture, something she knew would work, *it was not your fault. She has no power over you.* A change in Keiko. She was strong. Where were the years? The vampire mourned. A scuffle broke out at the edge of the march; there was shouting and insults; a Christian shopkeeper swore and her shop window was broken and the vampire was there. Shots were fired from the dark, and the Lebanese Army moved fast up streets to chokepoints in the East, funneling the marchers back. Snipers, they said, and the vampire was there. Eight quickly dead, among them Hezbollah's liaison with the army. A provocation, they said. A secret; an omen. Shi'a blood not willingly shed darkened the street outside the Electricité du Liban, surreally lit by benzene generator, a glowing icon paradoxical in the darkness while all about the blackout prevailed. In Jtaoui the dimmed Christ stared down. And the vampire was there.

He moved through the fringes, tunneling helplessly, passing the image of the death angel on the border of the Quarter, its face and his a blur, three blurs, Harold on his leash, his little black familiar. Past the small groups of the Christian young men, eyes bright and wired: At last a long-hoarded US$3K weapon had been used, at last a tamp on the slow bloody death of their world.

11 Une seule fin

"Don't say anything," Emmanuelle said. "Don't do anything straight away. He's okay. It's okay. Your father has had a heart attack."

She was at the door and behind the intense matter of fact was a sheet of desperation too tightly held. He looked at her and began calculating.

"Are you all right?"

"Yes," he said calmly. "I am all right."

"Okay."

"Where is he? What has happened?"

"Your mother called me. He had a heart attack at home. Men were visiting him. He has been taken to the Orthodox hospital."

She watched him.

"Do you want to come in?"

"No."

"Will you go?"

"Yes."

"Do you want me to come with you?"

"No." He gave her the dog.

"You look different," she said. "Are you okay? I could hear the shooting . . . " She trailed off, all her strength used up for this moment and no longer knowing what to do.

"I'll go there now. It's not far. Stay here and stay inside. Do you have food?" She nodded, and was glad to be told. "Stay here," he said, and the act of strength came easily.

"You have your color back," she said. She laid a hand on his cheek and whispered, softly, "*Trop, trop douloureux,*" and then he left.

———

The church bells were ringing out across the Quarter, and at the hospital ambulances were arriving from the march and there were grim orderlies rushing and outpatients handling their bandaged arms and legs carefully and eyeing everything from plastic seats and the place of trauma and there were gurneys lining the corridors. He was directed to the ICU and at the elevator passed a sprinkle of smoky blood on the linoleum tracked with the grain of rubber wheels.

Only Junko, only Joseph, and so frail and dependent, they rose and came to him in the empty waiting room with its dead TV and empty paper coffee cups. As soon as she saw him Junko's face became stern and tensed—she was being strong for him. They hugged and Joseph clapped his back.

"Oh Leon," his mother said irritably, a good show. "Why does he do this?"

"He is complaining already," Joseph said brightly, but his eyes wandered off and his voice faltered. "Complaining already . . . "

"What happened?" Leon said.

"Someone came, someone," Junko said, and then her face screwed up in an easier anger. "Those *men* came . . . "

"He was questioned. About—" tried Joseph, heartily, and stopped.

"Those men, they wanted him, those *weak* and *lazy*—" Junko's hand was to her breast and she was shaking her head, gone pale.

"He was questioned about—" Joseph was trying so hard.

"Can I see him?" said Leon, and when he spoke at last, they were calmed.

"Yes, but he's on drugs, Leon, Leon—" She started to cry but stopped herself and he put a hand on her shoulder and then hugged her. She shuddered hard against him, then stiffened and held him back to look at him. "My strong son. My *strong* son."

"Mama, I'll go see him," Leon said, and she nodded and just mouthed yes.

Against the whiteblue sheets he seemed moonlit, silver and brown and from afar much the same. But as Leon got closer he saw the bearlike shape of him was shrunken and the skin pulled tight to his white-stubbled cheekbones, each coarse and indestructible hair known so deeply, pale under a moustache of plastic oxygen tube. He saw the body of his father limp as it never was, never in repose or recline; his right hand dead upon the blanket, a great shunt sleeping in his knuckles.

"Papa . . . " he said as he lifted the chair up close to him. Abu Keiko's eyes opened slowly.

"Au, hello son," he said in an emotional murmur as he came out of his dream. A voice totally unlike his: soft and drowsy and okay: "Hel*lo*, son."

"Oh Papa," Leon said. He delicately put his hand under his so as not to tug the needle taped to the skin. Abu Keiko squeezed his fingers once and hard. He was struggling to keep his eyes open. He seemed foreshortened, shrunk, and humbled. "Oh Papa, are you in pain?"

"Nooo, *nooo*." He exhaled and drawled it softly. He tried to nod at the shunt, but the gesture was like a drunken man's, missing the mark. "The heart is, you know. *You* know," and he tried to nod again, but this time now just slightly left and right. He was alluding to an old joke of his—in the house he had a fez and a plastic novelty whip, and as children he'd make fun of Shi'a and the Āshūrā for them, and he would mock–self-flagellate, the whip over one shoulder, the whip over the other.

"Yes. Yes, Papa."

His eyes closed. He squeezed Leon's hand again gently and rested. Leon watched him until he came up again. This time the eyes were intense.

"My son, my son."

"Papa."

"Those creatures came for me—" His voice was husky. Leon gave him water from a cup and a straw. He took just one sip and spat the straw out feebly and stared up at him, shaking slightly, gathering the sentences. "Leon, *you have to leave.*"

"Papa, what has happened?"

"They came to me, I know them all. They accuse you. They won't listen. I said, not *my* son . . . " He coughed impatiently, a deep gurgle, and it seemed like his neck was weakened, could not even support his head. "They came to accuse you, and I told them, *not my son . . .*" and he began to cough again.

The fit lasted, and when it passed, Abu Keiko closed his eyes, struggling to think through the drugs. Leon waited. His father's eyes opened again, intense and bloodshot; a chemical smell rising off him.

"It's . . . *more* than them. There are others and they don't believe or care. They lie. There is no love. Don't—" he was shaking his head—"don't go out tonight, don't. . . . You have to leave." This seemed correct to him and he sighed an awful shuddering sigh and his head sank back in the pillow and his eyes closed again. Moments passed. At last he lifted his face as if in a realization. "They don't see farther down the road. They don't see past the first mountain. If they could, yalla . . . they would see . . . to the anti Lebanon. You." He lifted the shunted hand to press a finger on Leon's chest. "*You* don't know what you lack, but we . . . " and he moved the shunted hand to his own chest. The tube would not reach and tugged the needle and he winced late and slowly.

"Papa, *be careful.*"

"No, we . . . you see . . . *we* know what we miss." The glaze had gone from his eyes. "*They will not come into our area,*" he hissed, "*They will not* . . . ah, Leon!"—he pronounced it differently and he nodded intently—"You *have* to do violence. You *have to.* For a long time"—and he exhaled—"for a long time, I remember, it was fun. Playing in our own blood." He thought about this and stared across the room. When at last he looked back at Leon there was hatred. "*You.* I remember you down in the Hotel-Dieu in 1979.

You had that curly hair, and you were tying up their ankles with a washing line." He sneered bitterly. "You had a free hand with the quicklime."

"Papa," Leon said as if to a child in a nightmare. "Papa, it's Leon. That wasn't me."

"Do you remember that Palestinian vampire we pulled to pieces? I remember your ways, habibi." He sighed and his eyes unfocused and his face moved in small circles. The intensity changed again and he looked up into the air and murmured dreamily, "I did it *à ma façon*, it is the only way. *Une seule vie, une seule fin.* Leon," and he looked back at him, no less dreamy, "I took a road that was not finished. It narrowed and went rough and took me to a mistake, Leon, the wrong way, with no chance of reversing my course. Twenty years ago or more . . . I have taken you all with me, I'm sorry."

"Papa, don't. I do not judge what you did."

"Now," his intensity through the drugs was like an actor in good humor fighting to be serious, "you have to leave, Leon, for your mother. They won't listen, they are desperate. And weak. When Christian turns upon Christian . . . " He was croaking and the glaze came over his eyes again. "We don't care about things like we used to. You couldn't go on . . . I remember . . . a horse rearing . . . a horse plunging in the shallows off the beach of Jaffa . . . a horse . . . yes, I was in Israel! Can you believe? I saw a horse . . . let them . . . let them go and worship a black stone. . . . "

He receded for a while and then came up again. He remembered his mission. "Talk to Joseph. You must know. They will take the chance to . . . settle old scores. They are like that. Leave now. You see, I can't . . . ride horses up in the Mountain anymore. An old man needs a hammock. . . . " His eyes brightened slowly at the intruding joke.

"In the annex," Leon said. His father came up again further, smiling, nodding softly. He said, "*I'm* alright. I'm stro-*ong.*" Then he looked at his son, his eyes unfocused.

And he said, with a crooked forefinger waving over the folded hospital sheet, in a different, idle, incidental tone, as if his son were just one on this long list of tasks, going back twenty years or more, neutral and ticking him off, "*You* have to leave," and then he slept.

12 Pyr

The criminal and the victim alike return to the scene of the crime. There was a link to the video and the video was live. On the website of *Né à Beyrouth* from a year ago, he had found it. A reference to that one talk he'd attended at the Festival du Film Libanais, at the AUB West Hall, the talk from which he'd left too early and missed the vital information.

The night before he left, Leon sat naked and cross-legged on his neatly made bed before his laptop in the darkness. He rolled the two cuff links in one hand, then hit full screen. The video lit up the room, his silhouette with newly shaven hair on the wall above the full backpack by the door, the clean jeans and T-shirt laid on the chair, the passport on the document wallet on the bedside table.

The presentation was by a lecturer in film and media from the Maronite college at Kaslik. An Iraqi-Palestinian by birth, long resident in Lebanon and a sort of prodigy, a filmmaker, writer, and theorist. His talk was called *Since I Died Before Dying in the Interim Between this Death and the Last* and it had been about vampires.

He said that it was because the Armenian photographer was unaffiliated with any party or militia that he had managed to catch the only civil war photograph of a vampire, *pyr*, in the what must-needs-be-quote-marked — he had flexed his fingers on either side of the lectern — "flesh." And it bears repetition, the lecturer said, that this is the only extant civil war photograph of a vampire *ever*, despite their abundant numbers in the country at that time.

A frightening black-and-white photograph filled the Power-Point screen behind him. It was of the head and shoulders of a man in military fatigues seated at a grand piano in a ballroom. There was an automatic rifle lying on the dusty piano and the man seemed to be playing. He was wearing a sack on his head. It had tiny crooked slits for eyes.

The photograph dated from late 1975 or early 1976, six months into the war, after the Christians had occupied the fourth district, a tongue of land that extends from the Phalange headquarters by the port at the foot of the Green Line and stretches roughly a kilometer west along the coast in front of the St. George's Marina. This tongue of land was traditionally commercial and nonsectarian. It encompassed the hotels district, the soon-to-be monuments of the end of the Golden Age, of *Liban*-on-a-plate for American and European rich, the end of the Western myth of Beirut as the Paris of the Middle East and of Lebanon as un-Arabic, un-other.

The great hotels: St. George's, the Phoenicia, the InterContinental, the Murr Tower, and supreme amongst them, icon of icons, standing complexly beloved and vacant and scarred to this day, the most photographed empty hotel in the world, the Beirut Holiday Inn.

A small ironic hurrah arose from the audience.

The land was against the Christians, the topography and the urban design. Because low hills rise from St. George's and the marina up to Hamra and the great hotels are discretely spaced and sniper-friendly, and they preside over Downtown, preside over that sensitive tongue of land, casting great long shadows like blades about to snip it off. The Christians lost the Holiday Inn, and the whole fourth district, and the front line coagulated at the Green Line. But every impasse seems inevitable in hindsight. Perhaps a temporary blessing in a city so small and circumscribed that the war was confined for this early time to towers, this War of the Hotels, and managed in room-to-room purges. Soldiers who may have rampaged along streets of civilians so much more than they subsequently did instead lugged cannon, machine guns, and katyushas up forty flights of stairs to train them on the upper floors of other towers. All those forgotten awful little individual deaths were kept private in single suites, like their previous occupants' indulgences. Those snipers burned out with Molotov cocktails; those militia boys drowned in the water features; those raw recruits lost or left in retreats who hid in closets full of Canali suits with a bottle of the looted bar's last Crème de Menthe as the doors grew too hot to touch or the shots and bootfalls and hamzated verbs of Palestinian Arabic grew closer.

The crowd was shifting and not speaking or laughing now.

Leon paused the video. He could suddenly see himself onscreen: there in the West Hall, three rows from the front and the left, sitting alone at the foot of the terrifying photograph, facing away, perforce, from himself. Onscreen this younger self had turned slightly right in his seat, as if looking for something, or someone.

He picked up his phone.

3:30 AM.

His older self pressed play. The frightening photo on the Power-Point went to close-up as the lecturer recommenced.

The Phalange, as well as many of the other Christian militias, wore masks at this time because many of them lived in areas that were still multi-confessional. They wanted to fight and return home in peace at night. But everyone apparently knew this man in the photo from late 1975 was a French mercenary, so there really was no call for him to wear a mask—unless this picture was taken on Barbara Day, the Maronite Halloween, the day of second face. But the photographer, Harry "The Horse" Koundakjian, could not remember the date exactly.

There are many things that don't add up completely in terms of timing. The Holiday Inn burned near the end, before the first Christian defeat and the last retreat, so how was it he was on this largely untouched rooftop floor? But suffice it to say, the *pyr* is masked in sacking cloth with two narrow, drooping, darkened slits for eyes. He sits at the dusty grand piano of the rooftop restaurant of the Holiday Inn, and he plays, allegedly, Paul McCartney's "Yesterday," with his highly modified U.S. M14 with top-and-tail duct-taped magazines—"jungle clips"—lying before him on the shining, misted grand piano's closed lid. We see his dark and curly

hair about his mask, his slits for eyes, and his gentle tense of pos-
ture betraying the playing of his invisible hands. In the reflection
around his weapon on the grand piano, misted with dust shaken
from the new plaster of the ceilings, we see the black and milk-
white Lebanese sky through the window behind him.

The lecturer looked up and smiled.

And there is no reflection of him at all.

The younger Leon on the video was now twisted completely in his
seat, looking back at the camera.

Behind him the PowerPoint flicked over to a new message: *Civil
War 1975–1990: The criminal and the victim alike return to the scene of
the crime.*

But *pyr* have slept in the Lebanon for long, long before this, the
lecturer said. He was perhaps picked up—like a germ—by God-
frey de Bouillon and Peter the Hermit somewhere in the Serbian
forests between Belgrade and Nish on the First Crusade, accidentally recruited on the march toward Jerusalem. Suspicion and
the pogrom revive the *pyr* and give it vivid life. Any troop of soldiers with cynical leadership, a sacred cause, and little in the way
of qualms is the *pyr*'s natural habitat. The *pyr* is lost in time; he
haunts the present, and lost in the labyrinth, haunts all times.

In the front row on the video Leon saw himself rise from his seat.

There is substantial evidence that *pyr* had infiltrated the PLO
when the fleshpots were filled at the massacre of Damour in the
winter of 1976. The head priest of the town, a small Christian village arrayed across the hill-face overlooking the main highway
south of Beirut, was a Father Salaky. Three days after the epiphany

shots were fired on the village. In response to the sacking of the Karantina Palestinian refugee camp, a force was gathering in the hills behind Damour. It was comprised of PLO Fatah regulars, PFLP fighters, Japanese commandos of the Red Army, a couple of incongruously ginger-haired and sunburned IRA, and al-Saiqa, Syrian Palestinian fighters receiving their directives from Damascus. All were under the command of Zuhayr Musin, soon to be known as the "Butcher of Damour." When the shooting started, calls by Father Salaky to the Chamouns, to Jumblatt, and finally to Arafat himself were futile. Arafat rebuffed the priest with *pyric* elegance and economy: *Father, don't worry*, he said. *We don't want to hurt you. If we are destroying you it is for strategic reasons.*

In turn Salaky rebuffed offers of militia help from Etienne Saqr, the Father of the Cedars. He was resistant to the presence of armed militias of any stripe in his village. The Cain family was the first to be massacred in a siege that would last twelve days—the massed PLO and leftist forces were held off with hunting rifles and gardening implements. Under the eyes of their watercolors of Sharbel and the Christ, they were shot to death, the children's eyes put out, the men's genitals removed and placed in their mouths. The second twist in the spiral of retaliation, spinning out of Christian control, from Black Saturday and the purge of the Palestinians of Karantina in East Beirut—where now the abattoir and the chemical-industrial firms foul the little left of the river and the young dance inside a mass grave at Beirut's most internationally famous underground nightclub, designed by Lebanon's most internationally famous architect, Bernard Khoury's Bo18.

The massacre happened, as at Karantina, a cool concept but hot process coined in English as *exection*: execution and resection. The removal of the human organism that characterizes the place. After the fall of the Palestinian refugee camp of Tel al Za'atar the next year, her survivors would be transplanted into Damour, this haunted little town—Lebanon, this elegant Frankenstein remade of pieces of herself.

Haunted: even then. The power went down: House by house

and church by church, the PLO force exected the remaining Christian families who had not fled to the coast. The Saiqa, it's said, dismantled the human beings of Damour. Resisting Christians were captured and tied to Buicks and dragged to their deaths. The women were raped. The insanity, the passion required for exection was stoked with speeches, amphetamines, hashish. But *pyr* had risen, infiltrated: An al-Saiqa man shot a Fatah regular in the stomach in a dispute over hummus. He informed Musin himself, "I just wanted to watch him die."

In the cold nights that followed in the hollowed-out town, as the fighters took over the empty houses and the dynamited and despoiled churches, the signs of *pyr* began to multiply: a firing range in the nave. Eyeless children seen on the road. Fighters waking to find their comrades dead beside them; amphetamine overdose; a grand intractability. And here we recognize conclusive evidence of *pyr*: The process of exection extended to the dead. The Damour cemetery was invaded and it was a rout. They rooted out the corpsesnipers from the mausoleums, dragged the skeletonsoldiers from their elaborate Christian coffins, stripped them of their mortuary best, murdered their cadavers, pulling rib from rib, penetrating the vacant insides to locate and despoil and exect the very Christian soul. Many throughout the massacres were dressed to kill in furs and plastic masks, plastic faces with comedy moustaches, one even in Dracula costume. The lecturer looked up. *Did I mention it was cold?* We follow the Butcher of Damour to a warmer place, Cannes on the Côte d'Azur, years later, a few weeks after *Apocalypse Now* tied with *The Tin Drum* for the Palme D'Or. Here, on holiday and strolling the rue D'Antibes, Zuhayr Musin was put to death by persons and means unknown. Perhaps just by vacation.

But *pyr* does not die; he is not put to death.

The hot nights of the siege of the fortified Palestinian refugee camp of Tel al Za'atar mid-1976 witness full-blown *pyr* within and without the PLO: Civilians in the camps were kept from fleeing and used as human shields; infighting in the Christians maneuvering outside led to Phalangists blocking off the Guardians of the Cedars; the Red Cross and Crescent barred from entering and evacuating the wounded; shells falling upon ambulances; orders from Arafat to hold on to and tacitly to martyr the civilian population in the bunkers and hold out for the PR exercise of raising a sympathetic Palestinian body count profile worldwide and further sullying the Christian image with a terrible civilian massacre: obstinacy, hypocrisy, and bloodlust, the hot orgy, the wobble of the mind, the gasoline-soaked tunnels, the willingness to do all. This is *pyr*; we are legion.

It might be postulated that it was the Oslo peace accords that eventually stilled the *pyr* in Yasser Arafat: had he made no concession he might have lived forever.

The photo of the eyeless fighter masked in sacking cloth was back on the PowerPoint. *Yesterday*, the old song went. *Something, something was so far away.*

Who did this? the lecturer asked. Well, it was us.

Young Leon was holding on to the backs of chairs for support, leaving the lecture in some distress, approaching the camera so very slowly. In the dim of his darkened bedroom old Leon watched. He felt the change and the damage in himself. He messaged Emmanuelle.

Are you there?

She did not answer, she was not there, she was not there.

Young Leon reached the camera and he seemed to be grinning, grimacing, or crying, his teeth all black, almost swallowing the scene. His eyes were Keiko's, hazel-brown, expressionless. He passed beyond the screen and the video ended soon after.

Older Leon clicked on part II. The error message read:

[this video removed by user]

in the borderlands

13 10,452

No one will be named your name in this part of the world ever again. This is what we cannot bear, it is unbearable: our rage, our cap in hand. We fear nothing. We will remain here forever. Hezbollah have the Bekaa, the South, now inroads in the Chuf. Will you tolerate this? Clashes with the Druze in civil war fortifications on Hill 888. A rumor of Dany Aoun and a woman dead in a "horrific traffic accident." East Beirut is becoming destabilized and no mention of the shootings in the protest. More shooting in Tripoli and an Australian tourist is dead outside the SSNP offices and Future partisans keep the al-Masnaa crossing into Syria closed for the fourth day in a row. Speaker Nabih Berri gassing on about determination and unity. If Syria comes in, Israel comes in. This is Lebanese Light FM. We play Lebanon's favorites.

At first light he kissed his mother and walked down the hills through empty streets toward Charles Helou Station with just his backpack, laptop, and his document wallet. Ships left port today, in cool winds and a pale blood-orange haze on the Med. Wafik Chokr reinstated, the first of the governmental concessions. Downtown off the empty curving boulevards a couple of Sudanese and Yemeni laborers in dark-blue overalls lay on the manicured lawns of the empty gardens, where the flowers were chosen for the specific combination of their scents, where the bankers and lawyers strolled in the artist's impressions of what was meant to be.

He walked down George Haddad, passed rue Gouraud and Paul Café, empty too of all but journalists, passed in front of Phalange

HQ, and crossed the empty Avenue Charles Helou and took the street on which his sister died. Makhlouf's, *since 1969*, was open and he sat with nightshift LA soldiers and ate a sausage shawarma, cheapest on offer. He drank Arabic coffee and watched as outside, past a refrigerator full of éclairs and donuts and jellies and fruit salad, Makhlouf *fils*, a man of forty, hosed down and swept the street where she was shot, dragged out his same plastic chairs and tables. The radio played Western songs.

He finished his small last meal and crumpled the paper. He quickly inverted his plastic coffee cup on the plate. A plain thin trickle of black ran over the ceramic. He lifted it to examine the grinds. In the center a perfect nipple had formed smooth and flawless.

"Good," said Makhlouf's son, he'd seen him do it. "That's good luck."

"Good luck to you," Leon said as he left.

Makhlouf had seen the pack.

"Leaving?" He half-smiled, as if with pain. "Taking a trip?"

He nodded.

Makhlouf shrugged. He'd seen his own father die, his cousins emigrate.

"Good luck." An invocation, an observation, a question.

Charles Helou Station, just a parking lot in the concrete cistern beneath the motorway and one small office packed with men. Prices to Damascus had skyrocketed day by day: US$75 (up from $18) for a shared taxi doubled by lunchtime, for an epic old Buick reeking of lavender sachet with windows curtained on elastic tracks. All the drivers tense and visibly unhappy, and they were kept waiting, waiting to leave, all day, for hours till the car was filled with luggage, post, and illegally transported FedEx parcels strapped all over the roof—counting up the take, Daoud the driver, a moustached and crushed Druze with a famously trauma-tized father and a brother in Israel never to return, would make, on this one little trip, US$700 to $800, maybe, maybe more.

And at last it transpired, the passengers climbed in, and intro-duced themselves: Hassan, a gregarious, pudgy Lebanese business-man from Kuwait who'd come back to close up his house and got stuck; a sweet and pious near-mute brother and sister in their early twenties, Iman and Abdullah, Iman sitting on Abdullah's knee in the front passenger seat away from the other men in her mod-esty, in Abdullah's hug; and Anders, a six-foot young blond Dane who'd been visiting his student girlfriend, who took the middle seat in the back like a hero, his head bent under the thick Ameri-can velour; and Leon, hard right, jammed in the corner so his arms couldn't move and watching Daoud select caseless CDs from a vinyl file taped to his sun visor and watching though a brick-sized bit of window as they prepared to leave Beirut.

In the late evening in the old house of the night before, his mother had done her small tasks in the kitchen and he had sat opposite the sofa where his father sat with the newspaper, where his father always sat with the newspaper. There was that echo-ing emptiness without expectation—this house was so much his, and it was held together by him and his routines and his Pepsi and his swear words and his sense of what is right. *Here in my heart is love.* Leon had a memory of him showing him mutely and proudly the Aounist symbol he'd stuck with glue onto his wal-let. "Does it even mean anything Papa?" "Of *course!* Of *course* it does." The orange of Aoun, like Nike but in two curves, a tick on an exam: a short mangy streak descending left to right ("This is where we were—"), his finger traces the sketchy fall, thinning to a nadir ("—this is where the Syrians left—") then rises from that low point, solid and emphatic, even higher, wider than before, to widen, thicken definitively at the zenith. ("Of what, Papa? What we have now? Aoun finally gets to be president? What?" "The *future*, Leon. Always the *future*.")

His papa settled back, he sipped his Pepsi, thought, and leaned forward again and he grinned.

"Syria, you see, Leon, our bloody sister. She is a vampire. And we invited her in. This was the nature of the Ta'ef Accord to end the war. We thought the worst had come, but worse was yet to come. It was in 1989, when Jumblatt, Hariri, Berri, Frangieh, they all went to Ta'ef in Saudi, and they signed the invitation to the vampire. They said, 'Yes, your slut sister is Arab.' They said, 'Oh yes, your slut hates Israel.' They said 'Yes, yes, oh yes, please come in, sister Syria, and take care of your dirty, tired slut Lebanon, she cannot take care of herself. Change her laws, forgive who you want, imprison who you like, tax her money and her farms, fill her ministries with your flunkies, and run her house as you will.' And the music softly played and the pipes bubbled and they sipped coffee and sister Syria, *un vampire la plus terrible*, she said, 'It is not my custom to go where I am not invited, but since you ask so sweetly and so weakly, I will come in and take care of you. For you are my sister, with your tits for a minute, your legs for days.' And she came with all her terrible retinue and screwed us and bled us and pimped us out for fifteen more years, and then left us fucked and bloodied by the road to Damascus.

"Their soldiers, do you remember?"

Leon remembered. He remembered, as a boy, being stopped by moustached Syrian soldiers in their Russian helmets, men of twenty squatted in the shade of their tanks in the thick summer heat, sending him into West Beirut for beer and snacks and Bonjus. When he came back that first time without their supplies, they made him sit in the sun all afternoon, then kicked him once and hard in the small of the back and sent him on his way with a motion of a boot, when he was what? Ten years old? The Israelis? Once upon a time they'd fix your car for you if it broke down. Abu Keiko began to sound crazy when he got angry and talked politics.

It went better when Junko was around to calm him down. His numbers would get wild—70,000 Christians killed by the Druze in the Mountain in 1860 he'd claim. His back would stiffen, his eyes would get wide and empty, his rage was always there. Leon only realized he thought his father a little nuts when he was what? Twenty-five? Justified even then before the death of his daughter by the sirocco of his war, like those old laws that forgave crimes of weird passions in the Provençal mistral.

"Do you remember? You were too young." He sounded tender for only a moment. "Syrian lieutenants would grab a good Christian girl, a virgin waiting for a husband, put her in a tank with his six soldiers, and she would leave like this—" and he'd make a horrible gesture like an ape, with his hands hanging beneath his crotch.

"And she would have to go to hospital."

He would look at you as if you had to react to this nameless apocryphal horror.

"The General was the only one to say no to this, and this is why I fought for Aoun. He is military. He is Maronite but not intransigent and crazy like the mountain men. This is why they hate me now. He said, 'We are Lebanese, and we will not cede our country.' The slut has pride. We will not cede our sovereignty. And so they shelled him, sister Syria, they shelled us at the presidential palace at Baabda and everybody *let them. Helped them.* They shelled us to death and there was the inevitable ending. 1989. Fleeing in his pajamas to the French Embassy. And then to Paris. He abandoned us, but he had to. I was lucky, not like the boys who were left behind. Emerging defeated to the Syrian soldiers, wounded carried out on shoulders *Syrienne* to die. Hundreds of them, Leon. Executed, mutilated, disappeared. Rotting now in Damascene jails for longer than previously they had lived. I escaped, to my family. We were lost and left alone.

"So you see? That was Ta'ef. Syria is the vampire at our door, and all those fools invited her in. And she is always waiting. And whose fault is it? The US of A with their war in Kuwait, they needed Syria, and they made their deal and they looked the other way and Lebanon was lost. It was easy—they had given an eye already here when the marine base was bombed in 1983. Easy to wince and look away. The Christians were abandoned. The slut was left to make her own way. You know the Israelis thought we were like them? Some still do. We are Western. They are Western. Cultivated, intelligent people, who believe in democracy, in literature, in art. That is what we believed. And because of U.S. weakness now, we are a state not 'with an Arab face,' which is what the National Pact said, but 'with an Arab identity,' which is what Ta'ef says. So this is why I support Hezbollah. They are for the people. They are not like the other ones who have turned their guns on Lebanese. Their hearts are full of love for the Lebanese. They give the slut pride. She rises in her robes and finery, fierce. And when we rose up and kicked Syria out, sister left with our blood and our meat in her teeth. And Israel was sick of us. Israel did not care."

It was then Leon realized that he'd been drinking. As the contradictions multiplied, his thinking muddied and only the rage remained.

"The Shi'a believe that everywhere is Karbala! They are a defeatist people who can build nothing."

Leon said, "Democracy is just stable transition of power without violence. There is no difference between us and any other democratic state than guns. Everyone is corrupt. Some countries just know how to manage it better." A method for the control of hungry vampires. It was all too long ago anyway. Abu Keiko looked at him then with awesome pity.

"My son, you are too young to feel this way," he said, and laughed and then looked away vaguely. Thinking about another drink. Of Junko sniffing the Pepsi bottles. When had they held this conversation? The Hezbollah now killing Lebanese—maybe it was that, that strain on Ja'ja's bypass in there, funneling Hezbollah blood through his veins, Aoun's Memorandum of Understanding, the complicity in a filicide, that broke Abu Keiko's Frankenstein heart. Or was it his comrades, veterans, Christian brothers coming to the door as Iranian proxies to take his son after they had come as Syrian proxies for his daughter? Surely any one would do.

Destroy the body, and destroy the wall. *Here in my heart is love.* As if the family were flickering in scratched collapsing Super 8, trotted out for film students; some relic from a rusted unmarked can found stinking of the vinegar of acetate decay in the bins of the Sunday markets.

Junko had come in with tea on a tray and sat at the sofa's end. And they had sat in silence and he had listened to her sip.

Se—heee, poh. Se—heee, poh.

"Is the tea all right?" she said in Japanese. *O-cha o daijobu desu ka?*

His eyes moved over the crazed glaze of their coffee table. What was that tone in her voice? It was the tone of his mother before the first day of high school; it was testing, even mischievous, portentous: to steel them, making the lightest fun of her children's fear. Not something she needed to do when their father was there—this odd, young, light, and ironic quality in her came out when he was away.

"The tea is fine, mama. Thank you."

"Joseph gave you the money. You have enough for a while?"

"Yes, mama."

"There is another thing which will help you, I hope. Now I know—" Junko filled up the space of the room with her gentle and resistant whisper to defer demur, the soft and unpredictable rise and fall of pitch. She used her voice, her sighing Japanese, only when they were alone, and she used her quiet to refuse refusal. "When you were twenty-two, you remember going to the embassy? I had a choice then and I made a choice that might not have been your first choice—" When had she become so afraid of offending him? How pathetic and defensive had he been? "But the choice was made, partly because of the very strict rules of the government—" and she'd broken off then and produced the passport, burgundy and pristine. On the cover had been no cedar and no outline of the putative 10,452 km² of the Lebanon called for by Bashir Gemayel, and no Arabic, but two large kanji and chrysanthemum.

"It's Japanese."

"Because of the law, and because you had your ID card already, and that was all you need because we do not travel. For Japan, Leon, they're very strict—" Her voice had grown quieter and quieter as she explained the hard thing. "You could not have dual nationality. They don't allow it! It's my country. I love Japan. It is corrupt and imperialistic and it is too much in the palm of the United States, but it is your country too. And I had to choose and I chose and I'm sorry. But this will help you now. Won't it?"

The perfect passport had the very same picture of him as on his ID, at twenty-two, and his mother's name, *Shiokawa*, and the kanji and English and outlines of chrysanthemum, and it was almost but not quite the same color as the Lebanese.

"You had to choose."

"At twenty-two they changed the law and we had to choose your nationality. I wanted to give you that choice. Of Japan."

A long pause. Where was his Lebanese ID now? The Dahiyeh? In a file in a Hezbollah office, flipped through after the phone call came?

"It's okay, mama."

"Okay?"

And she sighed and then laughed a little and held her hand to her breast but differently from the hospital, in relief, and leaned back into the sofa. "Oh, *dear*."

"It's good, now, mama, isn't it?"

"Yes. I'd hoped you would see that."

A long silence had fallen and he'd flicked through the blank pages of his immediate future in reverse until he came to the Lebanese airport entry stamps on the first two.

"Mama?" He showed the forgeries to her.

"They are very good. Very good. Your uncle! You will be fine. Just be confident but polite and don't speak English too well." She laughed and then didn't and then shrank back into the cushions. "The address in Japan is in that new email." He went and sat beside her and put his arm around her and she sobbed, a cracking gasp, twice into his shoulder, and then stiffened again.

"Where will you go?"

I don't know.

"Tokyo."

"Good, good."

Another long silence, then a change in mood.

"O, Leon! The food. O, I miss the food so much. You can have *ohagi,* and you can have—"

She carried on a while and then she quieted. Then she said, soft, deep, matter-of-fact, "I'm afraid. I'm afraid that if he dies and now you're gone it'll only be me and I'll not ever belong. I'm afraid no one will be named our name in this part of the world ever again. I'm afraid there will be a war and I will have no children and no one will care for me here."

They zigzagged up the Mountain after they crossed Beirut River, a lesser road heading northeast, avoiding the Tripoli road, the Damascus highway, anywhere known where they might be stopped. They left the suburbs and traversed brief plateaus of developments in the Metn, skulls of ferroconcrete apartments and holiday houses for Kuwaitis and Saudis left unfinished in scars of excavation, to Rabtie and Majdel Tarchich and up through the Christian hills. Leon looked backward once through the small rear window, twisting awkwardly, apologizing to the Dane, for a last glimpse of the Lebanese Mediterranean. The steep drop-off, steepest in the Levant, to 1,500 meters in the Zahrani Canyon, he knew, and all he saw there was a brief glimpse of luminous steel, the sea at one with the sky in an endless, placid, silver ripple. They say that looking out there where you see nothing gives Lebanese people their moment of peace, *a hammock in the annex,* but Leon saw what he once might have seen: a great and lewd forgetful grandfather, spawning bastards to replace him.

The ivory seam of Lebanon mountain and milk sky, the white sun over seams of limestone rock in the scrub; abrupt gulfs and gulleys, the foreigners' half-built holiday houses like unexploded bombs in their craters of gradered earth, the stripped hillsides, winding up the slopes though one extended empty village, the brightwhite sundown Med bursting in the glass beside and behind, Daoud happy to be driving, lighting a cigarette, all-business, flipping down a CD from the file, choosing the music from the feel of the embossed label on the disk alone, Iman murmuring to Abdullah, his one arm on the windowsill, one around her shoulder blades, a big brown bicep, a strength, a love.

Lost Beirut, lost. Where wound abrupt plateaus of scattered trees, playgrounds amid, Syrian Social Nationalist Party posters nailed into the bark, Leon gently crying, turning away so the other passengers won't see.

Daoud turned off the music as they descended through the blasted suburbs of Zahle and onto the floor of the valley of Bekaa. Out either side of them fields were sprouting sprinklers, Rome's breadbasket filled with vineyards, lettuces, wheat, barracks of vinyl glasshouses and fields of contradictions, hashish and Hezbollah, Bedouin beggars and gunmen in bungalows. The road north to Baalbek and beyond, the Syrian border, was wide, so wide and straight and empty and uncambered, and morphed at either side from adequate asphalt to gravel and floc and then two parallel lines, like the last remnants of how many dead empires' dead convoys, of oiled wasteland and pieces of engine and rubber rags of stripped retreads. All along on either side the billboards rose, billboards and flags the size of drive-in movie screens, the yellow and green of Hezbollah and Amal every fifty meters like an aisle, a *via* into the new state. Daoud picked up speed and the old Buick on its soft American suspension floated fast up and into the north into the twilight and Daoud was hunched over the wheel and no one spoke, passing here a house made of tarpaulin, passing there a fence made of abandoned cars.

Far off to the right the dry and desiccated anti Lebanon hunched; its permeable rock they would cross at a pass in the north where the mountains dipped into the valley before Homs. They were driving away from Damascus to get to Damascus. (In the street outside the hospital, Joseph had pressed an envelope into Leon's hand. On the envelope was the address of a cousin of his in the city. Leon took out the US$500 and gave the money back to him, folded the envelope, and put it in his pocket and left it in his nightstand, later.)

They went on, a thousand miles an hour, floating over the debris, and even young Iman was feeling the tension, and the attention of the hills around about, the pressure of the ruined aquifer out there that now did not drain and hold the rain but sucked humans from its presence and people said, out there in the anti Lebanon, pockets of PLO still lived, civil war vets in tents still fighting the revolution high in the hills, gaunt and bearded and living on Syrian largesse. Leon watched the fields, the aquifer strong, like a migrainous throb in his forehead. They passed through the outskirts of Baalbek. They passed through Qaa and another awful, frightened border town. They came to where the road changed, shops appeared, the trash gathered. The Syrian border where a bright blue Pepsi sign fizzed and hissed.

Hassan and the Dane rummaged through their pockets for their documents. Abdullah and Iman unfolded themselves from their embrace and the car and stretched and looked around smiling as if this were just a slightly disappointing but nevertheless imperative tourist spot. Hassan and Daoud had been conferring and Hassan was emerging as either alpha or a boor—but it was he whom Leon asked.

"How much are we going to need?"

"Oh ho ho!" He laughed deliberately over-jolly. Behind him in the border office, beyond a horseshoe of a counter and under a portrait of Assad, the thickset and lanyarded Syrian border control officers swelled and sneered.

"I think it will be all right," Hassan grinned brightly and winked, and Leon realized his performance was for the immigration officers. He watched him and listened close. "If you give me your papers I will try to get us processed all at once."

The Dane was reluctant, aloof and goofy but seemed to realize he didn't have a choice. Leon gave up his new passport and the last roll of his cash and Hassan led the group into the office. The largest guard, his size some clue to seniority, entered the counter area from a back office and sat on a high revolving chair from the underside of which still hung, opaque with dust and age, ragged flaps of shrink-wrap plastic that had not been ripped from it completely. The guard ignored Hassan and watched the group in front of them until Hassan leaned over the counter and murmured in a tone both deferential and schoolboy naughty, a sardonic act to inspire conspiracy, and the officer laughed at something and took the proffered passports and the roll of U.S. currency as if it were just another task. Then they all stood outside and stretched and smoked and waited. They watched a file of Syrian workers leaving Lebanon on foot, dozens crossing unmolested the permeable border—ghostlike, moving, undefined, sketched on permeable rock—just supermarket bags of shoes and shirts and lunch remains hanging from their hands.

Their passports came back fast, and they all boarded the Buick and drove fifteen meters forward to a covered piece of customs concrete and stopped again. For twenty minutes Daoud, visibly terrified, negotiated with armed customs men, one police in camouflage, until a superior was called up, pissed off and smoking and drinking coffee. Everything was removed from the car. Daoud got back in and asked them for more money. "For benzene." They all refused. He got out, his eyes oiled and dark with defeat, and with no money for bribes was forced to leave all the illegal FedEx packages with the border guard. And then they left again, instantly in manicured fields emerging from the wasteland, then into Syrian suburbia, then swinging south again on a smooth and perfect motorway, mid trucks and infrastructure, streetlights shining, a portrait of Assad, *I believe in Syria*, and Leon thanked Hassan who shrugged, and then, staring out at order, a losing stream across the border, beginning to pick up speed, as the passage narrowed and the negative pressure increased, Leon fell asleep as if into a sink-hole, sucked into it, powerless.

14 The Old City

"We are here," said Hassan. Woken, gently, by his wide, concerned eyes, leaning up over Anders's lap and into his face. He was offering him a tissue and Leon took it without knowing what for.

"Where?"

"Bab Sharqi," said the Dane looking down at him with an expression of distaste, he thought, but who knew, who could read a Dane's face.

What had he said in his sleep?

"Damascus," said Hassan. "The Old City. The Christian Quarter."

Outside the old gate—an archway, and a rickety tower twenty meters high, a mess of different types of brick—there were piles of torn stone and ripped asphalt and black bloodstains and trenches dug in the street. There'd been artillery and shelling and rockets here to do this kind of damage. His thoughts were cloudy, panicked—he must move fast, he was at a disadvantage, there was too much to be done—he'd been in Damascus before but only at the cousins' when he was twelve. He didn't know this area, what time it was, where to go, where to stay that night—his geography was bad; didn't know where the danger was. He got out in the darkness, took his backpack from the Buick's great trunk and stayed close to the car for shelter. Traffic passed beyond on the boulevard to a great traffic circle. A light turned red and the line of traffic obediently came to a halt. He looked at a coil of plastic hose and looked back up the devastated Street Called Straight. He saw an excavator there. He stared at it for too long. And then alongside it a neatish pile of tile. There were pipes and wires in the long trench.

There was no battle; there was no shelling. There were only roadworks, oil stains, and excavations. A huge breath out left him shaking and weak inside.

"Anders, do you have a place to stay?"

Anders's voice was very deep and nasal for such a tall, thin man. He said he had a room at a hostel in the Christian Quarter and Leon said to him he would come along if that was all right with him. The Dane shrugged, irritable after the long ride.

They walked down the ripped-up Street Called Straight and turned off after a pizza restaurant and up an alley over boards laid to traverse the trench. Leon's thoughts moved slowly and he thought of what he'd thought—shelling in the Old City—and it frightened him. That this is what it felt like to lose, to be losing. An expensive vulnerability. To read phenomena differently than your companions; in self-protection to *see differently*, forever. It felt like a dangerous slip, going underground, and there was sudden hatred for that self-possessed blond boy, his bourgeois world, his pretty student girl, his refuge in his government, his country not a vampire or a slut like Lebanon, his backpacker's burden. *Yours is no real world; mine is the real and I, I am of it.* In the anger Leon felt suddenly real again, awake, and alert and as he followed him under the Virgin's Gate in the dark narrow alley, watching his thin back and his expensive backpack, he contemplated violence and wondered what possible implications there might be.

And found—he felt real again, a seeping peace—none.

At the hostel they were greeted by a squat Syrian who spoke Australian English. The man was bandy-legged, in shorts, and had lived abroad and expended unknown energies to convert an Old City villa abutting the city walls into some international hell full of Lonely Planets and Yahtzee, fuzzy CNN on coin-operated TV, and big dirty flags and dead old plants and lengths of dusty hose laid over the stone. Leon spoke to him in English, paid for a room, and gave him the Japanese passport to photocopy. He was given a Wi-Fi password and log-in, a key card, and placed in the only thing available: subdivided, newish, clad in PVC panels. It was only six foot high, narrow and long like a coffin, a single bed, a two-bar heater, lit by a fluorescent tube.

"I am backpacking through Syria," he explained as he was taken to his room. "I took the train from Turkey."

"Oh, what a great trip . . . " and the Syrian banged on about the train journey, the different rail gauges from the French and the Ottomans, what he could do tomorrow, until Leon said, and it shut him up, "Do you have any alcohol?"

"Oh . . . no. Sorry, everything is closed." It was awkward. Had Anders already said something about the taxi from Beirut? He had lied too early; he must get it right.

"How long did the Dane say he was staying?" Leon said.

"He said he is to fly out tomorrow."

"Be careful of him—he has lied to me already."

The Syrian looked confused and hurt.

"Um . . . we provide . . . we provide a breakfast for guests. . . . "

He needed sleep, he needed so much: a shower, a Lebanese smile, taste in clothes, a can-do attitude. He brushed his teeth in the bathroom and over the toilet misread a sign handwritten in English. IN SYRIA, it said, DREAMS ARE NOT TO WORLD STAN-DARD. PLEASE DO NOT FLUSH PAPER. He lay in the bed in the PVC coffin and told stories to himself, made his plans.

Three PM in the Old City in an old café behind the Umayyad mosque walls. Leon sat inside the French doors, on a polished-amber chair before a brass table like a brazier with a mottled ceramic surface no bigger than a dinner plate. A waiter in undershirt heated coffee in a *rakwa* over open flame. Five or six middle-aged men played backgammon. His coffee came on a steel water-splashed tray as big as the table, and as the muezzin began to call for prayers a nervous waiter ran to turn the music down and outside crowds passed in the marbled streets in noise and dust and light. But in the café it was dark and dim, tiled and shuttered and all male, and everything seemed all shades of tan, tobacco, and amber: the deep brown froth of the coffee's crema, the crescent over the oval boiler, pressed and hammered silver gone honey with age, brass fittings beneath the counter, old wood, the boney rattle of old ivory dice in the old backgammon sets as amber-gold as the chairs. All cool and quiet in the apple smell of nargileh. So scampering to turn the music down, coal fell from the tobacco tower of the nearest men's pipe, and the waiter dropped the nargileh tube and the plastic-wrapped mouthpiece melted immediately. But the small emergency merged back into calm. So very quiet before the muezzin—crack of dice and shuffle of feet, sizzle of coal in the fire. Outside the hot dry winds washed around the mosque and through the souk, the bubble-click of the water pipes, and another waiter swung an ember tray like an Orthodox censer to keep the coals alive. Beyond the French doors a younger boy, an eerie albino, stood watching the crowds passing up to the souk, one foot upon the terrace step, one down in *contrapposto*, his hand resting on an old man's thigh. He applied moisturizer and cologne as the old man offered up his soft tan neck and his hands. The boy saw Leon watching and rolled his wide pale eyes to him, and Leon smiled. In the Shi'a Quarter that afternoon, coming up from Bab Touma, getting his bearings, he had passed posters of Nasrallah and Assad paired to smile into a shared middle distance and some complex fantasy. He'd passed a poster of Arafat in the '80s and '80s Wayfarers and a poster of a grenade beside, wrapped in keffiyeh, a key hanging from its neck, THE 59TH ANNIVERSARY FOR AL NAKBA, it read. And he'd seen the Danish boy—still here?—in a bright new yellow Hezbollah T-shirt. The streets were full of tourists, the worm that sleeps not, and to Leon before this café, every crack a gunshot.

He left the coffee unfinished, thanked the waiter, and joined the crowds rounding the corner of the mosque walls. Twenty-four hours with no news of Lebanon. Too many tourists, and too many Syrian fops walked arm-in-arm in oil-shocked frozen fashions, tight silk shirts, moustached with slicked-back hair, flare-panted, panting loudly after women they turned and watched, then proudly turning back like they'd accomplished something grand. The crowds enormous and bloated. Under the great walls Leon sat in Roman ruins as the muezzin rose in chorus finale and watched a wasted young man who'd monetized the pigeons that lined the parapets. He'd laid out an octagon of twine and olive oil cans in the square and sat on a backless plastic lawn chair beside a table covered in seed packets. Occasionally he called, high and harsh, "Kai, kai, kai, kai!" and occasionally the pigeons would respond, condescending from the parapets of the mosque to his little arena, where he sold the seeds to parents of children and viciously fended off pubescent boys from his chair. Beneath the table the young man's bouncing foot, his biblical boredom.

Cafés were dragging out barrels of ice and chilled drinks as the crowds left the mosque. Leon headed back the way he'd come and turned into the spice souk. At the fountain stood a specter. An emaciated man of his height, fiftyish, and European. Desiccated and gray of hair and skin, he was dressed in shabby khakis hanging loose like robes. They met eyes and the man's widened instantly. Leon looked away but the specter followed. The man intercepted him at the corner of the souk and eagerly, desperately walked alongside.

"*Konnichi wa, nihon jin desu ka?*"

"No," Leon said. "I'm not."

"*Você é brasileiro?*"

"No. I'm English."

"Oh, you're English. English! Really?" His eyes were wide, pale, and empty. "I'm German," he said. "I work here for the EU."

"Oh?"

"Come back to my house for figs! For tea! I'll make you tea. I'm *German.*"

Leon laughed then outright at the sad stick figure. The German grabbed his arm tightly at the bicep.

"It's not raining," the man said urgently. "Look! Why don't you drink tea with me?"

"*Get off me,*" Leon said. The German's expression changed; he released his arm immediately, smiling.

"Oh, you're special," he said, surprised, pleased. "A very special young man. I, I work for the EU. You need to be careful." He began to whisper. "*Mukhabarat* are everywhere. Be warned. They are following jihadists and foreigners." The crowds around parted for them, people eyeing the two strangers at the entrance to the souk. The German stayed too close by his arm, leaning in close as Leon walked faster.

"I can . . . " The German was sniffling, frowning. Leon moved abruptly sideways to let someone between them. "I can . . . " But the stick figure dodged sideways with him. "I can . . . *smell* you," he said. "You," he sniffed again, "you're —" And then he said a word in German that Leon did not know and Leon stopped.

"Will you help me? Tell me where the gold souk is," said Leon, "and I'll give you a little cash."

"I show you where it is, and you will come for tea?" He said it proudly. "And figs?"

"Of course," said Leon.

The German led him through the souk. It was only a block away through the spices, safflower, paprika, dried lemons, Syrian pepper in woven sacks, and he chose the most heavily armored yet anonymous window, buzzed, a small sign at the door in English, in French, in German.

———

"I know what it's worth," he said.

"Ah," in English, laughing distantly. "You know what this is worth so why are you coming to me?"

"I know what it's worth."

"Oh I think you are . . . I think you are . . . misleading . . . "

The jeweler was shaking his head shrewishly, searching for the word.

"I think you are misleading *me*," finished Leon for him, and the jeweler grinned at that, but did not meet his eye.

The jeweler contemplated the single link—he hadn't looked Leon in the eye since meeting him at the door, and his silence since ("I have some jewelry for sale," Leon had simply said) had passed from impatient contempt to a studied blankness. He knew what it was worth.

"I know what it is worth."

At Leon's riposte he examined the jewel again with his loupe quite briefly, and then dropped it in a practiced palm. The link sat on the velvet tray between them.

At last the jeweler shrugged. "And so why do you come to me?"

What might he say?

"You were recommended."

"I see."

He was looking at Leon's clothes, hand-washed and wrung and sun-dried against this moment.

"In U.S. dollars," Leon said.

The jeweler made an ancient face of contempt.

"U.S. dollars?" He rolled his head on his shoulders as if in despair at this awful situation. "*Today?*"

Leon was silent. "Well, if not today, I'm moving on to Jordan tomorrow."

"Jordan! Jordan." He sighed as if the entire transaction cost him terrible pain. "Why go to Jordan?"

"I'm visiting Petra, and then flying out the next day."

"Oh? Where then?"

"Tokyo."

"Why do you want to sell this now?"

"I don't wear that kind of shirt."

The jeweler laughed at that and looked him in the eye for the first time.

"You say this is a Ugandan stone."

"Yes."

"I doubt it. You have no certification. What is the provenance? How can I sell it? There are sanctions. You know the Kimberley process. This hearts and arrows cut is very . . . unexceptional."

"Well."

"I can possibly give you . . . ten thousand for this."

"Ah, no."

"Well, then we cannot do business, I'm sorry."

"I'm sorry too."

Leon had once learned a trick from his father in negotiation—stay silent. *Don't* negotiate. Force the other to make a move, to fill the awkward quiet with a counteroffer. He stood and looked at the link thinking only about his breathing. The jeweler stayed seated.

The deal eventually done for $70,000, U.S.

Out of the souk and along the Street Called Straight through a maze of piles of brick. He followed the emaciated German, light and changing fast now. The specter kept turning to check him, walking quickly on, and then stepping back to match his pace, dusty as the road, pointing out the sights.

He showed him the house of Judas, and he showed him a Roman triumphal arch that resembled the bridge to nowhere in Achrafieh—perfect in itself yet connected to nothing.

" . . . and this is Al-Mariah Miyeh, Greek Orthodox Patriarchate . . . " he said.

The building was off a side street, a huge anonymous modern hump, this center of his church, the campanile beside, a car or two in front, a formidable fence.

" . . . it was burned down in 1860 and rebuilt in . . . "

"Take me in," Leon said.

The German winced and looked down the street. Leon gave him a second US$20 bill. Through the fence in the courtyard before the entrance, little children were gathered in a gabble, past a notice board razed of all notices. As they passed the children tried their French, their Greek, their English: "Hallo, hallo hallo!" As if calling into an abyss for the echoes. The German woke the caretaker in an outhouse who let them inside and left them there. The temperature dropped twenty degrees. He walked down the aisle past the German who stood hugging himself at the entrance, checking the street.

At the head of the nave the baubles of the racket all about: the double-headed Byzantine eagle a decadent symbol of a depleted gene pool, an incestuous deformity. Saints in the paintings foppish and pink and pathetic; the doomed Maria on her mule with a shrunken, feeble Christ in peasant purity amid the gaudy chandeliers hung low and secondary crucifi leaning precariously at the iconostasis. He walked through the chill as if returning to his childhood home in shame, seeing its smallness, the shabbiness and dirt, the things we absorb and forget, a great rage building.

"*Damawy*," said the German from the vestibule.

"What?"

"*Damawy*," he said louder. "It is the Arabic for bloodthirsty."

"I know what it means."

"Why do Christians thirst for blood?"

Leon stood up at the Angel looking deep into the weak, fey eyes of Cosmas and Damian. *It is not my confusion; it is not my sorrow that you have forsaken me—it is my content you are transcended and my readiness to be.*

The German was suddenly beside him, and clutched his elbow.

"Come back, anyway, come on, it is not good to be *ssss . . .* "

Leon had just touched the back of his hand to pull him off, but the German hissed and recoiled and held his hand to his chest and stared at him. The blood made his fingers form white ridges and ran fast and tapped quietly on the stone.

"What did you—" the German said, then broke off into German and held out the bleeding hand to him.

"O là," Leon said, "*desolé . . .* " and reached out to him. The German recoiled and backed into a row of stacidia, the high-armed chairs with their seats folded up half-trapped him there, holding his hand. He made a sound, a dreamlike effort at a shout, a constricted gasp and squeak. Leon saw the children moving past the open doors of the cathedral, and he reached to him again.

The German's cheekbone crumpled dustily, and he made another muted gasp.

"*Be quiet,*" Leon said, and he raised his arm and the German slipped down in the stacidia and fell over on the tile beneath the two-headed eagle. Leon reached for his shirt to pull him up and his chest sunk and he gasped and a puff of dust rose in the chill church with a burst of lavender and incense and something else, corrupt and metallic—his sickness.

"What's wrong with you?" Leon said. "You're sick?"

The German tried to speak and couldn't and sank back.

Outside the children gamboled and squealed, too young to understand their role in the world, to understand the dread mantle of the last Christians of Damascus—no one coming for them. Leon dragged the collapsed German into the sanctuary. Then he left, alone, out into the heat.

He sat in his PVC cell in the Damascene hostel counting his money till dusk came.

He packed his bag, he showered, he shaved. He used the hostel's little travel iron to smooth again his only button-down oxford shirt. He went to the office to ask the Syrian Australian for directions to a local restaurant.

The recommended restaurant was called, absurdly, *Arabesque*, and in the Christian Quarter just beyond Maria Miyeh. In a restored old Damascene family home, its staff all spoke near-perfect English, and its clientele were foreigners, aid workers, journalists. Now he had arrived, or departed.

"A table on the terrace, please."

He ordered zucchini soup and St. Peter's fish in a crust of almonds and a bottle of Ksara Le Souverain. And the food sat uneaten while the wine tasted of home, of sea, of Mediterranean blue on green weed of the lava rock off the Corniche, of young tan bodies leaping, shrieking *yalla*, into the water, of baking valley air, of rivers, of a dream of a girl in a bikini walking through the perfect waters up to her hips, trailing her fingers though the infinite reflections of a tree-lined gorge. He leaned back in his chair and stared up at Mount Qassioun of the desolate anti Lebanon, littered with lights forming a woman sleeping. So flattened, so very collapsed, the sleeping, like some total tragic failure, claiming her rightful rest. And the muezzin singing to her, forestalling her waking in a rage. Her heels tucked up to her buttocks under the mountain. Her arms lay out above her head, made by the headlights on the winding highway to Beirut. The Umayyad minaret of Jesus was at her feet; a golden minaret in the new city at her fingertips. The darkness over her shoulders was the military zone, the old Russian listening post, and over her hips a dark and spangled tattoo of military comms.

Fireworks fired somewhere near. He didn't lurch, he didn't flinch. A wedding; a wedding only. Lebanon was behind him: to insist upon it.

Minus the wine, the most expensive wine he'd ever tasted, the uneaten meal cost 1,500 Syrian pounds. A quick equation rendered this at only US$30.

He was beginning to think about the future.

———

He returned to the hostel late through the empty excavations. The outer door to the courtyard was closed and locked. He rang the bell. The squat Syrian-Australian owner opened it to him with a cell phone in his hand, avoiding his eyes.

"Ah, hello. Did you enjoy your meal? You did not stay very long."

"Yes, thank you."

"We are doing some cleaning. Please. I'm very sorry."

They entered the courtyard together but then the owner veered hard right into his office and sat down very deliberately and stared at his computer. Leon turned into the corridor to his room. There was a length of hose on the ground leading from the showers and there was a wooden trolley of cleaning products directly outside his door. He swiped his key card. It didn't work. He went back outside to the office. The door was closed now, and he knocked on the window. The owner inside ignored him, hunched oddly low and staring at his screen.

"My door won't open," Leon said through the glass. "My card doesn't work."

The owner entered something on his keyboard and hit return and swiveled halfway round and picked up another card from the counter beside and held it out to him without looking, feigning boredom or a familiarity he hadn't earned. Leon opened the door and took it from him. The owner swiveled away in his chair without saying anything. Leon watched him. Then he dropped the old card on the counter and walked quickly back over the empty courtyard and down the corridor. The concrete was dry both there and in the showers beside. The new key card worked. The door opened and inside his little room a thin dark man of about his age with a birthmark on his cheek, in stonewashed jeans and a black leather coat, was standing by the bed with a squeeze mop in one hand and the Brioni jacket in the other looking blankly straight back at him.

"Excuse me," he said flatly in English.

"What are you doing in here?"

"Housekeeping. Excuse me." He dropped the jacket on the bed and shrugged and stepped quickly by him into the corridor and disappeared.

Leon checked the room. Dust bunnies under the bed. Nothing seemed to have been moved. He removed his laptop and checked his clothes, lifting them from the backpack, laying them out on the bed, pitifully few. Then he pulled the metal U-frame from inside the padded rear lining of his backpack. He reached down inside. In the very bottom in the lint and grit the last link lay. When he went back out in the courtyard the man was gone. The cleaning trolley was where he left it. The hoses lay over the ground. In the courtyard under the flags of the world the office was closed up, the blinds were pulled down, and the lights off. The hostel was empty.

Leon banged on the office door.

"I know you're in there, little man. I know you're in there."

The Syrian gave no answer.

The next day he took a taxi from Bab Touma to Soumariah bus station and boarded a JETT bus for Amman. A new visa for Jordan in his passport cost him JD10 and seemed to somehow frank the foregoing forgeries. He crossed the border. The JETT bus passed a statue of dead Hafez Assad and a billboard of President Bashar greeted him there, then a huger poster of Jordan's dead King Hussein, and a smaller one of Abdullah II behind, the sons all standing on their fathers' shoulders as he would do no more, a Syrian-English "GOOD BY," crossing the desert as the sun went down, a dry apricot dust thirty degrees above the horizon.

15 The Jordan

Given time to think, there were two immediate options. The JETT station in Amman was just a vacant lot—there were taxis waiting with drivers who, with limited English and terrible confidence, sought out the obvious backpackers. He watched an overladen Canadian couple helped with their luggage from the bus's hold straight to a taxi's trunk ("Oh, no, thank, you, no, that's all right . . . "), their eyes widening in alarm. But as if possessed or haunted they followed and got in too, swept away by the rising tide of their lonely planet toward a hostel they didn't choose and couldn't locate and where the owner gave the driver his percentage.

Leon broke his Arabic into Japanese syllabics and got a better deal, at the Mansour Hotel on King Faisal Street. But there his assumed nationality had gotten ahead of him. Four young Japanese men were making fun of a young Jordanian who had a little of the language, and he heard them snickering as they taught him lewd phrases, as the young man tried to keep up. He received his room key from the owner, a shambling, unslept oaf named Ali, and as he passed he offered the young Japanese a rough acknowledgment the way they the young men do—"*Auss*"—on the way to his double room with its two single beds and ants all over the floor. Noting on the Japanese men his age their good trainers, their cargo pants, their bright parkas: how he should look; how he should sound.

———

Tomorrow, given that the Syrian had a photocopy of his passport and now, he must assume, so had the *mukhabarat*: the two immediate options, the two immediate, urgent ones:

Tokyo. The address for his grandmother-never-met was in the new Gmail he'd opened.

Or, once the question was asked, the most dangerous, the most *anti*, the most outlandish, unpredictable, the most far was the most near, he had the passport and there he would be unfindable: Why not simply cross into *Israel?*

And, once asked, *why not?*

That night he experienced the uncanny progression of the ants. He lay awake in the awful hotel with his money belt about his waist, listening to the padding of young feet, the clatter of keyboards. By 5:00 AM his bed was ringed with the ants, a column split around from the window on the way to the foul w/c.

They'd avoided his bed as if the castors were laid in saucers of kerosene—that old trick. But they weren't.

He got up in the night and naked but for the belt, stepped over the teeming streams of big black shining bodies—two streams, butting heads the way they do—from the window around the foot of his bed toward the bathroom. He followed their course. They climbed the leg of the second bed, swarmed, and roamed the old linen bedspread, gathered again at the farthest corner, to descend the bedhead to the dusty floor. The column then climbed the step of the bathroom and made its way across the tile and up the porcelain into the toilet bowl.

In the dark he could see: His flush hadn't worked. He turned on the light.

The toilet was filled still with his three meager turds, peppered with bodies of martyred ants, and the water palely bright with blood. DREAMS ARE NOT TO WORLD STANDARD. PLEASE. He flushed again.

In the predawn dark he washed and dressed and left his key at the bench where Ali slept behind on a chaise longue. He wrote an email to his mother, and then he left and sent US$10,000 back to her back to her by *hawala* at a Western Union. He bought all he thought he could stomach — three pastries at a patisserie, filled with cream and sprinkled with artificial pistachio.

He waited in the Allenby minibus to Israel for an hour at the bus station, watching the taxi drivers roughhouse and touch and grin, drink coffee, and smoke cigarettes, swaying curbside in the chill AM, gossiping brilliantly. His driver cleaned out the cab by sweeping all the trash out on the ground. This was a false alarm — they weren't leaving and they waited on. A ghostly African, seemingly there among the drivers by a common consent and a mild and somehow companionable contempt, boarded the bus with two handfuls of Armani socks and offered them sadly. He murmured, "Socks, please," to Leon, who said no, and then the African left to haunt the fringes of the drivers' clique. Trucks descended the highway under a pink and rosewater dawn over the collection of mounds that made up Amman.

He ate a pastry and waited easily. Poised and effective, immersing in the new identity; how easy, to be blank and imminent, to smile, to be an economic event and watch emptily all the Jordanian energy and generosity, a police presence of a puny, yawning two.

And when the bus filled up at last they were gone, west through the Amman hills, then descending into the Dead Sea depression, an underworld surreal; the highway cut into the face of the wall of the gaping wadi, his ears popping as they went so low. Before his eyes a NO SMOKING sign, and two slit tennis balls cut to straddle the poles of the smoking driver's mismatched headrest, borrowed from some other car, to hold it high enough for comfort.

Jordan valley flowers around the roadside now, orange and gay, and scrub and farmland at the bottom of the descent, flat out and mini-Edenic, moving through a low jungle—the size of a city block—of all that was left of the rich incredulity of the eastern Jordan valley. A mockery of what once it had been, but in the long view the desertification the lifespan of a bird. His guts beginning to boil again, he began to prepare a spiel for the Israeli border police.

The taxi let them off at the rear car park of a confused set of low buildings, and officials asked for passports and briskly segregated the tourists from the Arabs. He followed the Canadian couple, the girl distressed over a lost pair of sunglasses, through a maze of narrow corridor to a glassed window where he presented his passport again.

"Do you want it on a separate piece of paper?" They asked him about the exit stamp as if by rote, so he could travel in Arab countries without evidence of the Allenby crossing into Israel permanently in his passport. He passed as a tourist.

"Yes, sure."

And he took the Jordanian-stamped paper and his passport, exited the office through a courtyard of astonished, dusty flax, and to do obvious things gave a blank and practiced shrug as the Canadians got mad—because it was another JD12 to board another bus to cross the bridge, and another JD2.50 for every piece of luggage to go in the hold.

They waited half an hour, then the huge air-conditioned tourist bus just a quarter full shook into life, and left the parking lot to join the road, and there they were in the curve of the river, visible only by a narrow mess of scrub under a bleak Judean mesa crowned with razor wire. And then they were crossing the muddy cesspipe, all that was left a bare meter of the brown and sacred sludge of the Jordan River limping like a discredited prophet to the shrunken Dead Sea, over a bridge of immense low concrete bulk and gravitas, and then they stopped again immediately, their passports checked once more, and then sent on in the last motions of an economic ceremony toward the Allenby terminal on the Israeli side of something utterly abstract, the whole trip over in a few minutes.

16 At Allenby

The signs were everywhere outside Allenby, and as a foreigner he was sent to the prettified end of the terminal, and there separated from his backpack and laptop that were fed into the building by conveyor. The automatic doors led them into the foreign end of the concourse—an open void of linoleum with low benches for them to wait before the immigration kiosks. Beyond that, steel bars—twenty-barred revolving barriers of rough steel polished to a shine at the height of adult hands and to a lesser shine, lower, by the hands of their children—separated them from the mass of Arabs and the smell of desperate sweat, hundreds grouped in pools of extended family, all mostly older, the women in full chador and the men lugging great white jerrycans of Zamzam water from the Hajj.

Black Beta Israeli girls in army fatigues left their kiosks and sauntered over the tile, a hipshot shuffle, their webbing belts low-slung on their olive-trousered hips, walking low like barefoot, satisfied, and totally at ease like athletes at rest, teenagers after a sports meet. One entered a code by a door and they disappeared into the building. In the terminal the girls were all dark and stunning and in uniform; the men were all Shin Bet, twenty at least scattered through the terminal, all six foot two, athletic, and flush with health, in civilian clothes, another uniform: trainers and cargo pants and polo shirts; seemingly unarmed, their faces cryptic and generic and carefree. Then there were the psychics, who dressed the same but their faces wore their profession: gray and heavy with their gift. They patrolled the area behind the kiosks, before the X-rays and chemical search zone beside the Arab aisle, and in their faces he saw his sister, saw a mechanical prepared-ness, a gaunt function, the willingness to do all.

He was called up to the kiosk.

"Leon Shiokawa."

He went up to the booth and gave his passport to the girl and the psychic behind passed slowly, watched him with a massive brevity, pausing to converse with a Shin Bet regular, to laugh.

She studied his passport at length. She examined the Jordan stamp, the two forgeries, flicking back to the pages of his details, flicking back to the stamp. He concentrated on the U.S. M16 lay-ing in her lap. Thinking of an Abu Keiko story: how in the days of Tel al Za'atar, the Christians with their U.S.-Israeli arms thought the Palestinians were supermen—that smaller caliber, the Ameri-can 5.56 mm to the 7.62 mm of the AK-47—they'd fill the guerrillas with shot after shot and those men would keep on running, keep on coming.

He loved to kill Palestinians.

"Will you excuse me a moment?" the girl said. She toned it as a genuine question, and he said, "Sure." She entered a code and opened the kiosk door and she went to show the Shin Bet men his documents.

He should have said, "Yes," as if he wasn't quite sure what she wanted from him. Their faces were ciphers and American, like athletes discussing a play. The psychic frowned at his picture. Beyond them in the Arab area the gossip and misery went on, and a teenage Israeli guard shouted in husky Arabic at the nearest old woman, an ancient headscarfed *grande dame*, "Move *over* to the *left*," and shook his head in disgust.

The girl returned, shouldering her gun in a sense memory he had of that Hezbollah guerrilla, an everyday beauty he was sud-denly very powerfully passive and open to observe. But, on her, this weapon was more than half her height—she was only a teen-ager too, and, shyly, like a school prefect embarrassed of her new responsibility, she avoided his eye and reentered the code, climbed inside the kiosk, and sat down again. She typed a while and then passed his passport through the slit in the Plexiglas and said—their training was so very good—"I'm sorry, could you go with them, please?" Shy and smiling and acting the act of her age.

The psychic and the Shin Bet in the pink polo shirt came around the kiosk. There was a terrible vision of the Shin Bet man as flesh mechanic, wet hands and squirts of blood up his pink chest, a frown as he bent over something terrible in some terrible room, and Leon standing beside, Leon blood-mouthed watching his work.

I am Japanese.

"You don't have to worry about your luggage," the Shin Bet said in American English. "We'll get that for you. We just have to ask you a few questions." Leon could feel no body language at all. The psychic was like a man with a toothache: physically strong and able but hunched and slightly pale, concentrating, and he hung back as Leon walked beside the Shin Bet man toward an office door in the wall, opened it to a banal corridor, where above it another sign read, PLEASE KEEP THIS TERMINAL CLEAN.

More so than even the terminal, than the bridge itself—a concept in concrete—the office was a blank room, the blankest of rooms, the most generic thing he'd ever seen, a crucible for lies to be found out. It was the terrible room. There were gray PVC panels on the wall, stained office industrial gray carpets, three chairs, a desk like a crude and homemade weapon, and the Shin Bet man leaving left behind three human beings. A heavy big-haired woman, in the same clothes as the men, sitting behind his passport, pens, and a single piece of pad paper on the desktop, the psychic beside the desk, and he in front as if interviewing for a job.

She started by apologizing.

She shrugged. "I'm sorry, we just have to ask you a few questions."

"Oh, that is fine," he said in a light Japanese accent.

"You speak English very well," she said. He could feel the concentration like ozone in the air, like the shimmer of petrol fumes. The room smelled only of old coffee and stale man. The psychic seemed very far away, staring at the table, eyes flicking to Leon only once so far.

"No, no," said Leon, listening to his mother in his voice, mimicking her quietness perfectly. "For so much school, it's very bad."

She seemed to contemplate an acknowledging laugh, like an actor looking at a playwright's line.

"Why do you want to come to Israel?"

"I'm backpacking in the Middle East. As a tourist. I want to visit Jerusalem and Tel Aviv."

"How did you get here?"

"I crossed from . . . " he described the route carefully and told the basic truth.

"Who do you know in Lebanon?"

He said no one, told her of three days at a famous backpacker's in Gemmayzeh, of the conflict, of leaving.

"I'm sorry, we have to ask these questions."

"Yes, of course."

"Do you have family in Israel?"

"No."

"Were you given anything before you came here?"

"No."

"We have to ask these questions."

"I understand."

The psychic was watching him longer between breaks of staring at the table and he seemed to grow in sadness, seemed so tired. What was he doing? The woman was growing bored, did it seem? Or was this an act? She got robotic—

"Did anyone give you anything in Syria?"

"No."

"Were you given anything in Jordan?"

"No."

"Do you have family in Syria?"

"No."

"How did you get from Syria to Jordan?"

He explained again.

The psychic stood up and came to stand beside and slightly behind him. "Excuse me," he said. "Do you mind—" His voice was hoarse and he cleared his throat. The question had no interrogative. Leon was aware of the woman watching him as this happened, and he imagined the conical fall, how going limp might let him through the narrowing gap, and he smiled and he said, "No . . . ?"

The Israeli psychic placed a warm hand on his shoulder.

"Do you have any family or friends in Israel?" the woman asked blankly.

"No," Leon said gently. "I'm visiting as a tourist."

"Where will you stay in Israel?"

"I want to stay at a hostel in the Old City in Jerusalem. But I haven't made the booking yet. I am worried that they may be all—" He took a chance and went too far. "I don't know the word—no opening?"

Her face didn't change.

"Booking. No booking. I am worried about."

The psychic's hand drew a firmer grip on his shoulder, and then he felt the touch and warm tickle of the psychic's hair against his, as the man placed his head against him like friends or men mourning a death of a daughter, a sister.

"Just relax," the woman said. "It will soon be over."

"Yes."

"Did you meet anyone in Damascus?"

The man was whispering something in his ear.

"No one."

He didn't understand what he was saying.

"We have to ask these questions."

"I understand."

"Why are you worried about your booking?"

"Because . . . because I have none."

Then the head against his was gone, the hand on his shoulder was removed.

The psychic said something in Hebrew to the woman. She received the information implacably.

Then he left the room and didn't close the door.

She looked after him, then she looked at Leon's passport.

"What did he say?" Leon said. He felt like laughing.

"He said 'either ice masquerading as fire or fire masquerading as ice.'" She looked at him with something sardonic. "What do you think that means?"

"I don't know. I'm sorry."

"We know what you are. Your entry is denied."

"But why?"

"We know what you are."

And instead of what he did, instead of returning to Amman and taking another bus on Route 15 south through the Jordanian deserts, fields of stone, of Toyotas and canvas tents, herds of absurd sheep, to Queen Alia Airport, the vampire might then have been led out to join the seething Arab queue, and his bags given back, X-rayed and swabbed and analyzed. He might have been released outside to the car park in the bright foreign sun, surrounded by Palestinians with containers of holy water, the buzz of a drone overhead, the razor wire round Allenby a net for torn and clouded supermarket bags like ragged flags of factions of a future state. Instead of standing in the airport lounge watching on a TV screen in the corner puffs of smoke rising from far Beirut and the Corniche Mazraa, and watching a helmeted and flak-jacketed reporter standing on the empty rue George Haddad, only a few meters down from the Paul Café where he'd passed by just the morning before last, outside the Kuwaitis' empty apartments, where Abu Keiko would have, should have, stood and paced, and instead of what he did—practicing watching the footage blankly, practicing the unrecognition—the vampire might have paid U.S. dollars for the minibus, and ridden the highway through the Judean desert west though the hill country, past Jericho in the distance, watching the wave forms in the rock rip, impermeable and waterless, shantytowns in the wadis built of plank and corrugated iron and ripped old canvas, and eventually through the tunnel under Mount Scopus to emerge on the dual carriageway above the valley of the navel of the world, the first city quiet and arrayed beneath then gone, and he could have disembarked at the Damascus gate bus terminal and then maybe walked the Old City walls to the Jaffa gate and entered there and found the Petra hostel, an old Ottoman shuttered building overlooking David's Citadel under the late afternoon sun, a golden sarcoma bleeding under the skin of the white sky.

Instead of checking his new email for the Japanese address there from Junko—her mother in the country somewhere—and writing a six-word email never sent to Emmanuelle, *I will come back for you,* and at 9:00 PM boarding a British Airways flight for Tokyo, the vampire might have climbed the old stairs of the Petra past a money changer hunched in a booth to check in in the dim up there, free and franked and processed as a Japanese backpacker, and a grand and dour African in crimson and full ceremonial dress and a U.S. accent could have taken his U.S. dollars and led him upstairs to a cool cave with bare rock walls, a low double bed, and shuttered windows out to the citadel where on ladders they were weeding the walls of the Tower of David, and one clear panel in the midst of a wall of marbled panes on the east side by the barely plausible toilet with a view over a wastewater-filled wasteland to the sun-scalded Dome of the Rock and the vampire could have left his backpack and gone upstairs to the roof where you could rent tents or sleep rough for cheap in the summer with U.S. students and spiritualists and madmen with 360-degree views of the Old City and piles of mattresses and ashtrays in molasses cans and the urge—so strong—to leap, and seen the small house up there where the African lived and outside the house children's toys and dead herbs in pots and a little cage and in the little cage the African's little baby standing nude and holding the bars and screaming at Jerusalem.

But it was not to be.

in Japan

17 United Nations

White bones of the outlands of the airport under purple skies before the train went underground, an hour into Tokyo. 成田. Staring bloodshot-eyed at the newspapers of the passengers, able to read some of the kanji of the headlines: *Zengakuren* protests close Keio University; students rioting in the streets. Just his backpack at his feet. 八千代台. Alone, the vampire could smell himself; three days out, the same cargo pants, the same parka. The other passengers ignored him. 上野. Did he pass? He passed, here. He passed.

青山一丁目.

And he emerged at Omotesandō, 表参道, exit B2, on the wide boulevard of Aoyama dori in massive ambient heat and the line of skyscrapers extended down the road implacable. The streets were close to empty but back behind him at the intersection with Omotesandō dori the barriers rose and beyond that the shopping went on and the traffic unperturbed. He touched the wooden joints of the Maruyama building as he passed, cool in the heat. Ahead toward the UN University, opposite Aoyama Gakuin University, there were fires and a steady chant.

Their banners were in Japanese and English and the protest was in its last stages. Trash everywhere from a long sit-in, like bento boxes and chopsticks and empty tea bottles, all over the shining tile concourse off the dori and before the looming ziggurat of the UN University building. The great fascist stepped pyramid of a structure seemed to move in the light from the protest fires, its shadows flinching and flickering.

Before it were only twenty protesters, non-Japanese, and the banners and placards read of Burma, Burmese prisoners of conscience, Gaza and Palestine, Japan–U.S. relations, World Bank and IMF corruption, exploitation, 10% unemployment, the American air base on Okinawa, and thirteen million out of work. The trash suggested there had been many more. The group chanted slogans at the building, which was darkened and seemed uninhabited, the UN logo as big as a car, the earth in its wreath of olive branches, above the storm-shuttered central doors. They faced it like an idol or an altar. On the dori two police cars sat in darkness. Whatever had happened was winding down for the night and he went to a twenty-four-hour underground McDonald's for his dinner, iced coffee and inedible fries with airport yen, as the night sweated out.

In the early dawn the sun hit the concrete. The air was salty and stultifying immediately, brackish in the back of his throat. He emerged from the McDonald's and the protesters, almost a hundred, were preparing for another day. Most were very young. They stood about in loose factions gossiping in the closed-off street. They were highly organized and there were trestle tables piled high with massive stacks of red plastic helmets and wooden staves, a sports ice bucket filled with whistles. The Burmese group had formed again, reinforced with others, not all Burmese, but Arabs, Koreans, and they stood apart, their ages and despairs discrepant, receiving occasional ambassadors from the students.

He walked around them to a boy in socks on the pavement who was circling a huge and empty white paper banner between two long battens laid out on the road. He had a wooden rule and a cardboard box of poster paints. Leon watched him lay the rule a foot from the top of the banner, padding onto it with a pot and a brush, consulting a wrinkled page of notes. Leon stood beside the banner and watched as he wrote. His technique was precise and practiced and he recognized the style his mother sometimes wrote in Japanese—firm, deliberate strokes with no corrections, paint fading as the stroke grew long, like the Aounist symbol in reverse, working steadily from upper left to bottom right, each character the size of a manhole.

"It's difficult to get the right balance when you write big characters," the calligrapher murmured, and laughed.

"Yes, it's so," said Leon. The first character was simply *end*. He dipped the brush and precisely wiped each side on the rim of the tin, and Leon thought of Samir and his slow smoking. The boy painted the first stroke of the next in a mechanical artistry, and lost in his task he murmured on to Leon as he worked in the rising heat of the day.

"I did some practice with my *senpai*. Gradually we made them cursive."

"Cursive?"

"Joined together. Your Japanese is very good!"

"Thank you."

"The more you practice, you can write the characters easier, with no need to do outlines first."

End Japan

He stood and looked at what he'd done. Then he laughed gently and turned to Leon.

"Oops. I made a mistake. But I have paper. I can fix it." He resumed work and the message grew, rising simply, elegantly, stark and clean on the white. It took an hour. As the message progressed, he expanded the characters from a foot to two feet to three. He changed paints from black to blue to red to express the intensity. *End Japan's complicity with the U.S. imperialist occupations.* The groups of students in front of the UN University grew and the factions were coalescing, joined by more students arriving from across the dori who were already helmeted, spurring those early to form a line to the trestle and suit up. The boy finished up the last character, filling the banner, and stood and contemplated his work.

Idly, he said, "If I wanted to soften the impression I would use rounded edges. But for this event I imagined powerful, beautiful letters. Sometimes I make them more beautiful . . . or sloppier." He laughed again, self-deprecating, boyish, hoarse intakes of breath. He looked over the massing crowd of students. "See there?" He was pointing to an older man in a group at the periphery, with a small film crew, a sound man, and a camera operator beside a band setting up, four long-haired boys in black and sunglasses, a drum kit and amplifiers, guitars in hard cases. "That is Wakamatsu Koji. He's an old radical leftist who makes porn movies now." He laughed again, then looked slightly embarrassed. "Excuse me. You are Palestinian?"

"No, Lebanese."

"Oh good." He nodded urgently. "We need to extend the breadth and reach of the struggle and link up with other resistance movements. I—" His cheerful murmur became duller, rote but still unhesitating. "I will keep on fighting until the people are liberated. If I didn't do it, it would be a betrayal to all of us here, it would be a lie to everyone. It would be a mockery of our youth. It would turn what I'm doing into a lie, into art, and I would have to live with that forever. Like him." He pointed to the director. "I'd rather die."

The gathering group was being formed into lines by lieutenants.

"Shigenobu Fusako's daughter will speak at the protest today."

"Shigenobu Fusako."

"She is half Lebanese. She was the leader of the Japanese Red Army. She went to your country to fight the revolution. She is a hero. She had a child with a Palestinian freedom fighter there in the civil war. Shigenobu May. Now she is back here, May." He seemed a little embarrassed, thinking that Leon didn't know this. He laughed again, his adolescent, hoarse, good-natured barks. "She is really hot, though, her daughter."

"She is half Japanese?"

"Yes!" He seemed pleased his country was involved.

He knew about Shigenobu, but not about the daughter. "What kind of Palestinian freedom fighter?"

"No one really knows, but the rumor is Jojihabashu, the leader of the Popular Front for the Liberation of Palestine. It's a secret they keep."

It took him a minute to understand the Japanization of the Lebanese name.

"George Habash?" Habash, the old Palestinian leftist. Born in Lod where Ben Gurion Airport was built, where the Japanese would come, Shigenobu's young men, with their violin cases full of automatic weapons and grenades. Was that symmetry something they discussed in bed? Like a lovers' vow? Habash was dead in Amman these five months and Greek Orthodox, like him; like his father. *Going down to the party, your father called it. He loved to kill Palestinians. Are you going down to the party . . .*

"He died of a heart attack even though he had cancer. He was killed by Mossad. The mother is in jail here now. She was a hero." The young man checked Leon then—as if this were clearly difficult territory. "Her daughter—she is a journalist for Asahi news. And she teaches English." His grating laugh again. "You should talk to her!"

He began to seal the pots of paint and wipe his brushes clean. "My older sister worries. She says, 'Hurry up and quit and come home now.'" Bark, bark. "My brother says, 'Man, you always do interesting things.'"

It had grown harder to breathe—the air was thick, brackish, and salty. The students were all helmeted, hand towels hanging from the helmet straps to wipe the sweat, to mask against the tear gas when it came. They looked happy and very young and they stood in serried columns that stretched from the storm barriers of the UNU back through the troughs of municipal plants and across the dori to the hedged walls of Aoyama Gakuin opposite. The Burmese and the other foreigners arrayed in front of them seemed of mixed reaction—some were shouting in sympathy, some looked perplexed, because the noise was growing huge: The student leaders stood in front of each column holding a little microphone connected to a loudspeaker held by a lieutenant, and they were shouting different things to each column and each column was shouting back, reacting differently to what they heard, blowing their whistles, the noise echoing back off the building.

Then something happened and the groups were led off and began to move but there was too little space and too many of them and too many different columns, so they began to march in looping serpentines, merging in and out of each other's columns, linked arms and four abreast, chanting, whistling, and unable to get anywhere of any significance, they were bouncing on the balls of their feet like joggers stuck in a crowd trying to keep their heart rates up.

They slowly circled for a while, and began to feel the impotence of it, and began to jostle, and the foreign group was pushed closer to the impermeable barriers of the huge UN edifice, and a young man with a camera tripped and his camera was dashed on the tile, and he was pulled to his feet again. Down the dori reinforcements had been made to the police presence, four more cars walling off the street at either end.

The calligrapher and his group assembled at the battens of his completed banner, and began to raise it up. One of the columns of students was merging with another right beside them and two of the protesters, two young girls, were pushed onto the paper, falling in a heap on the message, and as they raised the banner it ripped around their fallen forms, and the calligrapher's group screamed insults at them. Leon pushed his way to the outside by the Oval Building, and stood with a small group of bemused salarymen who'd come outside to smoke in the gardens—most had stayed inside and watched through twenty-foot plateglass windows.

"Excuse me! *Excuse me.*"

There was a very small, shaven-headed young Asian woman behind him, amongst the men; not Japanese, his age or older. She was speaking English.

"Yes?"

"Are you Palestinian? Are you protesting?" She was totally un-Japanese, tough, even angry.

"No. Lebanese."

"Oh. Lebanese Palestinian? Lebanese? Are you an artist?" She seemed pleased, somehow.

"Uh, yeah. Lebanese. Filmmaker."

"You are in the Culture Center! I am there too." She had formed a total focus on him while the protest still swelled, the student mass heaving and calling.

"Yes. I am . . . just arriving."

"I am Kim Ahn. *I am a Vietnamese musician.*" She was shouting and she offered a hand to shake quite formally and she was so obviously different from the Japanese girls—a great stillness about her, not a peace but a compression of some huge rage—and another loudspeaker rose then, this one playing a military march and the students howled in anger. Down the dori a large black bus came into view, armored, great red kanji on the side. The salarymen around them abruptly stubbed out their cigarettes and went inside the Oval Building doors. The girl turned, her physical gestures precise and controlled, and moved her attention from him to the scene like moving a needle on a record. The parade music was so loud it was tearing at the edges and distorting, and the students now caught between the van and the silent UN were screaming back at it. The van was the rightists, nationalists—but the point was the dori had been barricaded, so the police must have let them through. Balance, Leon saw—it was all about balance.

"I'm Joseph," he said "Can you . . . " he was going to ask but the students broke column then and rushed toward the van, a peeling movement, the instigators running toward it, a tearing of the edge of the group, then their lovers and their friends then everyone rolled toward them and the bottles and staves began to fly.

She stepped toward it, her chest rising, and then said, "Come *on,*" and she took his hand, then dropped it, and he felt his heart rate fall sharply, and he followed walking with a feeling of great power through the edge of the students, past the Burmese and on down the two-lane alley beside the UNU, and they passed the rear of the Oval Building and in the loading zone was a police van blocking the way round and a police car behind that and beyond the riot officers with shields and nightsticks were massing behind the building out of sight. *"Come on,"* Kim Ahn said loudly, and dragged his arm again, left, back of the UNU, a weird semidetached set of utilitarian buildings at least as high but narrow. She swiped her passcard but the automatic doors were locked. They stood there with their backs to the huge closed glass doors until two baffled office girls caused them to open from the inside. They ducked into the long, cool, high foyer of shining tile lined with international flags on plastic sticks and when the doors shut again the office girls stood and stared and the noise went muffled and the air-conditioned chill maintained. In the high quiet his heart rate pumped up and up and Kim Ahn stood frowning at the doors.

"They will now beat them and teargas," she said, "and then it will go quiet, and then it will happen again this afternoon. They won't come inside. It would be *impolite*."

"This is the Culture Center?" he said.

"It is part of the UN building so it has embassy status. Have you checked in?"

"Yes," he quickly lied.

She looked hard at him. "Are you exhibiting tomorrow?"

"No . . ."

"You just arrived. I can't get satisfaction loudspeakers for my performance," she said and turned away. "It will be silly." She looked quite furious, five foot tall, every inch of her full up to her skin with the anger and adrenaline, glowing softly ochre-red, eyes wide with it. "Come up to my room and let us have a drink, for goodness' sake." She looked at him without expression. He almost laughed.

"Okay. Okay, sure," he said and she snorted disgustedly and stalked away to the next set of automatic doors, furious, fast, expecting him to follow.

18 In Kim's room

He stayed in her room for seven days and nights. The rains came. Thunderstorms and torrents that did not flood the streets like Beirut but flooded the floor of her kitchen with rubbish bags that bulged with the ramen cups and sushi trays of all they ate, disposable chopsticks puncturing and unseaming the plastic sacks so they collapsed and leaked sachets of soy sauce and grainy ramen broth. Whiskey bottles lined the floor by the sink. He paid for everything—returning from the convenience stores that were everywhere with bags full of food and alcohol. They ate and drank and talked in her room at night and she let him sleep on the floor on a yoga mat. She worked in her studio by day, a free space given her on the terms of her scholarship. He told her his passcard was still being prepared, and she loaned him hers, so he could get out and explore idly, like he was on holiday, returning each night by 10:00 PM when security came on. He figured out how to get what he needed at Japanese internet cafés—unlimited coffee and a private booth—and stayed in them for the daylight hours, anonymous and fading. But on the seventh day something happened.

She went to a studio meeting with the staff of the Culture Center and the fellowship artists who were to present or introduce their work. She'd told him about one, a filmmaker and installation artist who'd shot stills of the residents of Tuvalu, a sinking Pacific Island, in the style of '50s Italian monster movies, shrieking up to an empty sky in hypersaturated distress.

"The artists here make their shapes with Lego, their funny films, their animations, and their shapes from trash. And they say they are *interest* in this, they like *this*. They interest in *that*. What would they *suffer* for? Where even first is the *craft*? I am a classically trained musician. It is not *potent*."

They sat on the floor in there, 4F of the Culture Center, and drank Japanese whiskey from plastic bathroom counter cups. The walls were bare, beige; the carpet beige and industrial. The room was bare, and the building's two floors that belonged to the Culture Center were also bare. They had taken a bare, beige elevator to a beige lobby, and there off an office was an umbrella stand and a fire extinguisher and nothing else besides. Down the long corridor of the artists' rooms there were full vertical blinds arrayed the length of the building, which stirred slightly in the air-conditioning with a quiet *clack, clack.* On the other side it was lined with the doors behind which the young artists worked or slept, like prisoners or hotel guests creating something out of only their minds, revealed utterly by this blankness.

There was nothing in here to tell of her: a single bed and brown comforter in disarray, a single desk and aluminum Mac laptop, an open suitcase messy with use in front of an empty wardrobe. By the entrance one door led to a single kitchen, with its single set of crockery and cutlery, a single bathroom with its single set of towels. Cross-legged they faced each other over the bottle and pair of cups.

She gestured out the window.

"These protesters—their methods are too old-fashioned. You see they use the 1968 leftists as their example; they are already doomed to failure. They need to think about the future. Very organized but very flexible, passionate, ruthless. The road gets only harder. The Japanese are like the world but more: addicted to the middle class. And they have no international understanding because they cannot get an outside perspective of themselves. They know nostalgia, safety, isolationism. Economic dependence. Design. *Art.* They need to grow rice, not concrete."

"The rooms are so bare."

"I have a studio too, and I can put anything on the walls because I am a visiting *artist,*" she said with contempt, "and it is just *art.* So I don't. The speakers are no good, so I keep the music to myself."

She never softened as she spoke, just adjusted her barriers. He couldn't stop looking at her: the tiny individual black hairs of her shaven scalp, her mauve and fractured lips swollen and rich, her eyes dark and distant and angry, her eyebrows shaven into shards, the high rise of her skull and fontanel visible in the thin but coarse hair. An awkward pause.

"You make films?" she said.

"I made a film."

"Tell me about your films."

He said this; he said that. He explained the film basically. What could it hurt? The subtext was all and she couldn't know it unless he told her. He smiled a lot as he lied. He talked about Lebanese political history. He told her his mother was sick, his father was dead, he'd had to leave his little sister alone behind in West Beirut with the cousins during these recent troubles, all those famous Lebanese cousins, but that she—little *Hind*—knew he would return, he would return. It sounded like any other story. All the Lebanese bullshit. He told her about music: Fairouz and Majida el Roumi. He told her a story he'd heard from the '70s; how he used to catch river snakes in Beirut River and then sell them for the price of a cinema ticket. There were no more snakes in that river. Any kind of Beirut, heartbreaking, metropolitan, agrarian, was plausible. They were flirting.

"I am married to a man," she said levelly, a test. "He has a job. He is stable. I have a young daughter."

"Are they in Vietnam?"

"They are in Hanoi."

"That must be hard, leaving them there."

She made an amused, hurt face. "It is not so hard. I get to think. I get to work. I am thirty-five now."

She looked caught between expressions and emotions. For a moment poised there, seeing if she were to suffer judgment, rejection, boredom. If he didn't understand she didn't care. Then she got bored at her own waiting and changed the subject.

"There are strange visitors who come here. A Burmese woman comes looking for the Burmese photographer, who is one of the guests here. She stole in. It seems to be easy. She hunts for him, knocking on the doors at night like a ghost. He doesn't explain. He only says he comes from a quiet village and shows us pictures that look like a tourist book." She drank, and seemed happier with this story. "I don't mind the knocking. They come in here looking for a dissident—" she pronounced it de*ci*dent, "and we don't know if they are junta secret police or a protester." She smirked. "The Australians get nervous."

A white-noise roar was rising outside the window behind the gentle clatter of the blinds. She looked up into the corner of the room and listened to it.

"It is raining again. So it will save them from beatings."

"The rain?"

"The new rain. Out of season for monsoon. It is too hard and no one can do anything. They lose interest in political change. Weather changes, and changes us."

She got up and went to the window, a window that took up half the room's wall and could not be opened—these were converted offices. It looked out on the vast, bare, empty, tiled concourse of the inner courtyard of the UN building. He got up and leaned on the sill beside her to watch the rain turn the lamplit tile to a quivering mirror.

"My father was a violinist," she said. "In the sixties he played violin with the Viet Cong and he played violin for the soldiers in the tunnels. Debussy, Brahms, the *Sonatas and Partitas*. He played violin in the jungle for the men who conquered Dien Bien Phu. And that is where they try to get into," she said pointing into the courtyard. "They burn for it, are gassed and beaten. And only the artists here know. There is nothing there."

On the seventh day he stayed in. He checked his new and empty email on his laptop using her Wi-Fi log-in and drank coffee and read the newspapers. The artist's work she'd described had sparked some familiar scorn, and a memory that was fond and painful. He turned and tasted it as he browsed. And then he looked for it. He searched videos, using the most obvious terms: *Soldier of Fortune, video game, reenactment, rooftop, real life, battle, Lebanon, Pascal, Etienne, Georges, Leon.* A slew of captures from the last iteration of the old game was all he found. So he signed into YouTube as *leonelias* to find it under his old favorites.

In 2000 Pascal had bought a video camera. In 2000 they'd all been students, with university computer privileges, and they'd all gamed and they'd all played the old PC first person shooter *Soldier of Fortune.* Pascal had started filming everything with the new camera, but he shot architecture, he shot buildings and billboards and signs and symbols, static and abstract things. It had been Etienne's idea to make something with actual people. *I get it,* Pascal said. *It's a metaphor. Yeah,* Etienne said rolling his eyes. *It's a metaphor.* There had only been four of them—Georges, Pascal, Etienne, Leon—so Leon had asked Keiko to shoot it. What he remembered was her goofy unfamiliarity with the camera, the warm ease of the day, that simple thrill that felt like the habit of art of childhood—her excitement, her pleasure in the idea, in the *doing* of something no matter how silly and undergraduate. She was twenty-seven, an intelligence officer in the army, the same age as Leon was when she died. They shot the film on the rooftop of the old house. Three stories up on the hot rough tarmac amid the TV aerials and bird droppings and the water tanks for the three apartments sandwiched into the building; children's bikes grown out of and stiff tarpaulins and odd lumber, with the same views as Georges's and Lauren's apartment, away from the South and Hezbollah, over the dun east neighborhoods of Achrafieh to Bourj Hammoud and Christian Jounieh.

Soldier of Fortune. Georges, Pascal, Etienne, Leon, dressed up in military gear or as near as they could find: combat pants and cargo trousers, boots and gumboots, real military webbing, winter balaclavas—ragtag stuff brought from their homes, and from Abu Keiko's closet in the shelter. They used water guns and water pistols. Ragtag—instead of elite special forces or professional mercenaries they looked like the hash-crazed recruits—teenaged, sunglassed, and grinning over the grips of .50-cal machine guns—of one of the real militias in the old photos and TV footage. Keiko roamed about the rooftop in the bright sepia sun, bent over the camera and dead serious now—shooting weird Dutch angles they'd find out later, but she really hadn't wanted to let them down for this last silly project. The boys, armed and suited up as if for battle, mimicked the *Soldier of Fortune* impasses of the inexperienced.

Georges approached a wall in commando crouch, rifle raised and professionally aimed, and then walked directly into the wall. He jumped and jumped against it for a while. Behind him Etienne with a huge knife sidled covertly around a cistern, then turned and walked directly into him. Without acknowledging the collision he backed up and then walked into him again and tried to jump on him. They shuffled around each other in a slow-dancing nuzzle. Pascal slowly approached Leon, rifle cocked, then turned abruptly away and ran into a corner of the rooftop to bump against the wall. He stayed there twitching slightly. Etienne turned in one direction, then another, slashing at the air with his hunting knife in startled spasms, unable to start moving forward. Georges in a gas mask bunny-hopped around the roof in circles.

Keiko had filmed it all deadpan, but when they had watched it on laptop it was the last time Leon could remember her really belly-laughing out loud, with her eyes open to them like she did, like she was amazed at them, how funny they were. Helpless and teared up while the boys assessed their performances and criticized each other.

Leon smiled at its innocent two minutes and fifteen seconds. Twelve-year-olds might do it now if game engines even allowed for that kind of incompetence in a first-time player anymore. They'd called it "Beirut conflict." Uploaded at last in 2007, it had 149 views, five likes, and no comments. The sidebar's related videos showed thumbnails of footage from the civil war, and from fighting on the Corniche Mazraa just days ago. Georges, Pascal, Etienne—what were they doing now? In what kind of trouble and how protected was Etienne?

Leon went back to his Gmail and there were suddenly hundreds of emails. A dark wall of emboldened names and subject lines and times and dates where there'd been just three pale read messages, from "Gmail Team" and from his mother, before. He stared at the inbox in the silent Culture Center room. Messages, multiple new messages: May 13, May 14, May 15: bold and unread, from his mother (nearly tech illiterate, she was the only one who knew the new Gmail address, was its sole real correspondent); from his father (*Elias, Didier*: who did not use computers; who could not type: *Please call, son, Urgent, What the doctor says*); from Joseph; Pascal; from his bank (*Urgent, Please contact*); from Samir who had no email address at all he knew; all fake, all faked; but Etienne (*Call me, Hi Leon, Urgent*); Georges and Lauren's combined address too—*Call us, Hi Leon, Urgent, We Want to See You soon.*

He read the names of all those he loved. The cursor lingered over his father's name. Then he slowly moved the cursor across the page and clicked. But he missed the icon for his face and moved the whole window slightly. He had to do it again—log out. He'd been there nearly three minutes. YouTube had automatically signed him into his old Gmail.

The Skype connection was granular and dropping frames. Joseph's image was frozen like a screen grab, yet his voice continued. It was easier in snapshot than in movement to see how haggard he was; weight dropped off, unshaven, hunched forward to his computer. Leon's laptop had no cam—Joseph could not see him.

"He is well, he is fine," Joseph said. "Just fine. In the hospital. Flirting with the sisters."

The Skype struggled, and then suddenly Joseph's image came alive and sped to catch up with his voice. Fast-forwarding revealed his tics. Joseph pulled at the lobe of his ear; he adjusted the fall of the belly of his shirt again and again.

"It's terrible but then again, it's not so bad. We've seen worse."

He laughed mechanical; a semaphore; a gesture.

"And mama, Joseph?" Leon said.

"Oh, she is fine, fine," he said. His lips disappeared, the slack flesh at his neck protruded, his eyes closed, and he nodded and nodded and sighed through his nose. "You know, she is strong. Your father is strong too. It's me who is the weak one. I've no stomach for this: sickness, ill health." Was it something about watching himself on the webcam, with no image of Leon—he was speaking oddly, confessionally. "Your father never gets sick." He sighed as if at his own cliché. "Not a day in his life."

"Are you all right Joseph?"

His image froze again. Paused, he was looking off into the corner of a room Leon could not identify—the wall behind him was blank. His voice came thin and pixelate. "Oh, absolutely fine," he said in French to emphasize it. "Just tired. I've always been the weak one, you know that."

Leon stared at him. The subtext was complicity. His uncle as he always did was implying that they were the same, hiding from any possibility of being accused of doing so, and asking for a reassurance he'd reject if it came. But his frozen image looked away—not needy, distracted, uninvolved. A long silence was broken only by his sigh.

"You would tell me, wouldn't you?" Leon said.

There was another long silence—it was impossible to know if it was digital or his uncle pausing. When his voice came again it was far-off, mechanical, and dropping syllables. "Yes, I would tell you."

"You're sure?"

"Leon." His image caught up with him again. He was leaning into the screen, staring as if at Leon, but he was looking at himself in the feedback of his own cam, suddenly sincere. He no longer seemed to be speaking to Leon, either. "Without your father we are nothing. And we would be nothing now. I would tell you. He is a true man and a good man. Didi has fought forever. He knew before anyone what to do. Not just what to do but that it *had* to be done. That is why I am nothing now. I stayed out of it.

I got tired easily of fighting and weapons. I want bread and life." Leon didn't answer. The image dissolved and a snapshot of Joseph formed; frozen, pale, grainy, looking off into the background. "He was always different. I only saw chaos. He understood it better. Chaos left me behind."

"Joseph, come on. Is he all right? What's happening? Have you heard from my friends?"

"Yes, yes." He was getting irritable, enjoying his speech. "But you have to understand how to see things. Now Karantina at the beginning, and they say he was a hero and he *was* a hero. The cedars, the cross, the cause, and all of it. It was *right* to do as they did. But Leon, you know, it's my burden to know, and leftists and some historians will tell you, the belligerents were a small detachment of PLO guarding the camp. Not so many. The rest of them were Palestinians, yes, but Kurds and Armenians too, civilians, refugees, and poor families. We had nothing against them. But did they have to go?" His image resolved into another frozen still; dead eyes, following something off beyond the laptop. "They had to go. You have to do violence and you have to do it all the way. At Karantina your father killed a lot of people he said. He regretted it. But they couldn't leave them there could they, in the middle of a Christian neighborhood like a serpent waiting for its head to return? Could they? No they couldn't, so they did it all the way. They ate the snake. But not me. Without your father and the men like him we are nothing. Gone from this country. But I don't have the spine or the will for that. I never would. Killing Armenians and children."

"Yes, Uncle Joseph."

"Christians now are pathetic. Christian upon Christian. Fighting with everything they have, giving everything away. To what end? And though I tell you I was glad of what I did, you pay a price, and I got left behind. You don't know war. War is a natural event like a flood. If you don't make a decision you are swept away. If you make a decision you slightly reduce the odds of being swept away. But you soon find out. Didi had the whole war until it was decided for him. He made the right choice, morally right, but he was sold out by the fucking mountain men who killed his daughter, who play in our blood, who sleep with Syria and lie about it—"

"Joseph—"

"There's no other way really. Ja'ja', Aoun. There's no way."

"Joseph . . . have you seen Etienne?"

"Who? Who?"

The video shuddered and Leon watched Joseph come alive and fast-forward through the gestures of his long speech. He leaned into the computer and out again, gray and haggard, his unshaven jowls hanging loose. His eyes constantly flicking and flickering, following someone moving in the corner of the room beyond the cam. The connection had resolved.

"Etienne Suleiman, Uncle Joseph."

"Etienne? Etienne . . . ? Your friend. Your friend was in an accident, Leon. Ah, I'm sorry. He hurt his face."

"His face?"

"How is Cyprus, Leon? Are you enjoying your holiday? You will be coming back soon?" His tone had changed; he seemed elevated, mirthful.

"Joseph?"

"'Are you to be trusted,' Leon. Do you remember that?" He laughed properly now, and leaned back in his chair grinning, looking away. "'Are you to be trusted,' Leon? Do you remember that?"

"'Are you to be trusted?'"

"Yes."

"They would all say yes," said Leon. "Is there someone there?"

"They would *all* say yes."

"Yes."

"*I* say yes, Leon."

"Okay."

"Do you understand, Leon?"

"I think so, Joseph."

His eyes flicked to the corner of the room again. Then he

straightened his back and assumed a defiant expression. "A hammock in the annex, Leon. Don't send any more money." Footfalls on the floor echoing in the audio.

"A hammock in the annex, Joseph."

"Here we go."

He laughed again and then he flinched and then the connection was abruptly cut, the freeze-frame of his face looking across the room in a wince disappeared, and the time elapsed was indicated.

There was someone else in the room.

Leon turned and Kim Ahn was standing in the doorway.

"Are you to be trusted?" she said.

"What?" he said, and took off the headphones and closed the laptop. "Hi. How was the meeting? How long have you been back?"

"Are you to be trusted?" She was looking at him with a huge smile.

"What?"

"You were talking to yourself. You were saying Joseph, Joseph, like in a dream."

"Oh." He laughed. "Talking to myself. Yes. No, it's my uncle who is called Joseph too."

"Your uncle Joseph. I see. Are you to be trusted?" She was still looking at him with that smile, gone blankish now.

"It's a joke between us. An old joke. It's a riddle."

"A riddle."

"Yes."

"What riddle?"

"If half the people lie and half the people tell the truth, what do you ask someone to find out what kind of person they are?"

"Why not just tell them all to go away from me?"

He laughed softly, appropriately. But she kept looking at him that way. "Look," he said. "Do you want to do something with me? I need to do something. A trip?"

"A trip. Like a fall."

"No, like a journey."

Hongō Sanchōme Station, by Tokyo University. The remains of the protest there were all about. Empty streets, staves stacked against the old brick walls of the campus. Banners everywhere. Solitary police cars cruised the narrow perimeter roads, but there was a line of riot vans parked and prepped in the back streets. And it was easy to enter the dead and vacated university. There was no one around. Megaphoned voices far away echoing and eerie through the arches and across the cobblestoned paths, finding their own way in the humid silence before the typhoon.

The early students were gathered before the old Yasuda auditorium, factioned, columned, some already helmeted, practicing, waiting for the sieges to begin again.

He asked a harried academic, who gave them directions to the department he wanted, third floor, Faculty of Engineering Building No. 6. The corridors were filled with staves and pipes and posters and empty of people. He'd expected it to take days at least, but a solitary amiable grad student eagerly took on the task of grading the diamond; the professors were striking in sympathy and there was nothing to do.

The student left them in a staff room off the labs. Empty but for a group of four motley students alongside them talking about HTML. Leon listened for a while. Then he leaned toward them and greeted them in formal Japanese.

"Excuse me," he said. "I am very pleased to meet you."

They rather sullenly returned his greeting, the equilibrium of their conversation upset by the different levels of formality. He plunged on.

"Please give me favor. I am a filmmaker." *Boku wa eigakantoku desu.* "I am working on a screenplay, and I have a question, and if I do a lot of research on Google it will always only be a Google answer."

The two younger students seemed all right. The bearded one watched him with a slight hostility. Leon moved his chair sideways to face both tables at once. Kim was watching him, not having heard him speak Japanese before.

"So in my screenplay what I need to know is this. Could a suitably powerful organization trace a person's whereabouts, like the country or city, from the IP address," he transliterated it, in hope, as *aiupii adoresu,* "of a computer or network he uses, if they were monitoring his email account? If he logged on accidentally?"

The Japanese he'd used was quite formal and stilted, but the language had relaxed them somewhat.

The bearded one made a face of reserved disgust. The youngest one, who had a mole tufted with hair on his cheek, spoke first, and their English was astounding.

"I think the answer is a cautious yes."

The bearded one turned on him sharply and said to the other side of the room, "A suitably powerful organization can presumably do whatever it is suitably powerful enough to do, especially in the context of a *movie.*"

He used the term like someone older might have used "computer game."

The very quiet one, short and thickset to the level of dwarfishness, said quickly, "We do that every few seconds in Quova. IP address in, region, country out."

They started speaking faster, looking at their table, at the walls of the gritty staff room.

"It's how regional access works in ICS, in fact."

"If it's a webmail account though—" The young one looked quickly at Leon, who didn't say anything and he looked away again as if Leon had already replied. "Isn't the originating IP address that of the webmail server and not the local machine?"

"Depends how sophisticated the webmail system is, I suppose," said the bearded one as if he were tired. "Standard one that just sits on top of POP3 or IMAP I suppose will return the server address, yes."

"As long as it's for personal use."

"Sending from Gmail does not include the originating address."

"Sending from my personal ISP's webmail account includes gate dot u tokyo dot ac dot JP. Which is our outbound IP, I assume."

"Google Analytics," said the bearded one tonelessly.

The whole table said simultaneously, "Oh!" as if this were enormously impressive.

"Simple."

"Google Analytics is able to get down to city level based on IP too, so that must be possible." He turned to the dwarf who it appeared was senior. "I think it's probably a more expensive Quova option than the one we pay for."

"I'm assuming the suitably powerful organization may be prepared to dig into their pockets to pay for Google's services."

"I was assuming said powerful organization *was* Google."

Leon broke in. "It's not Google. My character logs on to YouTube and it automatically logs him in to a Gmail address he'd been avoiding. Can a trace like that still be done?"

It sounded rude and abrupt, but they seemed to appreciate it.

"No."

"Not without a subpoena to Google."

"If they couldn't plausibly raise a subpoena valid under U.S. law, then it's unworkably unlikely."

The bearded one had seemingly forgotten him and spoke rapidly in Japanese. "Sounds like he doesn't really want facts at all, he just wants to run Magical Movie OS, where hackers hit keyboards at random and log-in screens look like video games."

"The short answer is no."

"But if he wants to run Magical Movie OS, he needs to accept that's what he's doing and not pretend otherwise," said the young one.

"Anything that makes nerds scream is probably worthwhile."

"My character," Leon said, "suspects that somehow this organization knows where he is. Is following him."

The short one spoke to Leon in English again. "If he's using his own laptop, they could have installed some malware which reports back whatever the current IP address of the laptop is."

"Actually, that's a highly plausible method. Yes."

"Personally targeted malware is well known to exist in the wild."

"Yes, if he's silly enough to trust Windows."

"So a random malware-bearing stupid game can in fact be a keylogger just by installing?"

"It would have to say, when you install it, *This program has access to,* and a bunch of stuff."

"But most non-techies don't read that stuff."

"This program has *too long; didn't read. Click here for dancing pigs.*"

They chortled.

"Yes, that's exactly it."

The bearded one glanced at Leon's lap and said in very low, fast Japanese, "I suspect Middle Eastern guys are unlikely to play with pigs."

They'd all leaned forward or back but the dwarfish one sat still as a hunter. He'd figured Leon for what he was. They carried on for a while, until Leon said, "So if someone else had access to the laptop for some length of time he could install the malware?" They pronounced it *maru-eea.*

"Of course."

"A minute."

"Less."

Ginza was clean. Stripped back like a dredged seabed, raw concrete steaming in the sudden sun. Leon's scalp tingled, the follicles prickling in the stagnant and electric morning of the storm.

He chose a jeweler named Tanaka, utterly unlike the scene

in Damascus. No English and no other languages, local, friendly, open, white, and modern. A young man in a fine suit and spectacles who spoke politely to him in Japanese. Who did not bemoan the lack of provenance or Kimberly certification, only gracefully took the diamond and the student's Tōdai grading back through a keycoded door. Kim examined watches and rings. The young man returned twenty minutes later with his own grading and a figure on an invoice. Leon simply nodded. They left with a blank envelope of yen he exchanged most of at a Bank of Tokyo–Mitsubishi branch for a bank check of US$300,000 and $5,000 in a slim packet of $100 bills and change.

They walked through the debris of the riot in front of the UN building, past the Brazilian street workers cleaning up. He picked up his laptop, and they took a back road and crossed the barricades. They began in Omotesandō. At BAPE they bought T-shirts; at Donna Karan, sunglasses. They bought silk scarves and Yankees caps at tiny Harajuku boutiques, Suicide, and Chicago, a huge secondhand warehouse where all the clothes looked new. At Chanel he bought her a silk shirt and they picked at sushi, smoking Mild Sevens, at a streetside restaurant. Hachiko intersection by the station was a stifling, salty, festering thing. On the LCDs of the Tsutaya building thirty meters high it read 39 degrees Celsius and 90 percent humidity. A ticker announced another typhoon, Betsy, was on her way. But the streets were emptied by the threat of violence just blocks away up Aoyama dori, and in a vacant Parco where the staff loitered and gossiped she bought some sandals and from Mitsukoshi he bought a silver crucifix to wear around his neck. He told her it was his father's cuff link he'd sold; an inheritance from when he died. She seemed to derive a kind of contact high from his act; this tragic temporary insouciance implying some great sadness. Her eyes went wide and crazy and watchful.

They went underground, to Shinjuku to continue the binge, in sunglasses, hands full of shopping bags.

It was uncomfortable on the trains. A salaryman sighed through his teeth as they moved to the doors on the Hanzōmon line, watching them with unfeigned disgust. They were stared at or ostentatiously ignored by the few who'd ventured out: a pale Vietnamese girl with shaven head; a foreign, half-caste, ambiguous man.

She whispered in his ear, "They think I'm your victim. They think you're a *sex tourist*," and she giggled and almost laid a hand on his knee but didn't. In Shinjuku he finally found a hardware store, five stories tall and all for a screwdriver. He split his laptop open and gouged out the hard drive, and he laughed to try and make her laugh as he poured sugary coffee inside both and dumped the machine in two separate bins outside a pachinko parlor called Green Beans. He bought a camera at Yodobashi Camera. He bought a new MacBook and told her a history of the shitty old Compaq, and how he'd been waiting a long time for this. She didn't ask why he didn't sell it or give it away. She acquiesced as she'd done the whole day. She watched him distantly. They ate steak at Pepper Lunch: *Japanese Fine Steak, Sizzle It Your Way!* They walked skinny back streets as the sun set hard in the typhoon-cloud red like a bleeding muscle. She'd stopped using his name, *Joseph*. They drank beer in the dusty parks in the screams of cicadas.

"So when will come the time to reveal your film?"

They were coming round the back way to the UN buildings, around the Oval Building's AM/PM convenience store. It was late—one o'clock, two o'clock in the morning. After a long silence she'd finally spoken.

"I don't know, I guess . . . the next open house," he said.

"Uh-huh."

"Yes."

"They call them open studios. Not houses."

"Oh, yeah."

"When is it?"

"The next open studio?"

"Yes."

"I don't know."

"It's this week."

"Oh."

Outside the convenience store the ¥100 umbrellas were stacked for the storm that suddenly broke. The rain began with one or two spits and spatters then became huge, a grisly, shaking, heavy thing and they sheltered there—the Culture Center building just twenty meters away.

She was smiling at the rain. She was drifting away from him. He wanted to explain, to reach her and touch her and tell her the truth entire but it was simply not a thing that ever could happen. The rain filled the tile and made it live. Figures splashed through the storm and joined them in the shelter of the AM/PM's open veranda. Shoppers hurrying from the store abruptly stopped and made sighing sounds, small jokes. Even those with umbrellas sought cover.

An old man said appreciatively, "*Sugoi ame*," and a few in the small bedraggled group laughed.

She turned to look at the old man with that abstracted air, like he was sculpture, a sheet of music, a scene.

Leon watched her. "He said, 'good rain.'"

"But it's not, is it?"

"He means it like it's impressive."

Then she elegantly bent and shucked off her new sandals and scooped them up by the straps in two fingers and holding up the rear of her skirt ran suddenly out into the downpour leaving all the shopping behind.

He half-started, looked down at the bags and boxes, then up to her and the time taken to calculate that he couldn't carry it all was long enough for her to be halfway to the after-hours entrance in the side of the building. Running barefoot in the rain, calves flashing in the lamplight, up to her ankles in it, soundless in the roar. She touched the card reader—she spoke into the com—he realized she had the passcard and he didn't. She was almost gone, holding up her skirt in one fist. Thirty-five years old, a classically trained violinist leaving her daughter behind for this. He could let her go and disappear. He could remember her, like her, have to tell no more lies. Then he remembered—upstairs, in Kim's room, his passport.

A few voices shouted after him as he left the bags behind and ran into the cataract, instantly drenched in the rain the same temperature as his skin, as his eyes. She was heaving at the big steel door, she was ducking inside, it was closing on her, closing, handleless, a featureless slab of beige steel subsiding into the featureless wall of the building, closed and soundlessly sealed before he was even halfway there.

There were just barely three or four inches of some putative shelter in the doorway but the rain rung ricochets and splatter from the flooded tile as high as his thighs and it was near meaningless. He was locked out with no way of calling. All he had on him was money. Upstairs were his two changes of clothes, his backpack, his passport. Before him was a metal cabinet the size of a bedroom vanity with a red bulb, a metal grille and button, a pad for a card reader. It was hours after curfew and security required a passcard, a visual, and a verbal greeting to show a visitor was not under duress.

He pressed the com button to call the security guard. A few seconds—the speaker crackled and squealed. A voice emerged.

"*Hai.*"

"*Ohaiyo gozaimasu,*" he erred and corrected himself. "I mean, *konbanwa.*"

"*Konbanwa,*" the voice replied after a few unreadable seconds, and nothing more.

A story; a lie.

"*Ano, boku wa karucha sentaa no aa-tisto desu,*" he tried. "*Gomen nasai, chotto, chotto tasukete. Ano boku no passu kaado wa, ano, rosto, desu ne . . .*"

Um, as for me, I'm the Culture Center's artist. I'm sorry, a little, a little emergency. Um, as for my passcard, um, it's lost, isn't it . . .

The intercom was silent but for rattles and hisses. He bent close in the roar of the rain.

"*Ano, boku no tomodachi wa, Betonamu no Kimu Anu desu, passu kado ga imasu.*"

Um, as for my friend, it's Vietnam's Kim Ahn, has a passcard.

"*Gomen nasai.*"

I'm sorry.

He looked directly into the camera. The com was silent. Then a rapid series of hushes and static rushes culminated in a few words he couldn't understand.

"*Gomen, gomen, wakarimasen. Daijobu desu ka?*"

Sorry, sorry, I don't understand. Is it okay?

Just enough lack of fluency might let him through.

Then the com came clear as a bell.

"*Chotto matte kudasai. Kimasu.*"

Just a minute please, I'm coming.

The security guard wore a security guard's uniform, elaborate and almost marine. A military blouse with epaulettes, and embroidered badge of rank at his upper arm with a coat of arms and the words in English: *security guard*. A webbing of reflective vinyl, a buckle at his shoulder, a peaked cap cocked back in tiredness, in black-and-white serge. The uniform was loose on him, a compact, wiry man in his mid-forties.

He led Leon down the back corridor leading from the after-hours door, past a bathroom, a small kitchen, past an alcove full of vending machines. Leon heard the hum of the building all around, the flap of the guard's sandals, the drips of his wet clothes. At a side door the guard checked him once just barely, that he was following. They emerged into the main foyer, lined with international flags. The guard shuffled toward the reception counter at the end of the foyer leading to the elevators up to the Culture Center. Leon turned toward them.

"*Ne, chotto matte, chotto matte kudasai,*" the guard said then. Leon stopped. The guard had a flattish, resigned face, long ears, a smooth mole at one eye, another at his jawline, a precise military haircut. A face like an aged infant. He was stopped and looking at Leon, and his hand was on his utility belt where hung a flashlight, buckled pockets of black leather, a nightstick. "*Mibun shoumeisho misete itadaitemo ii desu ka?*"

Do you mind if I saw and reviewed your information?

"I can just go and get my passcard and come straight back to show you," Leon said. There was a separate doorway from the elevator directly into that small kitchen and the back corridor—he could get up and he could get straight back out again, disappear.

"*Ii, ii, ii.*" The guard was shaking his head, looking down at the floor before him. His demeanor had shifted with the small challenge, his shoulders squaring. No, no, no. "*Okake ninatte kudasai. Yoroshiku onegaishimasu.*" Please take a seat. "*Dozo.*"

He gestured to a small chair in the corner just beyond the reception counter, neither that for guest or guard; another border. Leon, as if propelled, went toward it. The guard followed him with his left side. When Leon sat he moved behind the counter, remained standing, leaning to the computer screen, reaching for a mouse.

There was a litter of paper under the counter's overhang and out of sight of visitors. Leon could see a sooty line of dust millimeters wide that followed the seams of things: the in and out trays, the monitor, the ancient telephone and fax. The guard's seat had the seat back jacked right back. His shoes were neatly paired in the back corner of the space, aligned on the industrial carpet at the foot of a huge beige printer. There was a thermos flask on a small card table, a paper bag, two small black bananas, like the ones his mother brought him, brought his father. There was a miniature TV playing a silent game show. None of this could be seen until you came this far. Scattered among the pages and pages of kanji all over the counter's lower tier were perhaps a dozen faxes with mug shots. The guard was clicking in some ancient software, Windows-esque, all gray and pale blue boxes. The cup from his thermos was full of milky tea and sat on top of the faxes. The mug shots were mainly of Burmese and Southeast Asian faces, women and men, all late twenties and early thirties. He could see his blurry photo taken from his ID card, taken at twenty-two. It was on a faded fax on shiny paper with a Lebanese Intelligence header, kanji in the frame but the body held in broken English a description, mentions of theft and transportation across international borders, and it was more than plausible the guard had not seen it. Under his plastic sandals he was wearing pilled gray Reebok socks.

"*Ano, Kimu Anu-san ni boku no passu kaado ga aru,*" Leon said.

Ah, Kim Ahn, my passcard she has.

"*Chotto matte kudasai,*" the guard said peering down at the screen, moving the mouse very slowly and deliberately. He clicked an icon forcefully, holding the mouse button down too long. "*Chotto matte kudasai,*" he muttered again.

Leon stood. The guard looked sideways at him, right into his eyes. Leon looked right back. His were deep brown, tired, far away. He looked down again briefly, then back up at Leon. They were both realizing something. Leon smiled and stepped toward him. The guard straightened and stepped back. His eyes widened. He reached again for the mouse in an absentminded semigesture. Leon pulled the fax from the pile. It tipped the thermos cup over and the tea spilled over the Burmese faxes and ran to the floor, soundlessly spilling on the stained gray carpet. The guard started, but did not move further. His eyes moved around the enclosed space as if for help. Then Leon crumpled up the page. The guard's understanding was near visibly forming, coalescing around the information. He reached for the printout, and grabbed Leon's wrist, his grip uncannily tight.

"*Tasukete,*" he said croakily, as if to some absent authority. Help me.

Leon grabbed his wrist too.

Leon shook his head no.

"There is a coup d'etat in Lebanon," he said in English. *"Rebanon no kuudetaa ga arimasu.* This is political."

"Tasukete," said the guard louder, looking down the empty foyer, past the plastic flags of the nations to the walled-off automatic doors. Leon pulled off his hand. "No," he said. "This isn't fair. This isn't right. I want to claim asylum." The guard listened, then reached with his other hand, automatically but awkwardly, to the nightstick on his opposite hip. Leon shoved him, two hands to the chest, into the corner against the great printer. They stood and looked at each other for a second, as if disbelieving in this moment. Then the guard rushed at him messily, any training he had deserting him but knowing he was alone, shrieking something, and Leon held him off with his forearm and with his other punched at his ribs, roundhoused crudely at the side of his ducked head. A voice was saying in French, *non, non, non.* The guard's body seemed alive all around him, suddenly incredibly lithe and strong. Pushing him back, pulling on his shirt. Leon charged him back against the wall. The guard's hand came up, scratched across his face with a ripping that felt anaesthetized. Leon pushed him down the wall with his weight on him and they collapsed behind the counter. They were grunting and puffing. As if experimentally Leon punched him in the face. *"Be quiet,"* he heard himself say. *"Don't."* The guard went still beneath him for a moment, then with awesome strength heaved up against him. Leon punched him again in the sudden knowledge gained from the first strike, a strange intimacy. The man paused at the blow. Leon punched him again, looking for the temple, aiming. Methodically and systematically he worked the man's writhing arms beneath his knees. The guard grunted and heaved again. *No,* Leon heard his voice say, *no.* Then *shh, shh.* He bent down closer to hold the man down; the crucifix dangling from its necklace swam across the guard's face. *No, shh,* he said. The guard heaved up against him. Leon put his hands around his neck and strangled him for a while. The guard kneed him in the back and scratched at his thighs. His hand caught in the belt of Leon's jeans and pulled and pulled. Leon let go of his

neck and held his head and slammed it against the ground. The guard writhed, trying to dislodge him. Leon pushed the side of his face down hard against the floor. His neck was stretched out, ribbons of muscle striating in the caramel skin. A ream of paper from the printer poured down on them in a fluttered clump. The guard's face was snarled up in his black polished shoes. Holding his whole skull in his hands as if to pull it from his body. His uniform ripped somewhere. His knee punched into Leon's back again. There was little noise: grunts, shuffles, scuffles, flat meatpacking sounds. He was trying to bite Leon's hands. There was blood on his teeth and he was hissing something. Leon dipped to his neck and bit deep to the molars. There was a crunch and wet pops and a spurt of lubrication, and the guard squealed beneath him and bucked and heaved and Leon bit again, and again, until time passed and the squealing stopped and he sighed and came to rest.

She was sitting down at her laptop and the gray light filled the room and lit her young-old face. The room flickered as she moved windows, and he stared at her and was suddenly nauseous.

He tunneled and was standing by the bed. She pressed the spacebar and started her song and from the laptop's little speakers came the bells, a carillon. He watched as in the center of the room a puddle, gray and dead, formed in the carpet around a bottle of whiskey and their cups. He reached out for something to hold and checked off the contents of the room, to slow it down. The door, the kitchen door, window, desk, and bed, a suitcase, roar of rain, and then came the first drip from the ceiling, *spit*, onto the carpet.

He turned his head to her and he had tunneled again. He was looking into the kitchen, at some cabinets. He was washing his scratched face, looking at a toilet cistern, nauseous, a yellow flower in a toothbrush holder, a toilet bag. He turned deliberately and went back out into her room. There were three sharp knocks at her door, and a murmured voice. He tunneled again.

Beside him, Kim Ahn rose from the desk and went to the door's peephole. The music changed, the sound of water, and her screams in high kilobits per second MP3 treated to a quaver. He was between the desk and the bed, his back to the rain and it was growing too hard to hold on to the present, too hard and silly and tiring; the beige walls of this cell in the pouring rain outside were dark and moving constantly.

"Who is it?" she said.

"It's me," Leon said, and moved his face to the peephole to show her and she opened the door. The blinds behind in the corridor shifted in the dead air, with a *clack clack*, and he came back inside the room.

She went to the desk but did not sit, just banged the spacebar impatiently to stop the music. The puddle in the middle of the carpet had grown and formed a sheen and her head turned away, looking at the bed, then into the corner of the room. "I need to sleep. Oh." He tunneled and raised a hand to the wall to steady himself, but touched her instead.

"You look different," she said.

In the corner of the room in a yellow wrap, her arms moved like waves before her, rippled over with the rainy window's tremors. "I have to dominate my passion," she said. "I don't know to trust what you say."

"I don't want to tell you lies," he said.

"I love my husband," she said very softly. "I don't lie. What makes you lie?"

"What can I do?" he said.

And she answered, "What makes the spider spin her web?" and she looked up into his eyes and as he told her the truth, told her everything, her expression changed and she began to transform, her eyes began to drain of color, the deep brown paling to a hazel, yellow, white like a pure glaucoma. She tasted so bright and he held her with all his strength in abeyance and yet there, so bright and full of rage he carried her down the river.

19 The saltwater river

The train pulled into the station late in the smoking rain. Water poured from the carriages' eaves as he disembarked. He passed the next doors. A grinning homeless man who'd ridden with him all the way from Yokohama fiddled with his fly and began to piss out the carriage onto the platform. It was a small, local train, and the driver waited till the man had finished before sounding his warning, closing the doors.

The rain a gray master over the little town. He left the station by its single ticket gate on to a narrow street. The restaurants were all shut up behind unbilled garage doors; propped against them were empty nets where they once dried the octopus long gone. A withered sign read BRITISH PUB with a monochrome Union Jack inside an arrow. He stepped over a child's smashed umbrella, pink with yellow elephants, tip up into the streaming of the gutter. It showed no signs of letting up. It was an immense white noise, a roared sound like *crush*, a super-whisper. The only lights were a series of ancient vending machines. Their windows were full of faded plastic facsimiles of cans of Wonda coffee and yellow C.C. Lemon gone white with age, leading to the only thing open, the town's single 7-Eleven.

He ran.

A boy mopping the floor in there sold him an umbrella and directed him to the koban around a dank corner. There, a stiff-backed and skinny policeman no older than twenty-two consulted Leon's printout, gravely stared at a huge wall map of the tiny town, and gave him the directions. The policeman stood at the open doors of the koban as Leon went out, and had still not given him his back when Leon turned onto the road by the river that gave the town its name.

With the salt encroachment the old cement walls of the river had grown their coral encrustations, their ripples, ridges, and blades of filthy mauve and violet still visible at the banks, but the heavy rains had brought the river to flood, and it was now a black-brown heaving maelstrom frothed with suds and algae and in the darkness yet still visibly mottled with leaves and blossom and supermarket bags and floating fragments of the coral bed torn up. White-waterless, near silent, it moved past him at imparseable speed as he followed the narrow road up the valley. The salt river to his left, and on his right beside, the precise and lichened high fences of the old houses here, where no lights showed through the sliding doors, where in sagging, sodden webs the spiders cowered in the downpour.

The house was up a spur off the valley, above the river, beneath the tree line. The fences were riddled with and worn like robes by a wisteria. The garden was in near ruin: It had a well under a flagrant persimmon, and a brown pond frothed in the rain and merged with the surface water of the mud that covered the area in front of the house. Slippery shards of flagstone formed a subsiding path to the two long, wide steps beneath the *fusuma* of the front doors. Beside them a scooter huddled under a tarp. He knocked and waited.

The rain on his umbrella drowned everything out. The sliding door simply shot open, and his grandmother stood barely five foot tall in socks in the doorway, baggy peasant trousers and a quilted shirt, but perfectly crystal blue pensioner's hair, waved and shining. Her eyes were alert, suspicious, and silver, and the first thing she did was check behind him.

"*Ne, konbanwa,*" she said in a low whistling wheeze, just as if to say what do you want. Then paying closer attention saw that he was foreign; she focused on him.

"*Konbanwa,*" he said. "*Shiokawa-san desu ka?*"

"*Hai, Shiokawa desu,*" she said automatically.

He said, "*Ano, ore wa . . . Junko-san wa, ore no okāsan desu. Shio-kawa Junko.*"

She stopped blinking and examined him. Then she reached inside the door and turned on the outdoor bulb. She made as if to strike him or stroke him, and grasped his chin between finger and thumb and pulled his face into the light. She stared at him, raising her chin, the ripples of brown crêpe-paper flesh of her neck leaving their own perfectly permanent creases.

His Japanese was stilted. "My name is Leon. Mama gave me your address. From Lebanon."

She absorbed this information and released his chin and looked him face to feet and back and then she seemed to slightly wilt all over, her stocky five feet shrank just slightly, and then she lunged forward and suddenly hugged him, banging her head on the frame of the 7-Eleven umbrella, ignoring it, and he dropped it, and she hugged him, then held him back, to look, not crying, her eyes wide, then she dragged him out of the rain and then she called him an idiot.

The house was ancient and she pushed him ahead down a wood corridor and into a tatami room. There was a small TV blaring in an alcove beside a bucket for drips, and newspapers and tea things all over the recessed table in the center of the floor underneath a hanging fluorescent light. She turned him around.

"Shoes! Take off your shoes," she said angrily but then her face changed and she looked for a moment lost. He bent to take them off and she shuffled fast out the room again, and doors opened in the corridor and she returned with a towel, and he took it. He grinned tiredly at her, and she looked at his hair and stood, as the rain roared on the roof, with her hand to her breast and only then did she begin to, just for a moment, cry.

———

The little kitchen was in the darkest part of the house. There was an iron tub and wooden bench and incongruous Hitachi extractor fan yellow with age, a rice cooker. His grandmother boiled water, pulled a bowl and chopsticks from an iron dish rack sealed to the counter by its rust, pulled a second, third, and fourth bowl from a cabinet she had to heave to open. He stood in there and watched her as she prepared the little meal, as she grunted companionably when she pushed past him; her odor of damp straw and strong tobacco, her shining, perfect blue hair. She ladled rice from the cooker into two bowls, squeezed miso paste from a plastic envelope in the little fridge into the other two, added water, then cracked an egg each on the hot rice. She placed it all on a wizened tray and added two grizzled persimmons from a cane bowl.

"*Boku no kaki*," she muttered to herself. *My persimmon.* "*Onegai, dozo*," and then again grumpily and impatient, "*Dozo*," and literally elbowed him. He saw what she meant and dragged open the reluctant *fusuma* into a disused and stuffy tatami reception room, an empty, dusty mirror of the other but tableless, and she placed the tray in the center of the floor and pulled up raffia blinds and drew aside the sliding doors. They opened on a yard out back he'd not seen: a wall of rain on a small gnarled willow, a patch of lettuce and radish, stumps of trees sawn down, a stone well with a bamboo cover tied in ancient twine. The ingrown remains of a traditional suburban garden of fifty years ago turned to subsistence.

"*Dozo*," she motioned. He sat down.

She sat too and moved the dishes, muttered, then she took off her wig. Beneath, her skull was wispy with sparse lines of hair like old cobwebs, boney, veined, and gray. She scratched her scalp thoughtfully with both hands, then replaced the wig, and seemed surprised and irritated he hadn't begun to eat.

"Please, please. Quickly before it gets cold."

He used the chopsticks awkwardly, picking at the rice around the still largely transparent egg.

"No, no, no," then she laughed, ancient and croaking. "Stir it in, son. Stir it in like so." She showed him; broke the egg with the tips of the chopsticks, stirring it briskly through the hot rice where it formed a pale yellow sauce, cooked lightly in the borrowed heat. A proteinish odor rising off it; cheap nutrition, poor people's food.

He ate. She wolfed hers down fast, a utilitarian shoveling-in, the bowl held high to her lips.

The rain roared down and they ate until they were finished.

She said something complex, and he asked her to repeat it and she sighed grumpily.

"What do you eat in—" and she said a word he didn't know until he did.

"No," he said, and smiled at her. "Not Arabia. Lebanon."

"Ah, so it is. Lebanon." She followed his pronunciation quickly. "You don't eat any Japanese food?"

"No, but mama talks about it. About *ohagi*—"

She made a terrible wince, her head fell sideways, her shoulders hunched up, and she cried again.

He didn't know what to do for her. He sat and watched her, hunched. He got to his feet and sat down beside her, hugging her rough old shirt, the smooth hair of the wig on his cheek. Then she stiffened and straightened.

"Okay. You go back over there now."

He almost laughed, got up, went back.

"So," she said, and sighed the last of her cry out. "I have a *lot* of questions for you. But are you full of food now?"

"Yes, Grandma. Thank you."

"Then have a persimmon from my own tree."

"Yes, Grandma."

"Your mother ate persimmons from that tree when she was a little girl."

"Yes, Grandma."

She looked away out the garden where the smoking rain poured on. Then she got up and went out into the kitchen, boiled the jug again. In the alcove there was a low mahogany cabinet. On top just a rough pottery jug and lying the length of it a piece of narrow branch, fuzzed and indistinct with dust. It was the only decoration in the room. She came back with green tea in Arabic-style, handleless cups, but lacquered and large.

And he tried to explain it all in his bad and broken Japanese. He told stories of Abu Keiko that were flattering and strange, with exhausting childish gestures, arm flexes for strength. "He is—he was"—and fluttering nunchaku to explain—"champion three." That his father was a good man, a strong man. She didn't seem to understand or distinguish Lebanon. He left out the war completely. He called him *my father*. He didn't know *security*, so he said *police*. She nodded seriously, her only response. He wanted to make her happy, and she seemed so or at least she seemed quiet when he said it, *police*, mimed a door, mimed standing in front, mimed on guard, mimed the last Christian of the Lebanon.

Out of nowhere she asked, "How old are you?"

"Thirty."

And she sighed and whistled for the years. "You are big and strong. You are a man." She thought. "Do you like *sake?*"

"No, thank you."

"Whiskey? Maybe I have some old whiskey. I don't drink it."

"No, thank you, Grandma. Thank you."

"No, no, no," she laughed without pleasure and looked in the corner of the room. "Your grandfather liked to drink. Does your father drink?"

It was the same word for drinking anything. *Otou-san wa nomimasu ka?*

"No," he said. It was easier, more or less true.

"That is good. Your grandfather. He would drink half a bottle of whiskey. I cried. I laughed about something, and then I thought of it, and I cried and said, it's too much. He—"

She said something too complex.

I don't understand, he said for the nth time.

She got irritated again. She made a gesture like a man pissing and flapped her hand at the tatami.

He nodded; some accident.

"It was his death." She looked hard at him. "But your father does not drink."

"No, Grandma."

"That is good. And you do not drink, that is good."

"Yes, Grandma."

"And Junko-chan is happy in Arabia? She is content."

It was almost not like a question, but a prayer, a propitiation of old, old pains. He tried to summon replies, but she bounded up and shuffled out into the corridor, and there was the hiss-*clap* of sliding closet door again. She came back with photo albums.

"Ray-ohn" was how she pronounced his name. "This was your mother."

She was impossibly young. Barely twenty, so very much like Keiko, eyes straight and full of ruled rage into the camera. She wore a military uniform, sexless and bereft of insignia, and she stood in Japanese mountains with a wooden rifle. She was thin, certain, full of focus, like a Hezbollah.

"This is the last one before she left. We said she left her home to fight and that is good. But then there were crazy Japanese in Israel doing things, in North Korea and in the mountains here. Nothing from her. I have always been scared she got lost."

"She did not write?"

"Never. But we think that is very brave." Her face was blank. Then she said, "There can be more to life than only to survive and reproduce. In my time we had no such choice. Only survive. She was a protester and I argued with her and her father argued with her but I was still very proud. And she went for what she believed in, and then—" She made an open hand; a gesture of nothing, diffidence, acceptance, he couldn't read.

"Now, there is your father, the Arab, and Junko, and you."

He owed her—they owed her—honesty, history.

"And I had a sister."

And then he had to try and explain.

When he was finished he was flushed and hurt and sweating, from the gesturing, the struggle and absurdity.

She had only occasionally repeated a word, grown distant and still and cool. Not as if in response to the warped facts but to him and the difficulty. The rain poured on and he felt he might vomit and there was the long white noise, the whisper-roar, the cool air from the garden. She stared out past him. He didn't understand it, not enough—how much or what kind of sorrow she felt. What right to bring this to her house, this quiet house in the trees and in the rain.

"Your grandfather," she said very quietly, and distantly, at last— not *my husband*, but *your grandfather*—"put lights up all through the trees out there when your mother was just a little girl, and we ate our dinner outside in the garden in summer. Hanging—" She made the handshape automatically for him and pointed to the light. She waved out there. "Everywhere. When he died I took them all down. We had not used them for years anyhow, and they were ripped and old, but I took them all down. The way things are lit is as important, almost more, than the things themselves. A tree must only be a tree this way." She smiled at him. "Difficult, *ne?*"

She made a handshape of a tree; her other in a fist expanding, the sun rising over it, then clenching, falling, behind. Then the fist that was the falling sun came before on the sunrise side of the tree and expanded; the shadow, rising.

"The darkness, *ne?*"

"Yes."

"This way the darkness can be a hand, a devil, an animal, a laughing thing. A face of a child. A black fire in your life. Out of control. Laughing. To shine a light on it, that thing, which is your knowledge of things outside your knowledge, is to tell a lie and to kill the world back to yourself." She tapped herself on the nose to show the pronoun meant her. "This is why I took the lanterns down. For the—"

But he couldn't understand the last word. He was too red, too hot. "Now it is bedtime."

She got up and came over to him and kissed him on the top of his head and hauled him up and put him to bed, a dusty futon in an empty upstairs room, the only room at the top of the stairs. He heard her shuffling around beneath him till he slept.

At last the rain did stop. He was woken by the silence. Other sounds came up out of it: bullfrogs in the fields, call of an owl, ticking of water from the eaves. A ticking sound in here: a clock. He reached for it and felt it, faceless, the thin sprung hands read ten o'clock. He dressed and opened the door and moonlight filled the steep and narrow staircase.

Halfway down on the stair was a blackened dinner knife.

The feeling was like his heart being pulled down in his diaphragm, a great silver-lead dread, a terrible abstract weakness leaving his body capable but unable to be moved by a conscious want or volition or will. A psychic end-space, trapped up in the room. He went back up and closed the door, lay back down upon the futon.

Being eight years old. Being in the basement. Being with Keiko, each with an AK-47 in their hands. Being as bad as they could, sitting cross-legged and facing one another, she with the bullets, he with the jealousy and the youth. Pointing the gun at her, firing at his sister with all his arch will and ignorance, and the unexpected clap of darkness, the heavy thing alive in his hands. Keiko's wide eyes toward him, eyes he'd never seen so big. And then turning, and turning, and then she getting up, walking so slowly over toward the wall, fingering the missing piece of concrete, turning back to look at him.

These things will always be there. Why not be brave and go out into it? Simply say yes.

They unloaded the guns with religious seriousness, put them away together, locked the cabinet door. They went upstairs and watched TV and waited for Junko to come home and they'd never once spoken about it again, never been so bonded and true. There were times when she came home in uniform, aged about thirty, just a few months to live, and her eyes would come up out of those late things, manifesti, districts, municipalities, severance and reaction, cool wars and shooting wars, would come up bright and full of the opposite of tears, that thing between them, true secrets, that true secret, love.

He got up again, and opened the door and the dinner knife was still there. He went down the stairs and picked it up and put it into his pocket. He slid the waxed *fusuma* silently open and stepped out into the storm-washed garden. The scooter's tarp poured water off in pockets as he lifted it and crumpled it into a silent pile. He walked the bike over the flagstones to the top of the street, walked it halfway down the hill where he jump-started it, and rode quietly to the river.

The river was utterly drained. The coral held the detritus of the flood, bags and rags, a shopping trolley, a shoe, a bike, all leaking weed and long stuffs downstream as if facing into the brief lull of a great silent wind. There were concrete obstacles like jacks as big as a man forming barriers at intervals down the bed. Clothed in dead coral like freakish starfish growing in all directions; draped in huge dead jellyfish like collapsed clouds sprawled on the weir. He turned up the river, away from the station, fast along the tow-path on the little bike.

She has no power over you. Ah, but she does. Emmanuelle's hands out either side of him, cupping into the wind. Leaning hard against his back so she could let her hands go free as they raced along the river. Her thighs on his; jammed in behind him on the bike. But already she was receding: one hand flattened into a fin, feeling the weight of the wind, finding the fight then the lee, the easiest way through. He had money. He could do whatever he wanted now. He could take her on a trip, tell her meet me *here* and *then*.

She tightened her body into him, and he felt her helmet against his head. Her hand cupped the wind again and dragged her back and he heard her make a hard sound in the helmet, scared and excited, felt her hand clap on his chest, her hard lean on his back.

She whispered, *Slow down, I can't hang on, Leon slow down. . . .*

Her hands went limp in his lap. He looked down once and at speed and saw the wired ties around the narrow, tan, Vietnamese wrists, and his heart went dead again, *it will always be there*, and Zakarian whispered in his ear, *If you're going to fuck me, fuck me now*, and anything was better, to fall better than to be wired to this future of endless then, and he let go and leaned back and the scooter's front wheel rose and wobbled and the scooter veered and crossed up and he fell and skidded and rolled. A quick and violent clutter. Hands limp to offer no protection. Any violence to escape.

But gravity has its way.

He lay in the rough, wet road staring across the gravel. Feeling the hot rise in his skin all over, very still and painless—something dragging at his foot? He looked down and there was nothing there—just his grandmother's scooter lying in the middle of the road, one indicator blinking, one smashed, on the wet gravel, a wall of trees behind.

Fuck your mother.

This is what it is like. *I only drink whiskey or gin.* At every moment unbidden, a bottle cap flies to the corner of the room, a boy runs after it, Leon trips on the threshold. A rabbit's foot; a hammock in the annex.

See that? One punch.

Bent over Bashir in the waste ground of Mkalles, Bashir holds up his hands, says, *Please.*

Help me, he whispered into the road. *Someone, please.*

One punch. He loved to kill Palestinians.

Please.

Keiko palming herself away, down the road, screaming at her gone foot, and looking at him in Makhlouf's behind the plastic chair, her face bereft of recognition. *What do you ask? How can you know?* And just the silence, and then the man coming down the hill not looking, that man with the sword, wearing the uniform of a security guard. *Death will come and it will have your eyes. Now and forever and to the ages of ages.*

And then there was no more and then.
To be eight years old, and forgiven.
But I am now who now I am.
A losing stream, playing out.

He got up. He righted the scooter. It was still running; those eternal Suzukis.

He rode it back into town, and the front wheel was crooked but he held the handlebars slightly left and it rode straight. On the silent main street was the sign, BRITISH PUB. He followed it down the road to another that read THE FRANK GOUR.

A weird hybrid, a mahogany bar with British ales and Guinness on tap and a wall of Scottish single malts. Through the door behind a Japanese kitchen. High stools and tables, and a tatami space too, like a dais in the corner.

He ordered a beer and sashimi. The young owner was briefly pleased to be serving a foreigner, poured it perfectly, indicated a table, he'd bring it over.

"*Sumimasen. Daijobu desu ka?*" he said it quietly when he sat the beer down. *Are you all right?* Leon looked down, at the stains on his trousers, the gravel rash on his palms. Yes, thank you. The marks would always be there and that had to be all right. A television was mounted high in the corner of the room playing soundless footage of the protests in Tokyo. Over the helmeted columns marching and the riot vans in smoke firing water at the crowds, there were mug shots or passport or ID photos flashing up inset in the corner of the screen and the kanji beneath them played too fast to read. They were arrests or deaths or wanted pictures. They brought him his food. The voices were quiet in here. He noticed Almaza, Lebanese beer in the fridge. The sashimi was *aji*, mackerel. Small dominoes cut from the flanks of the fish and arranged in three neat arrays cupped in an arc of the fleshed fish itself, which was skewered from tail to head in a sedate arc around the meat, the wound giving on to what was removed. He thought of the Lady of Lebanon at Harissa over the bay of Jounieh. Kim

Ahn's face appeared inset in the television screen and was just as quickly gone. He recognized the kana—ベトナム, Vietnam—on the ticker below the image, then the screen filled with the banners of the multinational groups on the dori before the UNU. Then Shigenobu May, child of the revolution, was giving an interview. She held the microphone, speaking soberly of Palestine, of citizenship and equal rights for Palestinians in Lebanon, of her mother, her mother's jail term, nonviolence, the future. No, he realized, Shigenobu was the interviewer. The camera panned away: She was holding a microphone, talking to a games developer at a gaming conference, a reporter for Asahi News. Her other job. They'd changed the channel. It was quiet in here. How long had he been here? How long had he watched? He looked down at the food. The fish was twitching. Though dead and fleshed it had vestigial reflexes; it shuddered slightly, and twitched. The barman was still behind him with the remote control in his hand, watching the TV. He noticed the twitching sashimi.

"*Ne, chotto genki desu ne*," he said and laughed. Still a little bit of life left in it.

20 in Beirut

The fighting had all but stopped.

Israel had not come in. Syria neither. East Beirut remained untouched. The meeting was held in the capital of Qatar, and from all over the Middle East they attended. *To resolve the Lebanese crisis.* A president was elected. *The parties commit to abstain from having recourse or resuming the use of weapons and violence in order to record political gains.* Electoral districts were gerrymandered or rectified, depending on the point of view, and the opposition gathered additional veto powers. A new balance, or in other words a new stultification, was achieved and people went back to work. The streets filled again, the road to the airport was reopened. Business resumed. The ATMs refilled. The port reopened; the abattoir pumped into the river again. Streets were swept of stones and cartridge shells. People began to plan for the tourist seasons to come; calculated the hit they'd taken on the summer. What is the collateral for an exhausted quarry? Exactly that removed from within. The shooting at the march was ignored by Hezbollah; risen above for the sake of the new reality they'd manhandled into being. Sunni moved north of the Corniche Mazraa. Shi'a families moved north and east into the Chuf. Though they with immediacy and imminence outnumbered the local Druze and Christians, they were not yet able to vote: Municipal suffrage was based on origin. The women got pregnant again. People would soon begin to call it "the little war." Numbers but not names of the dead were tallied for news reports; names were tattooed in secret on cerebella. Some wondered if it was not best to forget; to adjust. The carousel was restarted and the children got back on because the Luna Park was open again, and when the Kuwaitis returned with their $1,000 a month pedigreed pets their apartments on the eastern side of the Place des Martyrs were reopened too, each less one Christian, one security guard.

But along with those numbers and names of dead that for the young were added to the store of rage and for the old that of the great and familiar impotence and love for this, this very moment in the sun, was added, too, the knowledge that things had changed and that the dog in the backyard they'd finally let into the house—that dog bit not only strangers.

that was the river, this is the sea

isolar

I am now who now I am.

Four beautiful Maronite men stride into the Cloisters, coats even in the heat wave flowing as they sweep around the corner of the installation. Their leader grabs the shoulder of the man we've hired to show them in, a comradely, dominating touch, and kisses him, and they pass by to their assignation at the back of the hall, impeccably groomed and impeccably tanned, the harpsichord they pass some incredible antique. All cheerful, terribly focused, and glad; they, small mountain men at ease in the city, at the peak of physical fitness even in middle age, with their stocky muscular legs, bowed in fine chalk stripe worsteds, sleek Italian shoes, emanating capability, strength, and ferocious, jolly, good cheer.

I am with Albert by the side of where I am to speak, next to the grand piano and behind the fan of seats for the orchestra. North Cloisters of the University College London Wilkins Building is divided in three spaces: orchestra, seating, and the gallery area at back where the guests hover uncertainly before some take their seats. They are a little unsure of the progress of the evening despite the fact the program explicitly states the recital will be followed by the talks, then refreshments provided during the time allotted for the guests to mingle among the art.

Albert can, I think, tell that I am nervous, and he is grinning a little over-gregariously, standing a little overly close.

"So they came," he whispers through his grin.

"Of course."

"It looks as if you've passed inspection."

"Of course."

"Of course. And you're ready for the Q and A?"

"And how is your son, Albert," I say. At this for the benefit of anyone watching he grins yet wider, as if I had been witty.

"Oh, he spoke his first word! You simply wouldn't believe it."

"So young. A genius like his father. What was it?"

"Yes! Well, I rather attractively broke wind, and gravely he pointed to me and pronounced, 'poo.'"

Albert is German, and the most stereotypically English of men I have known in London. A consummate actor and chameleon. A young man out of his time, overeducated to be so underpaid by me, accentless of his native language, fluent in three more, on a highly skilled migrant visa, funny, efficient, and smart. He will manage the Q and A fine for me.

The leader of the four Maronites, Antoine Gemayel, is looking to catch my eye. He is a squat and shiny man, tan, he smiles and bows and I reply likewise. In amongst the guests roaming the art at the rear of the seated area the émigré installation artist Raymon Boch is pale and emaciated, is standing alone. Amr Saffari, six foot four and moustached, is watching distantly.

Albert is the kind of man who introduced me to the phrase, "getting smashed with panache." He stresses his drinking but never gets drunk. He is a stellar statistician as well as a good political mind. How many Germans might I meet who would drop a shot into a pint glass and enunciate in Sloane Square English, "Try this one for size, Fritz. Depth charge."

The poet Emile Khoury is here, telling endless jokes. Etienne Saqr's younger daughter, the singer, is here. A large contingent of LSE international relations postgrads, the majority Arab, is here, and there are Palestinian scarves amongst them. My mother is sitting in the second row from the front, waiting for the speeches. Her long hair gone quite thoroughly white, as long as Emmanuelle's, wild and dark to her breast, beside her. My wife, bent beside my mother, both heavily made-up and dressed up, silver Mitsukoshi crucifix at her neck, in deep conversation, smiling gently and calmly as if by rote at every exchange, then subsiding into thoughts her own.

It looks as if it will be standing room only, and this, I suppose, is good.

The banner is only medium sized and in a restrained and ser-iffed font: DIASPORA AND RETURN: GREEN LEBANON IN THE TWENTY-FIRST CENTURY.

Someone always has to make the leap. Someone has to push the pendulum back hard enough, too far, to correct an historical error, to enact a new error. This movement will in time itself be corrected, but only partially, and through its self-sacrifice, through the breaking of how many men, a new equilibrium is attained; the error is shifted. Two steps forward, one sideways, and one back. This will in time be called inevitable. The job is to make the inevi-table occur. The recital is thankfully short. The guise under which we have gathered journalists, clergy, diaspora leaders, and repre-sentatives, is, in fact, no guise—the first speaker is on water. He is one of Fors's old students too, Yani Habbab, a resource consul-tant who begins with a quip on the European heat wave and then treats of the end of snow in the ski resort of Rabieh in a speech entitled *It Never Rains. But it Pours.*

The mood is dour and low in the hall. Michael Armitage of the *Financial Times* is reading his BlackBerry. The *Guardian*'s Toby Manhire stares at me throughout as if I am something he is consid-ering the merits of eating or no. An *Independent* journalist leaves to take a phone call. There is fidgeting only somewhat calmed by his slides of the dam and reservoir at Aramoun. Antoine Gemay-el's smile is still directed at me but is there, could there be, some-thing of a glaze of disappointment? *Just don't leave.* Habbab winds up on a pessimistic note of rising temperatures and falling rivers and critical thresholds in the Bekaa. It is allayed only by a short anecdote. The so-called Cedar Island Project has been canceled: a Dubai-esque series of artificial islands to be built in the shape of a piecemeal cedar tree—weirdly akin to the Phalangist cedar—off the coast of haunted Damour, for residences, beach houses, a business park, and so on—so, for tourists—just a few kilometers south of the Shi'a slums of Haret Hreik. It was never our intention for this speech to be to the converted. We emphasized business; we emphasized investment. We played to Turkey, Saudi Arabia, and Jordan, but Bob Mitchell of the U.S. Embassy has come, and there is an Israeli attaché here and Idith Zertal, on a book tour in London, too. There will be a series of lunches over the coming days, where I will elaborate on my position. Habbab makes a dark quip about the Cedar Island's putative size being larger than that of the remaining cedar forests of Lebanon, to little laughter. It makes me sad, or it ought to, to know this kind of quip is that of the defeated, the rearguard left behind. The kind of quip that Henri Fors himself would never make, would not even understand. I see him more clearly now. He was a man for his time: when action is impossible, witness is imperative. But his time is past.

Gemayel and his entourage are here to make the decision as to whether they will clear the way, will *groom* me, in effect, for the East Beirut list.

Albert takes the podium and thanks Habbab to the kind of obliged applause, noticeable decibels and duration shorter than the last, that will not recur unless very much earned. The journalists were promised something special.

Albert introduces me at length. Am I something special? I am sweating slightly, yet feel nothing, not nervous, blank, frozen, not passionate. Galvanized, someone else might characterize it. Sealed, hardened. I *am* strong.

He starts the applause and the hall joins in, more hopeful and earnest than what Habbab received—we are so weary—and the play, the hint of the lie we fed, has excited many here and I wonder if this means they are the wrong audience for these ideas. Those whose secret fears and desires wish a voice are weak and have already capitulated, or can they too be turned, galvanized. I think often, as I watch Israeli films of their soldiers' doubt and struggle, of the Shi'a mothers in the South, screaming at the Israeli tanks taking their boys away to prison, *We will replace the young men*. And they do, and it is only electoral corruption—for that is what it is, what we rely upon — that keeps our corruption and our mothers and our children alive and in our homeland.

Albert steps away from the podium, with its single daisy in a vase, and we shake hands and grin and he leans in to my ear and whispers, "Are you ready to leap?"

I am.

"The Lebanese Christian situation is terminal. It is that of the losing stream, dribbling out in the sinkholes of Iranian and foreign influence, the Shi'ite demographic bomb, the usurpation of the Lebanese state by a proxy nonstate actor, and the sinkholes of Arab and Islamist disarray.

"I consider it one of my chief responsibilities as a secular advocate and leader of the Christian diaspora to rehabilitate the reputations and sacrifices of our fathers and the deplorable and untenable condition and future of the Christians of the Lebanon and elsewhere in the Middle East.

"And I wish to start with a man, whose daughter is here today," I nod to Pascale Saqr, who is stone-faced, "a Lebanese patriot born in the South who liberated Beiruti Christians from Tel al Za'atar in 1976 and is unremembered for this. Etienne Saqr, now in exile in Israel and under sentence of death in Lebanon, who once said, 'Politics is not the art of the possible. Politics, like all great art forms, is the art of the impossible. Otherwise there is no problem to resolve.' I have gathered you here today to contemplate and begin the process of swinging the pendulum, of generating the inevitable. Of resolving the impossible."

My model is water; this is to be the beginning of the flood. This is intended to be the first act that begins the reshaping of the borders and banks and becomes mere inevitability, what the Israelis call facts on the ground. Water is discursive; drawing to a point.

At the mention of Etienne Saqr, there are catcalls from some of the LSE students. I don't recognize most of them; they are younger, from after my time there. There is a terrible irony of which most are unaware — that Saqr killed Japanese as well as Palestinians at Tel al Za'atar. These are the ironies that must be imbibed.

"Saqr once also said, 'When you are fighting you either follow the cause and don't get the money, or you follow the money and lose the cause.' In Lebanon this is *triste*. For too long the Christian leadership and Christian elite have followed the money within and without the country, feathering their nests and squandering our future while diminishing our lifeblood: the vote. First generation diaspora *should have the right to vote in their country."*

The diaspora groups have been quiet till now, but raise at last a hoarse cheer.

"We may dislike confessionalism, but it is the board we have laid before us and we must play on it. The Doha Agreement sapped the Maronite presidency of its powers and devolved its prerogatives to the Sunni prime ministership. This is why it makes no sense to align ourselves with ex-warlords from the civil war era who scuttle after that nonposition, who maneuver with only one goal in mind, little knowing they long for the straitjacket. Let me reassure you. I was born Greek Orthodox. I am not qualified."

This raises a small ripple of laughter, not only from the converted. The speech here seems to settle, or is it the audience. It is here that I feel listeners, some hostile, but still seated, and that is all I need.

"For the Christians it was not until the latter period that it became a civil war. Ours was a war against occupation, Syrian and Palestinian, which goes on today. The current campaign for Palestinian naturalization in Lebanon is pushed for by Arab countries that refuse to shoulder this historical burden themselves and care not for the million-strong community of Christians in Lebanon. We are alone as usual and we need to admit as much and act as such. The Aounist alignment with Hezbollah is another categorical error. Not a durable model. We see this in the steady encroachment in the Chuf, in the buying up of Christian land by Hezbollah front companies, in Hezbollah camps on Mount Sannine, our last refuge. Who doesn't read these signs? Are you not tired of Lebanon bearing the brunt of Hezbollah's adventures in the South? What kind of state do you think the Party intends? Even their most senior imams know that the Iranian model is no future for our country. Yet they control us, hold the population hostage by generating events to which they can respond, like a fighting dog that wants to be whipped so he can bite, and knows only this. Balance is our model. And I want to, with you, redress the balance. For our native soil. For our children, for our parents, for 1,400 years of continuous settlement in that one place.

"This is our rage: our cap in hand. Our country is not a beach house for Gulf Arabs. Tourism is a death sentence for us. The discussion, to preempt the editorials, over Saqr's position, Ta'ef and Doha and the Lebanese Arab identity, is moot. The Lebanese face is Lebanese. The Lebanese character is Lebanese. The Lebanese identity is Lebanese. And I am proud of it."

It is strange to hear in my voice the ventriloquist's passion, my father's rage controlled and shaped. It is strange to say these words, to vocalize so vehemently, off-book and totally on. To maintain elegance and control, the appearance of liberality in these surrounds so conducive to such an appearance—the vaulted ceilings of the Cloisters, the cool tile floors in the ongoing heat wave. Churchlike; not oppressive but allusive; the borrowed air of reason.

The New Academic Building at LSE was the first option. It was abandoned not because of doubts raised by several Saudi donors and faculty there, which might have been maneuvered, but because of the air of the temporary, the transient, the discussion, the *talk*. Cloisters has history, humanity, imagination. Realpolitik is questionable here; idealism has a chance. Cloisters is a passageway, and it is where students conduct enrollment. It is a symbol; it is a tunnel.

"And our solution is water."

The sentence gets lost in the applause that is sustained and not unanimous: The boos are fewer but as loud, and there is a scuffle at the rear of the seated area the security guard calms with the restraint we pay him for. I watch ancient Henri Fors leave, stiff-legged like an old cat in his chunky brogues.

Albert takes the podium when finally the conclusion of my speech is done, to announce as much. Emmanuelle smiles at me, still applauding, the traces of gray in her hair quite visible under these lights. Albert shakes my hand and whispers in my ear, "*Congratulations. You've entered the mirror.*"

At last the Q and A is reached.

Albert outlines the rules and how one of my grad students will pass a wireless mic to the interlocutor. Arms are raised. The first is a young woman from the ThinkFirst poli-sci blog.

"Thank you. Mr. Elias, given the riots in Europe why ought we here pay attention to Lebanon now?"

"A good question, Ms. Howe." She's young enough to betray a brief blankness at the flattery of being known. "And my answer would be that Lebanon is the crucible of the world's religions, and to I hope pardonably mix metaphors for a moment, the weather vane for the future of the Middle East vis-à-vis the West. Historically this has always been so. Since the discovery of oil and natural gas in the Levantine basin, it is so now. It will always be so. You can't change geography."

She's young and hungry and unsatisfied by this.

"I can see you need a little more. An example. You are aware of the Syrian droughts of the last five years, and the critical state of the Euphrates River. Syria is witnessing a recurrence of the Byzantine Dead Cities of the fifth century, but the new ghost towns are Assad's legacy. The people urbanize. Only the Lebanon has water. This is true in regard to Israel as well. We are the last hope of both Israel *and* Syria, and what we won't give by trade and projects and mutuality will be taken by force or by guile."

The grad student takes the mic from Howe. Albert checks me quickly before handing it to the *Financial Times*'s Armitage. I feel my eyes go slightly dead.

"Ah yes, good afternoon, Mr. Elias."

"Good afternoon, Mr. Armitage. Michael Armitage of the *FT*, ladies and gentlemen."

There is a minor murmur from supporters, one quiet boo, for once on my behalf. I am one of Armitage's pet projects, along with wind turbines and expense scandals, and he must be handled. He is tall, thin, his face shiny and gaunt. His eyes deeply shielded, an experienced and ancient predator. He reminds me sharply now of the language poet, Peter Jensen, the vein throbbing in his forehead in the back streets of Shoreditch so many years ago after that reading; his rage when I attacked him so surprising, his wide white eyes and a kind of *affrontedness*, his poise put to play, the abrupt, stiff-limbed flails. He was beautiful, intimidating, hard; bright with his success at the reading. I broke him down to pieces.

"So, ah, Mr. Elias. Your, ah, accent seems to have changed."

"Too long in England, maybe, Mr. Armitage."

"Quite. You have so much confidence, yet so little experience."

It is, I suppose, good to get him out of the way as soon as possible. He looks at the pad in his hand then back up to me, and the attempt is to get me off-balance and has almost worked. I cannot respond with hostility, because it presents as hysteria, which is weakness.

"Is this your question?"

"No, I'm coming to that. I apologize. I'm coming to my question. Mr. Elias, you've written this extraordinary set of articles, the now-famous water paper in *Nature*, and your memoir."

"And a novel." I smile.

"And a novel also, I do apologize. But and yet it would seem that your memoir leaves out a great deal."

"I'm sure I don't know what you mean by that. Can you be specific?"

"I'll come back to that in a minute. My question is, who are you, Mr. Elias, a Greek Orthodox, traditional historical Muslim allies and leftists in the Lebanese sphere, growing up poor, as your memoir insists, in a multiethnic family with divided political allegiances in a Christian East Beirut scarred by the consequences of inter-Christian warfare, to now support and or be supported *by* rich Maronite Christian technocrats and speculators? How does this sit with your supposed activism for water rights, protection, and your various activisms? How do you respond to this reputation you have gained as a bully with a Messiah complex?"

Greedily, the boos and murmurs have been rising; many have

been waiting for the *FT*'s hit man to make his move. Gemayel's fixed smile is like a mirror. I am about to reply when, without looking up from his pad, he continues.

"And further to my earlier point, I should like to ask how you respond to accusations in regard to your involvement in crimes in Lebanon, theft and a number of suspicious deaths, presented in an article entitled, 'Lebanon's New Man: Who Does He Think He Is? Jesus Christ?' published in my newspaper June 6 of last year? Events conspicuous for their absence, even in the form of a denial, in the narrative presented in the section of your memoir dealing with your emigration from Lebanon, 'In the anti Lebanon'? And published, this memoir I'm referring to, we're assuming simply as part of this bizarre and elaborate PR campaign? Why do you want to join the *zaim* families of Lebanon? Why are they accepting you into their embrace? Where do you get your money from, sir?"

"You're referring to the article you yourself wrote?"

"Yes. Yes, indeed I am."

"Thank you anyway, for bringing up this point. But Mr. Armitage, you will not speak to the contents of today's speeches and presentations?"

"Well, I rather think I am. And I'm sure those attending here today as well as the readers of my newspaper would appreciate it if you answered my question."

"Your several questions."

"Indeed. At your leisure, sir."

"I will answer each of them, in reverse order to that in which they were asked."

There are other accusations: that I am gnomic in statement and persona. Rumors of drug use and disappearances. *"You're aging very well."* I wake with a pain in my heart that is constant, to the right of my chest, a pressure like a strained lung. *"When you lie, are you in fact even aware you are lying?"* I need more time. Accusations that I publicly advocate things like *memory* and *hope* to hide my lack of both. That I believe hope is a cheap thing. That I am a monster behind an alabaster mask crazed with cracks.

I return to Lebanon within the month. I am told I am guaranteed a bloc of votes in the next municipal election, which I will lose. In the subsequent election I will win and enter as the youngest-yet member of the chamber of deputies. These things have been guaranteed me. The death of my father wiped many slates clean, and I have been seen as someone to use, someone malleable and plastic, a blank and pale *masque neutre* to be drawn upon. I can feel them spray-painting my face already. For now, that is all right.

The word my grandmother used was *imagination*.

I am in the labyrinth, in the Lebanese mud, and I maneuver; I am in there and I am dirty, wounded and infected by it. And loved for it, by those who live there, the dirty, wounded, and infected.

We similarly long to wade out and be washed where the river flows into the sea.

Printed in the United States
by Baker & Taylor Publisher Services